TRIPLE
JEOPARDY

RICHARD SPEIGHT

TRIPLE JEOPARDY

WARNER BOOKS

A Warner Communications Company

Warner Books, Inc., 666 Fifth Avenue, New York, NY 10103

W A Warner Communications Company

Printed in the United States of America
First printing: July 1988
10 9 8 7 6 5 4 3 2 1
Library of Congress Cataloging in Publication Data

Speight, Richard.
    Triple jeopardy.

    I. Title.
PS3569.P442T75   1988   813′ .54   87-40405
ISBN 0-446-51394-6

Book design: H. Roberts

This book is dedicated to two people. My wife, Barbara, provided the love, support, and encouragement that enabled me to write it. Dr. Max Haskett provided the insights that enabled me to write it accurately. I thank them both, from the bottom of my heart.

Richard Speight
January 31, 1988

TRIPLE
JEOPARDY

CHAPTER
One

Judge Cullen Whitehurst awoke with a start when Tony Costello tapped him lightly on the elbow. No one could tell; the benign expression on his face never changed.

The judge took the small note from his court officer's extended hand. He unfolded it and read the terse message, tossed it facedown on the mahogany surface in front of him, then nodded almost imperceptibly as Costello withdrew to his customary position in the corner of the courtroom, next to the jury box. Costello smiled knowingly.

Judge Whitehurst hadn't actually been asleep. His mind had simply slipped away from the boredom of reality and wandered off on an aimless path of its own. It was something he did frequently, especially at times such as this when the trial over which he was presiding bogged down and the lawyers seemed to have nothing better to do than drone on, dredging up useless trivia as only lawyers could do. The quiet atmosphere and dim lighting in the courtroom lent themselves to such mental meanderings.

Whenever this happened, the judge's dark brown eyes always remained wide open; his slightly paunchy chin rested on one palm or the other, giving him the appearance of keen interest and serious contemplation. But his mind was elsewhere. The entire process was a defense mechanism—one of the few things that had kept him from going stir-crazy during his three and one-half years on the bench.

At the precise moment when Judge Whitehurst returned to the real world, Barbara Patterson was reading a medical deposition to the jury, a particularly stultifying exercise that she did with all the enthusiasm of a schoolchild reciting Shakespeare. Judge Whitehurst began paying close attention to her words, not because he cared what was happening, but because he was waiting for the right moment to interrupt. Ms. Patterson was nearly finished.

"Doctor, you have testified that your statement for services rendered in this case was six hundred dollars, and you have exhibited with your testimony a bill for that amount." The jurors looked as though they couldn't care less. "Doctor, is that amount reasonable for the service rendered, and consistent with the amount charged by qualified physicians in this community for the same services?" It was a boilerplate question, one that had to be asked in order to make the medical expenses admissible. She finished by reading the answer.

"Yes, it is. If anything, my charges are below the average in the community."

That's what they all say, Judge Whitehurst thought to himself. For once I would love a doctor to tell the truth, something like "That's high, but I'm worth it." He smiled at the thought as Barbara read the final line of the deposition.

"I believe that's all, Doctor, thank you." Barbara closed the deposition and walked back to her chair at the plaintiff's table. The defense counsel rose to read his brief cross-examination of the same doctor. He had taken only a few steps when Judge Whitehurst spoke.

"Counsel, the Court has some personal business to attend to. We are going to adjourn for lunch early today."

The young lawyer stopped walking and turned toward the judge. "Your Honor, I have only a few brief questions on cross-examination. If I might be permitted to continue—"

"Counselor, I am well aware of the length of your examination," the judge interrupted, drawing out his words, lacing them with mild sarcasm. "We all look forward to it with great excitement, but the jury will just have to sustain its level of anticipation until after lunch."

As he spoke, the judge stared right through the lawyer. Tony Costello smiled again, but the judge's comment drew only slight, uncomfortable laughter from the jurors.

Barbara Patterson felt sorry for her counterpart for the defense; he stood frozen halfway between his chair and the podium.

"Thank you, Your Honor," the young man said, controlling his voice as best he could. The judge then turned toward the jury.

"Members of the jury, as always, you are not to discuss this case among yourselves until you have heard all the facts and I have given you the law. You may go to lunch. Perhaps you can do a little shopping, whatever you want. We will recess until one-thirty; you should be back in the jury room at one twenty-five without fail. Adjourn court, Mr. Costello."

"Everyone rise," Tony Costello commanded, standing ramrod straight, his hands down by his side. A burly hulk of a man, Costello's appearance demanded attention, if not respect. When he barked out his instructions in the courtroom, people instinctively did as they were told. The sparse assemblage arose while Judge Whitehurst stepped briskly down the small staircase and disappeared through the door next to the bench.

"Court stands in recess until one-thirty," Costello repeated before following Judge Whitehurst through the mahogany door.

Barbara Patterson stood in place, slowly gathering her papers. Her adversary was still poised halfway between the small lectern and his place at the counsel table, his copy of the deposition still open in his left hand.

"I hate crap like this," he said as she approached him. "Did you know this was going to happen?"

"Not really," she responded. "I asked Tony when we would be breaking for lunch. I have some witnesses on call, and I didn't want them sitting around. He told me we might be leaving early, that the judge had something to do. I didn't realize he meant *this* early. But then again, nothing really surprises me in this courtroom."

"This is ridiculous," the flustered young man groused, glancing at the gold pocket watch he had pulled from his vest pocket. "We didn't even start until nine-thirty. At this rate this trial could take all week. It should have ended yesterday."

"Is this your first trial before Whitehurst?" Barbara asked.

"Is it that obvious? I've had some motions, and a few hearings, but no trial. I've heard the horror stories, but I swear this is worse than I expected."

"Count your blessings. At least you're working by the hour. Think about me. If this thing never ends, I never get paid."

The young lawyer snapped his briefcase shut.

"Look, let me give you some free advice," Barbara said, still feeling sorry for the flustered young man. He looked back at her. "Don't let these little things get to you so much. Whitehurst is a good judge. He'll be fair with your client. You can count on that. Just roll with the punches, and don't sweat the small stuff." Barbara's words held little conviction.

"Bullshit," muttered the young man as he yanked his briefcase off the table and stormed toward the door, almost running full force into Assistant District Attorney Bernard Fine.

Bernie Fine sidestepped the young lawyer, then smiled broadly as he walked toward the defense table, where Barbara was stuffing papers into her own briefcase.

"Whoa, there," he said. "What got into him?"

"Whitehurst. What do you think?" She smiled at her colleague. Barbara had been in court with Bernie Fine several times. She respected him. She also liked him.

"What brings you here?" she asked.

"I had hoped to have a word with His Honor, but I guess not."

"Write him a letter," Barbara suggested, only half joking.

"He's only hurting himself," Fine pointed out. "Does he think we're all going to forget this kind of crap at election time? And it's not just the lawyers, either. Jurors, litigants, everybody notices it. It's not right. Why should people have to pay for these delays? Some days we don't work more than four hours. And when we are here, we don't get anything done. Doesn't it drive you up the wall?"

"Of course it does. I try to overlook it, but unfortunately, it's getting worse. At one time, he was the best. He was tough, but at least he was consistent. What bothers me is that you can't count on him. One day he's on top of everything, and the next day he's lost in space. One day he goes by the book, and the next day he's totally arbitrary."

Bernie Fine held the heavy door open as Barbara exited into the busy hallway that bisected the fourth floor of the courthouse.

"He's totally unpredictable," Bernie interjected. "Some of the older guys in the DA's office warned me when I signed on. They said you can let yourself get to feeling comfortable with him, and maybe say something you think is clever, or even friendly, and the next thing you know he's zapped you, like he did just then. It's enough to make you dread walking in there."

A crowd had gathered around the brass elevator doors.

Barbara barely knew Whitehurst, but she liked him. She had seen him in the better days and admired not only his skill, but his grace and his dignity. She had seen him from a unique perspective, through the eyes of a young woman caught up in a painful convolution of lives in turmoil as she watched the dissolution of her sister's marriage. That trial had shattered Barbara's own idealistic fantasies about love and loyalty and commitment.

Cullen Whitehurst, freshly appointed and anxious to please, had been the judge. He had handled sensitive testimony with great respect and decorum; and he had likewise handled the frayed edges of their exposed humanity with kindness and gentleness. Not a big deal to the world at large, but big to Barbara, to her family, and especially to her older sister. Cullen Whitehurst had made a bad experience bearable, and in the process had provided Barbara with the last little push she had needed to make the law her chosen profession.

Yes, Barbara Patterson had seen Cullen Whitehurst in the better days. She didn't know whether he remembered or not, but she would never forget.

"The best course," Barbara said, "is to do things his way and hope your next case lands somewhere else."

The two lawyers stepped into the elevator together; the brass doors closed behind them.

Lorene Crosby always knew when Judge Whitehurst had left the bench and had entered his chambers. She didn't have to be summoned; whether by instinct, intuition, telepathy, or whatever, she knew. She had spent a good part of her lifetime anticipating his needs.

A trim, graying woman of fifty-one, she had taken on the job of secretary and confidante to Cullen Whitehurst thirty years earlier and had been with him through two different law firms and now the bench. Like her boss, she enjoyed the prestige of the judiciary. She was the judge's secretary, and they all had to come through her to get to him. She played her role of protector to the hilt, but with a remarkable degree of tact and charm. While Judge Whitehurst had his problems with almost everyone these days, it was impossible to dislike Lorene Crosby.

Ms. Crosby walked through the door connecting her office to the judge's. She placed a stack of pink callback slips on top of his desk calendar. Tony Costello was helping the judge out of his robe.

"Your wife called and said she would meet you at the governor's office. The governor's wife asked her to go to lunch after the press conference. The governor's secretary called and asked that you come early. Use the back entrance; the governor wants to talk with you a few minutes before the conference begins. The lawyers in *State versus Eisenberg* called. They want a conference; I set them up for eight-thirty tomorrow. The rest of the calls can wait. The mail is all junk."

"Who is on the Eisenberg case?" the judge asked, riffling through the call slips.

"Ted Conner and that Markham fellow from Powell, Goldberg."

"Call them back and have them come at nine," Judge Whitehurst instructed. "I don't want to see anybody that early tomorrow. I'm not going to start court until ten." Lorene Crosby made a quick note on her steno pad.

Tony Costello hung the judge's robe in the small closet at the far end of the spacious office and poured him a fresh cup of coffee from the pot he had brewed earlier.

Judge Whitehurst took the cup. "Is there anything you need me to do before I get the car?" Without waiting for an answer, Costello went back to the closet for the judge's suit coat.

"No, you go ahead, Tony. I'll be right down." Judge Whitehurst took the coat without putting it on.

Tony Costello slipped quietly out through Lorene Crosby's office and headed down the narrow hallway to a little-used stairwell. Judge Whitehurst was one of the privileged few with an inside parking spot; thanks to the fortuitous location of this stairwell, he had quick and private access to his car.

"How's the case going?" Lorene Crosby asked as the door closed behind Tony.

"Tedious," was the terse reply. Judge Whitehurst looked at his watch, then looked at his secretary. She backed away from his desk.

"Get your coat and wait for me outside," he continued. "I have a quick call to make." She knew better. There were no secrets between them, and no calls he could not make in front of her, in spite of what he might think. But she did as she was told.

As the door to Lorene's office clicked shut, Whitehurst slipped into his jacket. He walked over to the closet, opened the door, and stood in front of the mirror. He saw before him a rugged face, mature if not handsome, with tanned skin, a receding hairline, and a touch of gray at the temples that accentuated the darkness of the sparse hair that still remained at the age of fifty-eight. It wasn't the face he would have chosen, necessarily, but it was distinguished enough, even if his chin was getting somewhat flaccid and his prominent nose becoming bulbous and veined. He straightened his tie, then closed the door and returned to his desk.

From the bookshelf that lined the wall over his credenza, he withdrew three volumes and, fumbling in the empty space behind them, pulled out a cut-glass carafe. Without ceremony he raised the carafe to his lips and drank several gulps. The liquid burned his tongue and throat. The stinging feeling sliced a pathway down his chest and settled into his stomach just as the buzzer on his telephone intercom went off.

"The car is ready," Lorene said.

"I'm coming."

He looked down at his desk calendar. It was open to that day: Tuesday, September 24. There was only one notation: "Governor's office—press conference," written in red, and underlined. This was a big day.

He flipped the page to Wednesday, then took a final sip from the carafe before pressing it back into its hidden nook and hastily shoving the books into their place. With a tiny spray bottle pulled from his pocket, he covered any traces that might be lingering on his breath. Feeling renewed confidence, he opened the door to Lorene's office and walked on past her desk, carefully avoiding her glance.

"Let's go," he barked as she picked up her purse and dutifully followed him into the hallway.

CHAPTER

Two

The governor actually had two offices, both located on the first floor of the capitol, connected by a small hallway.

The larger of these was the office the public saw on television. At one end of the spacious room was a beautiful picture window overlooking the rolling green lawn of the capitol grounds, with its large old trees just beginning to change color in the fading days of September. Beyond the trees loomed the multicolored, bulky forms of the city's tall buildings. The governor's desk, a dark wood behemoth with ornate carved legs and decorative brass handles, occupied a position of honor in front of the window.

Around the walls, accented by decorative moldings, portraits of the state's prior chief executives peered down from gilded frames. The state seal was woven into the crimson carpet in front of the governor's desk. A pair of comfortable wing chairs faced the desk; beyond that, a massive conference table was surrounded by twelve leather chairs in a color that matched the wing chairs and blended into the overall harmony of the scene.

On this particular morning the governor's formal desk had been cleared of his personal memorabilia and covered with a bouquet of microphones. More than a dozen of the little gray-and-chrome bulbs seemed to sprout from the surface of the green felt desk pad, their black wires trailing off the desk and onto the floor like a small rubber waterfall.

The room was nearly full of reporters and cameramen when Tony Costello and Lorene Crosby arrived. Margaret Whitehurst had saved them seats. They spoke briefly with Madeline Foreman, the governor's wife, then joined Margaret in the chairs nearest the desk.

Judge Whitehurst had gone to the governor's other office. Shielded from the public eye, it was in this office that the real work was done and the real news was generated.

The "inner sanctum" seemed spartan when compared with the luxury of the public office. But it was more than adequate.

Furnished with comfortable, well-padded furniture and a commodious desk, the working office was most noteworthy for its unbelievable clutter. The desk was always covered with papers, the credenza and shelves constantly jammed with books and bric-a-brac. All of this had special meaning to the governor; his staff knew that the ultimate sacrilege would be for someone, anyone, to move anything.

Family pictures and personal mementos dotted one wall. Certificates, commendations, framed newspaper articles, and pictures of the governor with various luminaries covered any remaining bare space. Like most men with egos large enough to make them brave the risks of running for public office, Bradley Foreman enjoyed having his accomplishments on public display. The "wall of fame," as his secretary had dubbed it, was kept up-to-date. She periodically replaced the oldest articles with the newest, the least important honors with the more important, trying not to visibly disrupt the general order of things. The "wall of fame" presented the picture of a man on an upward track, a mover and shaker, one who frequented the councils of the mighty and who relished being part of that world.

It was said of Bradley Foreman that he was born to be governor. Certainly he looked the part. He stood a shade over six foot three. An imposing head of white hair crowned a ruddy face that accented the bright blueness of his eyes. From those eyes, wrinkles trailed upward and outward, giving him a look of perpetual merriment. Coupled with his broad smile, booming voice, and firm, ready handshake, the overall effect was pure politics. And yet there was a sincerity about him. People instinctively liked and trusted Bradley Foreman. They always had; he had made the most of that fortuitous circumstance all his life.

He and Cullen Whitehurst were more than friends. They had been part of each other's life for years. They went to grade school together and played on the same high school football team. While Foreman shone, Whitehurst had toiled in the trenches. They went off to college together and joined the same fraternity. Foreman was elected president his senior year; Whitehurst ran his campaign. They attended the same law school. Once again Bradley Foreman, always in the political forefront, promised change and was elected to head the student government—again with Whitehurst's help.

There was no jealousy between them. They fit together like tongue-and-groove boards. Whitehurst was a plodder, a detail man, the kind of nuts-and-bolts realist that a dreamer such as Foreman needed. He provided the direction necessary to focus Bradley Foreman's dreams, and the fuel required to accomplish them.

Each rejoiced in the other's talents and applauded the other's successes, but each had a definite goal. Bradley Foreman had made it known from the start that he wanted to be governor, an ambition born of little more than the exhilaration of youth. He was not only serious, he was obsessed. And Cullen Whitehurst, from the beginning, had believed in his friend and had let him know he would help make this dream come true. Whitehurst had also let his friend know, from the beginning, the price of such loyalty. His reward would be the power, prestige, and security of that most treasured of political appointments, a judgeship. The deal was sealed early on.

When the time came for the two men to go into law practice, it was only natural that they would do it together. Foreman, the rainmaker, brought in business. Whitehurst, the organizer, saw to it that it was handled with skill. The chemistry was perfect; the business flourished. Eventually more than fifty lawyers toiled under the banner of Foreman and Whitehurst. But the senior partners never gave up their dream. At the peak of his success, Bradley Foreman finally took the step he had been planning all his life. He called in his political IOUs, took a year off, and hit the campaign trail, cutting a wide path with his winning smile and friendly handshake. In spite of his apparent political inexperience, and in the face of the dire predictions of experts, he won. It was close, but he won. Six months later, a judgeship was bestowed upon his friend. No one was surprised.

Now, nearly four years later, it was nearing time to run again. That fact occupied most of Bradley Foreman's energy during his waking hours. Everything he said and did these days was geared toward that campaign. The presence of an attractive young challenger on the horizon made events such as today's press conference doubly important. Everything had to be just right.

Cullen Whitehurst was ushered into the inner office. Governor Foreman was seated in his comfortable old leather desk chair. He was coatless; his sleeves were rolled up. As his old friend entered the room, the governor extended his hand and spoke. His tone was friendly, yet there was unmistakable tension in the air.

"Cullen. How are you?" The governor gestured toward a chair next to the desk. "Sit down."

"Thank you, Governor." Though they were old friends, Cullen Whitehurst always used the correct title.

"I appreciate your coming today, Cullen. This is a big day for me. You, of all people, can appreciate that."

"You were kind to invite me," Whitehurst replied, still paying lip service to formality.

"Kind? I couldn't have passed this bill without you, and you know it. Hell, I'll bet half the fellows on the Hill still have sore arms from the twisting you've done over the last few months."

Governor Foreman smiled. He was posturing as usual. But he was right. Cullen Whitehurst's lobbying had contributed significantly to the crowning achievement of Bradley Foreman's first term, passage of the toughest drunk-driving law of any state in the Union.

"It was fun. Great fun," Whitehurst mused. "It reminded me of the old days, when you and I were wheeling and dealing. Believe me, it was nice to be able to get away from that judge's chair for a while."

"We've had some times, haven't we, fella?"

"Yeah," Whitehurst mused. "Those were the days. We were quite a team. . . ."

The governor propped one foot up on the front edge of his desk and leaned his swivel chair back as far as it would go.

"You were good, Cullen," he said, still smiling. "You were great, actually. The best I ever saw in court. No detail missed, no stone unturned. You had the instinct for it. Don't you ever miss that?"

"That sounds like a speech you would make at a memorial service," Whitehurst replied, only half smiling now. "You aren't trying to dump me, are you?"

"Of course not." The governor straightened his chair back up. "It's just that I always wondered why you want to be tied down like that. I never could see you saddled to the bench. Not really. You're too active." The governor studied his friend's face as he spoke.

"It's not so bad. Like everything else, it's what you make it. Anyway, quit being oblique with me. If you've got something to say, say it."

Judge Whitehurst wasn't smiling now. Neither was the governor. There was an awkward silence as the chief executive leaned forward and folded his hands on his desk. He was searching for the right words.

"Cullen, is everything all right?"

Cullen Whitehurst shifted uneasily in the soft leather chair.

"You don't look good, Cullen, and frankly, I'm hearing some things that disturb me."

"Like what?" Too loud, too quick, Whitehurst told himself. You sound defensive. He rubbed one palm with the thumb of his other hand, then shifted to the other palm, unaware of what he was doing. His eyes avoided the glance of his old friend.

"Reports. Just reports. I don't want to deal with specifics. Besides, it's not one thing, just things in general. They way you behave on the bench. The hours you're keeping. The places you've been seen in. And frankly, the condition you are seen in. It's not good. I don't know how seriously to take what I'm hearing, but it's not good."

"A judge has a lot of enemies, Brad. You know that. Lots of lawyers would love to see me fall on my face. In every case, someone loses. There will always be griping and backbiting. It's part of the game." He tried his best to sound casual.

"There's more to it than that, Cullen. I've talked to Margaret. She's worried. She says you're spending a lot of time alone, that you seem withdrawn. You're gruff and unpleasant. You're unpredictable. One minute you're on a high, the next minute you snap at her." He stopped for a moment to consider his next words. "She tells me that's what it was like before."

Cullen Whitehurst closed his eyes and slowly ground his teeth together. He couldn't believe this was happening.

"Really, I'm fine," he insisted, managing a weak smile. "I'm just tired, that's all. Everything's under control. I'm under control. Good God, you of all people ought to know what I went through. I'll never let myself get that way again." He looked his old friend right in the eyes as he spoke and never flinched. "I've got everything under control," he added, unable to stand the silence. "Believe me. I'm on top of this thing."

Foreman didn't flinch either. "I also know you aren't keeping in touch with your counselor."

Whitehurst stiffened. "How do you know about that?"

The governor paused before answering. "I don't. I just took a wild guess. Is it true?"

"Yes. But only because I haven't needed to. And I've been busy. That's all. My God, do I have to answer to him for the rest of my life?"

The governor rose and walked around next to Whitehurst's chair, kneeled down beside him and put one hand on his arm.

"I have a standing appointment," Whitehurst said.

"What does that mean?"

"I go when I need to. I'm always welcome."

"Who makes that decision? Who decides when you go?"

"I do. Who else?" Whitehurst tossed off his reply with the casualness of one responding to the idle inquiry of a total stranger. But a familiar tightness gripped his chest; a rapid heartbeat hammered in his ears. He was fighting a rising tide of anxiety.

"Isn't that dangerous?" Foreman asked. "Should you be making that decision alone?"

"My God, it's been eight years. Will anyone ever trust me again? What do I have to do to prove myself?"

"It's not a matter of proving anything, Cullen. You know that. It's been rough," he said softly. "It's been hard on all of us, especially Margaret. But what we did, we did for you, because we loved you, and wanted you well. We still love you, and all of us will do anything we can. You know that. But we have got to know the truth. You know that too, don't you?"

"Yes, of course." Whitehurst felt his voice tremble slightly; he struggled for control as the governor continued.

"Look, Cullen. I want to shoot straight. We've been friends too long to play games. I have two concerns. The first is you, of course. I want to help you, but I also have to think of myself. I'm not going to apologize about that. I am about to sign the most important piece of legislation to come across my desk since I took office. I promised the people I would do this, and I have done it. *We* have done it. Your name is tied to that bill just as much as mine is. If this fails, the public is going to react. Next year's election already looks tough enough. I don't need an albatross hanging around my neck. If you're having problems—and I mean any problems—tell me now. Don't let me stick my neck out and then chop it off. Don't do that to me."

Though the room was cool enough, Whitehurst could feel beads of perspiration gathering at his temples and running down through his sideburns. He fixed his gaze on a point between Foreman's eyes and stared straight ahead.

"I'm fine, Brad, really I am. You can count on me. I won't let you down."

The governor stood up, straightened the knot in his tie, and looked down at his friend for a moment. He teetered between acceptance and rejection, but only for an instant. "Let's go to work," he said as he grabbed his suit jacket from the coatrack.

Someone turned on the television lights just before the governor entered the large formal office. The temperature in the room quickly rose. Whitehurst, standing in the glare behind the governor's desk, was grateful for that small favor. His wife and close friends noticed immediately how flushed he looked, but he managed to convince himself that the heat explained away his condition.

Governor Foreman took his place behind the massive desk and began to read from a prepared statement.

"Ladies and gentlemen, I am pleased to announce that today I have signed into law Senate Bill one one six two. With this act, I have kept the promise I made to the people of this state on the day that I was elected. With this law in place, our state now becomes a model for every other state in this great land. With this law, we have made a clear and unequivocal statement."

Governor Foreman's voice rose and fell as he spoke, adding drama to his presentation. As usual, he was drifting from his text, embellishing the plain language, adding his own special flair. He was in his element now. This was what he did best.

"We have demonstrated to our people and to the entire nation that we will no longer tolerate the carnage on our highways caused by those whose abilities are impaired by the use of alcohol or drugs. We have spoken in a loud and clear voice to those who choose to drink and drive. They now know that they will be severely and swiftly punished—up to one year in jail for the first offense, five or more years for subsequent offenses. We have issued a solemn warning to one and all ..."

Cullen Whitehurst looked around the room as the governor spoke. The only other sounds in the room were the gentle whir of a lone movie camera sandwiched between the television Minicams, and the rhythmic clicking of the still cameras that were capturing the conference for the state's daily newspapers. He looked at his wife; like everyone else, she was staring intently at the governor. His eyes moved to Madeline Foreman, an attractive, dignified woman who looked as much at home in her role as her husband did in his. He shifted his glance to Lorene Crosby, then to Tony Costello. As he looked at the four of them seated together and listened to the voice of his friend the governor, his mind drifted back in time to a morning eight years earlier when, as now, they had all been together in one room.

It was more than déjà vu; it was a chilling reliving of a morning he would never forget. It forced its way into his consciousness at odd times, without warning. It was like an old film, a rerun, seen time after time. Only he couldn't look away or stop it or even speed it up to get it over with. It began as if by its own will, occupied center stage, and played on until it was ready to release him back to the present world.

This was hardly what he needed at a time such as this, but it was too late. The switch had been tripped; the show was about to begin. The intervening years dissolved like reflections in a turbulent pool, and there he was. Eight years ago.

CHAPTER

Three

*I*t had been a Sunday. That was a clear recollection. A cool, crisp autumn Sunday, the kind that treats the senses to a potpourri of delights—provided, of course, one's senses are working. His weren't. In fact, he had missed much of the day. He slept late, well past noon, not because he wanted to but because he was physically unable to do anything else.

The night before was part of the recollection, but only as a blur. He remembered a party. Not much detail, but clearly a party. He remembered arriving, having a few drinks, enjoying himself. He remembered being the center of attention; a feeling he always enjoyed, a position into which he frequently maneuvered himself.

He remembered being witty, entertaining, almost euphoric in his enjoyment of the evening. That's how he had felt at the time, until he got sick. The memory of getting sick stood out, but then there was a blank, a blackout, a gap in time where nothing existed. Then he remembered being home, being half-conscious, having his shoes and tie removed, being led to the bedroom by his wife, and being placed in his bed. An all-to-familiar scenario.

The feeling of nausea that had first hit him at the party was overwhelming by the time he was left alone. He remembered clutching at the edges of his bed. So violent was the spinning sensation that he had actually feared being propelled off, into some undefined void. He recalled throwing up repeatedly, and crying for help; he remembered that Margaret hadn't come. Unlike the other times, she hadn't come. Then finally, when he had thrown up everything possible, when he had retched until he felt he might turn inside out, when he had despaired of ever regaining his balance, he had stumbled into the welcome abyss of drugged sleep.

That was all he remembered about that Saturday; it was always the first memory to return whenever the switch was tripped. When it happened, the sensations returned so vividly that he felt that very same nausea once again, a real feeling, bringing him to the brink of losing it all one more time.

The first thing to return to him about that Sunday morning was always the smell. He had almost gotten sick all over again that morning and would have, except there was nothing left within him to come out.

In his mind's eye he once again pulled himself up off the pool of dried vomit where he had spent the night and staggered into the bathroom. He was a mess! His hair, his face, his clothing—everything was foul. Somehow he managed to find his way into the shower, fully dressed. He let the hot water wash off both him and his clothing. Only then did he strip and lather himself thoroughly, kicking the soaked garments into a pile at the corner of the shower stall. The clothes were ruined anyway.

As he dried off, the fog began to clear, and he realized how much his head hurt. His temples throbbed; the back of his head felt as if it were crushing his brain; his eye sockets seemed to be closing in around his eyes. He looked in the mirror. His eyes were red and difficult to focus, his face pocked with red blotches. His thoughts wandered through the possibilities, searching for survival, trying to decide what to do next.

Then he had thought about Margaret.

Where was Margaret? Why wasn't she there to help him? Anger welled within him now, just as it had then.

He had leaned against the wall to maintain his balance as he struggled into an undershirt, slacks, and slippers. He made his way down the sweeping staircase to the main hall that split the massive Georgian home into two sections. He was about to turn left through the dining room, past the breakfast room, and on to the kitchen. He was looking for his wife. That's where he expected her to be. But for some reason he turned right instead, into the living room. Perhaps he had heard a noise. Perhaps he was attracted by the light spilling into the hall. He couldn't remember anymore, but he always recalled vividly what he had seen when he entered that room.

Cullen Whitehurst was a self-made man, but not necessarily in the most enviable sense of the word. In truth his personality had been forged in a crucible of adversity; his character was a product of self-defense.

He was born in a small town some hundred miles south of the city where he now sat on the bench. His mother was a tight-lipped, sharp-tongued woman who seldom laughed, and never cried. If she felt affection she never admitted it, and certainly never let it show. She had rules for every occasion and restrictions that stifled every opportunity for joy. For her, everything was black or white. If her only child strayed across the line, discipline was quick in coming.

Discipline is part of the essence of love. Children need, expect, and want limits; they want to live within their capabilities, to be affirmed and strengthened by the gentle hand of loving guidance. That definition would be learned by Cullen Whitehurst later; it bore no resemblance to the kind of discipline practiced by his mother.

Perhaps it was her own upbringing. Perhaps it was her obsessive fear that she, and she alone, was totally responsible for holding the world together and making it possible for herself and her loved ones to survive. Perhaps it was her compulsive need for control. Perhaps it was some other experience, some dark secret she would never share, and no one would dare guess. Certainly the circumstances of her marriage lent the poor woman no support; she could depend on Cullen's father no more than could the son. Whatever the circumstances, her distorted view of loving discipline manifested itself as cold, aggressive, bone-chilling attack. With unfortunate regularity, it took the form of physical abuse.

Early on, Cullen Whitehurst learned his mother's definition of "right" and "appropriate" and "acceptable," not so much out of respect or tradition but in self-defense.

Thus motivated by fear of his mother, Cullen Whitehurst did what any child would do—what any child *should* do under such circumstances. He learned the formula for survival. Do what she says. Better yet, *anticipate* what she is going to say. Follow her demands to the letter, and peace will come. Fail, and misery will follow.

He tried, but didn't always succeed. A torrent of words and blows rained down upon the boy during his childhood years at home; an admirable list of worldly accomplishments mounted next to his good name as he sought to survive in the only way he knew, by blunting his mother's anger with hypocritical humor and ill-motivated success. To the outside world he was an achiever, a model child, a sure bet for success, the kind of child other parents held up before their own as an example. Had they been able to look beyond the slick, fabricated surface, however, his admirers would have seen an empty shell, filled with an astonishing mixture of fear, calculation, and determination. Succinctly put, Cullen Whitehurst was a frightened child, unwarmed by love, reacting blindly to life.

But at least his mother was consistent. That's more than Cullen Whitehurst could say for his father.

From the very beginning he recognized one important thing about his father. If you depended on him for anything, you were likely to be disappointed. He was a man of violent mood swings who could laugh and play the pal one moment and be withdrawn, sarcastic, or totally unreachable the next. Cullen never knew how the old man would react or what kind of mood he might be in. So at an early age Cullen quit taking chances. He quit bringing his friends home. He became quiet and introspective and spent as much time as possible away from their house.

It wasn't until many years after the older man's death that Whitehurst learned that his father had been an alcoholic and had probably been one all the years Cullen had lived at home. Having this revealed to him was a moving experience, one that explained so many things and brought out into the open so many feelings.

Chief among these feelings was relief. Like any child, Cullen Whitehurst had needed a dependable father, especially in the face of his mother's constant onslaughts. He needed a father who would do things with him and be his friend, but more importantly, one who would really *be* the father, draw reasonable limits, and make his son learn to live within them.

In his better moments Cullen's father had actually come through for the boy. The two of them had some good times together; not all of the memories were bad. But the real gap, the one Cullen never allowed himself to feel, much less deal with, was his need for a father protector. Cullen Whitehurst was more than fifty years old when he finally faced the unanswered question that had haunted him for years: Why had his father let his mother treat him that way?

The inconsistency of life at home was maddening to young Cullen. Anger and frustration naturally followed. In time Cullen Whitehurst grew to hate both his father and his mother. It was an undefined hate, one that quietly consumed him like an undiscovered cancer. Years later, once the truth about their own lives was known, that hatred could at least give way to pity and a measure of understanding; perhaps even love, though unrequited, and mixed with an overwhelming sadness and sympathy. But this revelation, when it came, was too late to change the bitterness of childhood that accumulated within the soul of Cullen Whitehurst all of his life.

It was at his father's knee that he had first learned the fine art of denial, of avoidance, of buying peace at any price. He also looked to his father to define for him the most important ingredient missing in his mother: affection. Cullen was deceived by the man's periods of placid acceptance, mistaking this for an outward manifestation of love. What the boy clung to as a substitute for affection was really no more than the fumbling, thick-tongued passiveness of a man driven into submission by his own private hell, and by the domination of the woman he had married.

Thus Cullen Whitehurst grew up and became a plastic man with no ability to give, receive, or even recognize intimacy, an empty shell with no sense of self-worth apart from the regard he might extract from others by the sheer force of his personality and the strength of his will. But in that regard he was a success; thus rewarded, he bent all of his efforts in the direction of being as perfect as possible in the eyes of the world.

In the process of surviving until adulthood, he became subconsciously convinced that parenthood was a curse, and that he, the child, was the outward manifestation of that curse. He could see no reason to inflict such a fate on himself or anyone else. He grew up a man who wanted no part of children—a fact that Margaret Whitehurst knew intellectually before they married, but one that her heart had failed to accept as irrevocable. She had firmly believed that she would change him. She had been wrong. The resulting void in her life was painful to bear, but she, too, had survived.

Cullen and Margaret Whitehurst loved each other. They really did, each in his own, inadequate way. She understood what he had been through, and although the emptiness of their nest gnawed at her heart, she stayed with him and supported him as best she could. Cullen understood little about their relationship and felt even less. Such affection as he could generate was all hers, and he did what he could to express his regard. But she mainly knew him as a demanding, hard-driving perfectionist who expected too much of everyone around him and even more of himself. He wasn't easy to live with when sober. He was impossible to live with when he was drinking.

Cullen Whitehurst would never have consciously chosen his father's fatal weakness. He was strong. He was in control. He was able to make intelligent decisions, to be moderate in all things.

Those were the same lies he had heard at home as a child.

Fortunately for him, Margaret Whitehurst was totally different from his own mother, who had looked the other way, unconsciously enabling his father to ruin their lives for years. Margaret saw what was happening. She was smart enough to find out what needed to be done, and strong enough to do it.

Strength didn't come to her overnight. It built within her brick by brick as she watched her husband's own strength erode, and his world slowly crumble. At first she was aggressive toward him, believing that he really could take control if he wanted to, believing also that if she pushed him hard enough, he would do so. As time passed, and as the situation became more and more hopeless, she sought help.

In Cullen Whitehurst's mind, Margaret was wrong. Everyone was wrong. Margaret's nagging was reason to do as he pleased, to quit trying. He used it as an excuse. If people would just leave him alone, he could take care of things. That image of himself was his legacy; that had been his attitude as he stumbled down the stairs that Sunday morning eight years ago and stood, weak and shaken, at the entrance to his living room.

All five of them were there, sitting quietly, waiting for him. Margaret, Tony Costello, Lorene Crosby, Bradley and Madeline Foreman. There was another man also, one he didn't know. They all six

looked right at him. No one said anything. No one introduced the
stranger. Cullen stood in place, feeling vulnerable, embarrassed, and
exposed.

Anger immediately boiled and rose to the surface. He felt as if
he had walked into a trap. This was his home, his living room, his
private life. Even now, eight years later, as he remembered the shock
of seeing them there, he felt the same anger.

His wife had finally broken the silence.

"Sit down, Cullen," she said in a steady voice. He would never
forget that voice. It contrasted so sharply with the tension in the
air. Yet he noticed the slight quiver, the smallest evidence of her
nervousness, as she continued. "We want to talk to you."

His immediate reaction was a strong desire to lash out, to put
her in her place. To put *all* of them in their places. But he was so
stunned by the circumstances that he did as he was told. His pulse
raced out of control; his mind skipped from possibility to probability
in search of answers to questions he was afraid to ask, desperate
to avoid the verbal assault he knew was about to come.

Once he sat down, silence followed. Cullen Whitehurst looked
around the room but avoided their faces. He tensed his jaw and
clenched his hands, trying to look calm.

"Cullen, our firm has lost two clients in the last month because
of you," Brad Foreman had begun. "At the luncheon we gave for the
loan officers from Continental Security, you drank too much and
became belligerent. You almost had a fight with Sydney Pollack. You
insulted him and embarrassed all of us with your tasteless humor
belittling the Jewish race. Then, at the exploratory meeting two
weeks ago with the Sunbelt Group, nothing you said made sense.
You seemed out of touch with reality. You tripped over your words.
Their people were incredulous. We never heard from them again.
The Sachs firm called day before yesterday and asked for their file.
Friday, two of our clerks found you asleep at your desk. They only
thought you were asleep. Truth is, you were passed out. I tried to
cover for you, just as I have been covering for you for years, but I
am through. I'm through fooling myself, and I'm through coddling
you. The partners have met and have voted unanimously. You are
not welcome back until you have gotten help."

Brad had selected his words with great care. It was one of the
most difficult things he had ever had to say, but that detail was lost
on Cullen Whitehurst at the time.

Whitehurst reacted bitterly. He tried to argue with his law partner. He denied the accusation, explained away the events, and chastised his old friend for discussing business in front of the others. But Foreman refused to be baited. His response to Whitehurst's raving was as calm and deliberate as his initial presentation. At every juncture he simply repeated what he had said before.

"You are not welcome back until you have gotten help."

Lorene spoke next.

"You have insulted me and hurt my feelings. When I first came to work for you ..."

Cullen Whitehurst scarcely believed his ears. The nerve of this woman! Let her quit. Quit, hell! He'd fire her! After all he had done for her! Now she was turning on him, telling him off, making up lies about him.

"... I cannot, and will not, continue to work for you until you have gotten help and straightened yourself out." Finally, she had finished.

Cullen barely listened when Madeline Foreman started talking. The cumulative effect of their litany was becoming too much. When she recounted embarrassing scenes he had created in the Foreman home, and told how they were ruining their friendship, he just simmered inside and stared at the woman.

It was Tony Costello's presentation that finally began to soften Cullen's attitude. Could they be right? Sure he drank occasionally. He even got drunk occasionally. But was it this bad? Was he really sick? Did he need help?

He hadn't realized how his conduct had affected all of these people. He had lived through everything they were talking about, but he had seen it only through his eyes. Had he really looked so foolish? Had he really been so thoughtless? So cruel? So crude? Surely not!

Finally it was his wife's turn to speak once more. This time he listened. He stared in disbelief as she laid her cards on the table, one by one.

"I am afraid of you," she began. "Twice in the last week you took a swing at me when I tried to keep you from drinking. You missed, but I cannot take that kind of risk. You might not miss the next time. You have embarrassed me to tears before our friends. Last night was only the latest time. You think you're being cute, but in truth you become loud, foulmouthed, and obnoxious. You are totally unpredictable. I get cold chills when I hear your car pull in the drive. I never know what you'll be like when you walk through the door. The tension in this house is driving me crazy. And I have cleaned up after you for the last time. I don't like the smell of puke any better than you do."

Her voice cracked as she emphasized that last point, but her steady tone quickly returned. On she went.

As he listened, her words touched him deeply. He felt her pain, her anguish, her agony. But it was her last words that made the difference, that turned him in the direction of recovery.

"Cullen, I love you," she said. "We all do. I want to help you. But you have got to accept the fact that you need help. You are a very sick person, and if you don't get help soon, you will die. I cannot cover for you anymore. None of us can. We all want to help you live, but we will not help you die. If you are going to do that, then you are going to have to do it alone."

Dr. Richard Maxwell then introduced himself. He was a psychotherapist who worked with alcohol and drug abuse problems at a place called Harpeth Bend, a cutting-edge treatment center nestled in a pastoral setting some forty-five minutes from the city. Cullen knew about the place; it was an isolated farm where helpless winos went to dry out. That was what he thought. In reality it was much more, but at this point, what Cullen thought really didn't matter. His emotions had been numbed; mere thought had become nearly impossible. Decision making, at least for a few minutes, was out of the question.

Clean clothes were already packed. The appointment at Harpeth Bend was already made and a room was reserved. The choices were clearly defined and carefully set before him. The decision was gently but firmly placed in his lap, and left there.

Cullen Whitehurst kept the appointment and stayed for six weeks. To acquaintances and business associates he was on a vacation. An unusually long trip for someone with a reputation as a hardworking, hard-driving practitioner, but a justifiable trip in light of his long years of service to the firm. Those who suspected otherwise accepted the explanation graciously, at least in public. What they said in private was something he would never know.

The experience was indescribable. His body was racked time and time again with the torturing pain of withdrawal, but that was nothing to compare with the agony of his mind as layer after layer of defenses were peeled away like strips of charred skin. Worst of all, he was forced to do it himself. He resisted mightily, employing every conceivable excuse. But finally, under the guidance of Dr. Maxwell, he began to expose the lies of his life one by one.

From that moment on he was able to regard pain as an ally. Honest pain is a part of life; denial and deceit had been his worst enemies. His only hope, agonizing as it might be, was to begin to face the truth about himself and to deal with it.

He remembered another day as he looked across the crowded governor's office at his wife.

She had looked different then, sitting on the edge of his bed, watching him stare out the window. There had been many turning points, but that was the one he always remembered.

"Thanks for coming," he said. He hadn't seen her for several days.

"I would come more often ..." she said, her voice conveying the same calmness and resolve she had maintained from the beginning. "Dr. Maxwell said this was best for now."

He continued to stare out the window.

"So how are you feeling?" she asked, killing time. He didn't answer. She watched him fold his arms tightly across his chest and stare down at the floor.

"About the same," he finally answered.

Margaret did exactly what Dr. Maxwell had told her to do, the same thing she had done on previous visits. She did nothing, just sat there, not pressing the conversation, not rushing things at all. If nothing happened, if everything was the same as it had been before, that would be okay. "He'll have to do it in his own time," Dr. Maxwell had explained, "and in his own way." So today, like the others, she simply waited.

"I haven't looked forward to this," he said as he sat down beside her.

"Looked forward to what?"

"I've dreaded the hell out of it."

She didn't ask again. He slumped down and stared at his clasped hands.

"But I know now. I really know. And I'm ready." He bit his lip and looked up; his face was red and strained with anguish. "God knows, I'm ready."

Margaret took her husband's hand. The gesture gave him the last bit of strength he needed.

"Margaret, I'm an alcoholic," he said, his voice cracking with emotion. "There are reasons for it, but there are no excuses. That's what I am, and I can't change it."

Tears welled up in Margaret's eyes. She stood in front of her husband, took his other hand, and looked down at him as his body gently rocked back and forth.

"I've hurt you so bad, and I'm so sorry," he cried out, as the river of tears that flowed within him finally broke through and began to pour out.

"I'm so sorry, please forgive me." She pulled him closer and pressed his swollen cheek against her chest. "Please forgive me," he cried over and over again, his body jerking with explosive spasms of emotion too long denied.

Though she couldn't express it at that instant, in her heart she forgave him immediately and fully. She rejoiced in the glory of having been given the opportunity to do so. From that moment on, she was his partner in the therapeutic walk. She became a part of the recovery process, an active participant, joining hands with her willing husband. She believed his words as much as she welcomed them; they became a team. When time came to return to the world, they met together with Dr. Maxwell for the final time.

"This is a big day!" Dr. Maxwell was seated in the chair he always used during their sessions, but unlike most of the other times, the serious times, he was smiling broadly as he spoke. His feet were propped up on the edge of a battered bookshelf filled with an assortment of paperbacks and pamphlets.

Margaret Whitehurst clung to her husband's hand; they were side by side on the overstuffed sofa that faced Dr. Maxwell's chair. There was no desk between them.

"Are you guys ready?" the doctor continued.

"We sure are," Cullen answered.

"I wish you could keep working with us," Margaret said, looking at this man she had come to love and respect so much over the past few weeks.

"You'll be in good hands," Dr. Maxwell assured her. "I've made the arrangements. And I'll keep in touch."

Margaret leaned closer to her husband.

"I've got a lot to do here," the doctor continued. "And besides, leaving this place, I mean completely leaving it, is an important part of the process. It's a statement that you make, a kind of 'I can make it in the real world' statement."

"That's a big jump," Cullen mused.

"You have my number. You can call me. But I'll bet you don't have to. I've got faith in you guys. And you have each other. Believe me, I've seen an awful lot of people walk out of here alone, headed down a mighty rough road. Those are the ones I worry about the most."

"Margaret has been wonderful," Cullen said.

Dr. Maxwell looked at the two of them for a moment, but he didn't say anything. One of the things Cullen and Margaret had learned in his office was to respect silence. Every minute didn't have to be filled with words; sometimes the quiet had a great deal more to say.

"You know when you started getting better, Cullen?" Dr. Maxwell asked.

"When I told Margaret the truth," Cullen answered, remembering that day in his room.

"You told her, and she loved you anyway."

"That was the first time in my life that I really understood that I am worthwhile no matter what, that someone could love me, no matter what."

"That's called grace. It's a gift," Dr. Maxwell said. "A gift from God. You are his creation, and he doesn't make junk. He made you into a good human being, and he loves you just like Margaret loves you—with no strings attached. You need to hang on to that, Cullen. You're not healthy yet, you're just getting there. And whenever you start denying the truth, whenever you start to try to control things again, I want you to think about that. I want you to lean back, emotionally, and let the love and grace of Margaret, and of me, and of God, support you."

Cullen Whitehurst had always been a religious person, in an outward sense. In one respect it had been part of the package he had created, his manufactured self-worth; in another it had been a part of his struggle, his search for answers to the undefined questions that haunted him. But he had never really understood the healing power of honest love—from other human beings and from God—until he met Dr. Maxwell. In his lowest moments, when he was stripped bare and exposed to the world, Richard Maxwell and Margaret Whitehurst had knelt down and extended their hands. They had loved him anyway. And so had the God for whom he had searched so long. His wife and his doctor had been, for him, the instruments of that love.

"You're in for a fight, Cullen," Dr. Maxwell continued. "There are two things I want you to remember. You've heard one of them before, but you need to hear it again. And the other one, well, I've been saving it to challenge you when you leave here."

Dr. Maxwell sat up straight in his chair and faced Cullen and Margaret. He was no longer smiling.

"First, remember that your addiction to alcohol is a disease. At one point in your life you weren't addicted, but the time came when you reached your point, and that was it. You were hooked. There's no going back. You can stay dry for a year, ten years, twenty years, however long. Then, one drink, and it will be as if you had never stopped. You can try changing to something else —pills or something worse—but it won't work. You're dealing with a deadly enemy. Never underestimate its power, or its determination to get you."

"I won't."

"Second, and maybe most importantly, remember the difference between a victim and a volunteer. You've dug up a lot of trash over the last six weeks. You've learned a whole lot about why you are the way you are, and how you got that way. You've done a lot of blaming, and you've done a whole lot more forgiving."

"And a lot of people have forgiven me," Cullen interjected.

"Including yourself. You've forgiven yourself, because you have come to see yourself as a victim, just as your parents were victims. That's the key to forgiveness, understanding that none of the people involved in this mess ever really chose to be there. They're all victims."

Cullen knew what was coming next. He knew it instinctively, even though the words had never been articulated before.

"But that was then," Richard Maxwell said, slowly and deliberately. "That was then. This is now. If you do it again, you're a volunteer. You've seen the truth, and you've felt the pain. You know the score. If you do it again, you're a volunteer."

Cullen Whitehurst's hand began to twitch involuntarily; he tightened his grip on Margaret ever so slightly.

"And Margaret," the doctor added, "that goes for you, too. If you ever lie for him, or look the other way, or do *anything* to enable him to hurt himself or you, you're a volunteer."

Dr. Maxwell relaxed back into his chair. "That's the challenge. It's as simple as that. Don't volunteer. Ever again."

Once he returned to his home and to his work, Cullen White-hurst was, indeed, a different person. He and Margaret enjoyed each other again. His attitude and conduct had changed. Following the principles ingrained within him during his recovery, he methodically visited each person whom he had hurt, at least all whom he could recall, and apologized. Each experience was a new cleansing; each succeeded in removing one more barrier to enjoying life once again. Success fed upon success. Cullen Whitehurst was a new man.

He dedicated himself to recovery, throwing himself headlong into the process, enduring the pain with the dedication and resolve of one giving birth to a new person. His appointments with his new counselor were regular at first, and eagerly anticipated. The harder he worked, the more he understood; the more he understood about his insidious disease the more he wanted to make things better and to make amends. Slowly but surely an element of joy returned to his life, and it spilled over into his relationship with Margaret. She shared that joy and for the first time in many years, felt the satisfying oneness of a true union of two lives.

He stayed that way, too, for more than five years. During that time there was the excitement of Bradley Foreman's campaign and the exhilaration of his victory. Cullen was so elated that he kept himself under control, but a nagging fear lingered. His visits to the counselor became less regular. Finally he quit altogether, convincing himself that he could return when he wanted to. He could, of course, but he didn't.

Three years ago, Cullen Whitehurst began to wonder if his cure were permanent. Unfortunately he stumbled upon a golden opportunity to prove to himself that he still could control his actions, that there really wasn't anything wrong with him and never had been.

Ironically, it was a doctor who planted the seed. Hearing White-hurst's casual comments about the tension in his life, he suggested a "toddy" in the evening before bedtime. Just one. Maybe two, but no more. Just to relax. Whitehurst dismissed the suggestion at the time, but the source it came from gave the idea credibility that it hadn't had before.

Then came the celebration his law firm held to toast his appointment to the bench by the new governor. The party was festive. Champagne, hors d'oeuvres, backslapping, laudatory remarks. Eventually the partners drifted off and he was alone in the firm's stately conference room with several admiring young associates—fresh-faced young men and women only lately signed on at the firm; people who knew nothing of his history. Glasses of champagne lined the surface of the credenza. He took one to join in the spirit of things. He hardly thought about it. It happened so fast. But the timing was perfect. He stopped at one; he had passed the test.

He was so proud of his control that he almost bragged about it to Margaret, but thought better of it in the end. She had become a fanatic on the subject, a crusader who still attended meetings and spoke publicly about alcoholism. He didn't want to stir her up. But this seemingly innocuous incident had freed him once again, for he now knew beyond a doubt that he could set his limits wherever he wanted them and could follow his own restrictions to the letter. There would be plenty of time to tell her later—or so he told himself.

Unfortunately, months passed, and the impulse to share his news quickly dissipated. The wisdom of such a sharing had been debatable anyway. Much of his time now, and even more of his psychic energy, was devoted to preventing discovery. He became more and more obsessed with finding opportunities to test his own strength without being discovered.

"... Judge Cullen Whitehurst, my good friend, whose advice, counsel, and effort were instrumental in helping me formulate this important piece of legislation and secure its passage."

Whitehurst's mind was yanked back to reality. He looked up just as Brad Foreman motioned him to step forward.

"Judge Whitehurst," the governor continued, "the people of this state owe you a debt of gratitude, and so do I." The cameras clicked with renewed vigor; the governor beamed with pride as he vigorously pumped Whitehurst's hand. The two men turned toward the battery of cameras and smiled.

The press conference lasted another twenty minutes. Through with his prepared statement, the governor allowed questions from the press, after first reminding them to limit themselves to the subject at hand. Governor Foreman was ever careful not to expose himself to ambush by arrogant reporters. Though glib and quick of mind, even the most agile thinker would be hard pressed to deal spontaneously with all the issues facing the chief executive of this sprawling state. Better safe than sorry, that was his credo.

Even with this restriction, the questions were blunt and disquieting. One of the more pointed ones was directed to Judge Whitehurst. It came from a reporter from one of the local television stations, an abrasive chap not noted for his sense of decorum.

"Judge Whitehurst," he began, "a number of commentators have suggested that the governor's bill has been watered down, by Senator Burroughs's amendment eliminating mandatory sentencing. One columnist recently wrote that to leave sentences to the judges' discretion adds a weak link to the bill, one that will eventually destroy it. Perhaps you read the column."

The reporter held up a scrap of newspaper.

"The columnist puts it this way: 'It has always been true, and it always will be, that there is a double standard in the judiciary: one set of rules for friends, another set for everyone else.' "

The reporter lowered the newspaper column and peered over his reading glasses at the judge. "Do you have any comment about that?"

Judge Whitehurst bristled inwardly. Of course he had read the column. It had been written in response to a case in his own court.

"I know about that column, and I know why it was written. It involved a case over which I presided. I really can't comment on that part of it, but let me address the issue as directly as I am able. Bear in mind that I cannot speak for judges generally; I only speak for myself."

Judge Whitehurst stared straight at the reporter. "I am fully aware of the public perception that judges do not always administer justice with an even hand. That is what the columnist thought, and it is obviously your opinion as well. Unfortunately, the public must get its information from you gentlemen of the press. Rarely do they have all the facts known to the judge who is faced with the responsibility of making the decision."

It was a mild dig, but an effective one.

"As for this particular piece of legislation, I can assure you that the Burroughs amendment will not change a thing. From the very beginning of the long process that has resulted in this bill, I have been dedicated to ending the carnage on our highways. While not intending to prejudge any situation, I can assure you that no person will receive special treatment in my court. This excellent new law will be followed to the letter, and violators will be punished. I have given Governor Foreman my promise, and I give it to you as well. And I believe my fellow members of the judiciary feel exactly the same way."

Margaret Whitehurst and the governor both smiled in approval. Whitehurst remained solemn and dignified as he retreated to his place behind the governor, but inwardly he too was smiling.

"Next question!" the governor barked out, pointing to a reporter in the front row.

CHAPTER
Four

The Cambridge Club was an impressive place all year round. In the days before Christmas, it was spectacular.

The main building had been a private home for many years. Its impressive grand staircase served as the centerpiece of the club's facilities, just as in bygone times when genteel ladies had descended that same staircase to greet nervous gentlemen callers waiting with hats in hand.

Festive decorations of the season added luster to the spacious hallway. Red balls hung from the gleaming brass chandelier; a live fir tree, gaily lit and festooned with strings of cranberries, was set against one wall. Fresh green garland was wound around the polished wooden banister and draped along its gentle downward curve; the newel post at the bottom was bedecked with bright Christmas ribbon.

From the beautiful columned porch, where the city's well-to-do could be dropped off without exposure to the elements, one could see down the entire length of the driveway that stretched nearly three quarters of a mile to the highway beyond. On either side of the long drive, a well-manicured golf course was nestled amongst hundreds of old oak trees, most of them predating the house itself. The lushness of the course spoke eloquently of the wealth of the Cambridge Club's members, who included in their number most of the movers and shakers of the city.

One wing off the main hall consisted almost entirely of a huge ballroom, the most beautiful in the city, host to some of the area's most prestigious events. Across the hall was a dimly lit bar.

On this particular December evening the Cambridge Club was hosting some of the city's most influential and controversial men and women at the Bar Association's annual Christmas banquet. Liquor flowed freely; smiling faces and glad hands were commonplace, belying the intense professional jealousies that simmered just below the surface in the competitive legal community.

From his position near the entrance to the bar, Tony Costello surveyed the gala scene. His height enabled him to scan the milling crowd easily, allowing him to keep an eye on Judge Whitehurst without being obvious. It wasn't his favorite part of the job, but it was an important part. Judges were easy prey to the lunatic fringe of society, many of whom consider themselves "victims" of the legal system. In this community, as in many others, court officers were far more than traditional courtroom bailiffs. They were unofficial bodyguards as well, staying with their charges all during the working day and accompanying them to their more public social engagements. Armed, trained, ready; sometimes by their judge's side, but always nearby, prepared to take action if necessary.

Tony Costello was well suited for his role. At six and one-half feet, his imposing frame towered over the crowd. He had the countenance of an Italian pugilist. Looks were deceiving, however. His battered face and misshapen ears were a gift of nature, not a product of battle. Tony Costello was no fighter. Indeed, he was gentle as a lamb, loyal to his friends, and sensitive to the needs of those around him—particularly Cullen Whitehurst's.

Though they had started out at the same public high school, Costello's career had been devoid of the magic that surrounded his friends Cullen Whitehurst and Bradley Foreman. In spite of a marked lack of aggressiveness, he had been a fairly successful basketball star, thanks mainly to his height. But he had dropped out of college after a year. By the time the Foreman and Whitehurst law firm had opened its doors, Tony Costello had already drifted through a series of unsuccessful jobs and two equally unsuccessful marriages, the second of which was redeemed somewhat by the presence of a son, who was now eighteen, and whose existence was one of the few real joys in Tony's life.

Cullen Whitehurst had rescued Tony Costello from obscurity by exerting influence with the county judge, who appointed Costello a deputy sheriff, a position that paid poorly but carried an element of prestige and permitted the exercise of considerable power. Thus well-positioned in the courthouse, Costello found himself in the perfect spot to move up to the fourth floor when his friend became a judge.

Costello felt great sympathy for "his" judge. The good he did seemed lost in the shuffle. Not even his efforts in support of the drunk-driving bill had redeemed him from the scorn his recent conduct in court had earned him amongst his colleagues. In the three months since that law had been placed on the books by Governor Foreman, in the ninety-one days that had intervened since Judge Whitehurst promised to enforce it to the letter, little had happened to make the legal community change its mind. It was business as usual in the hallowed halls of the Seventh Circuit Court: short days, unending sarcasm, erratic behavior, and capricious decisions.

Arrests had been made under the new law; some of them had ended up before Judge Whitehurst. But those cases had been plagued by the same problem that now marked all of the judge's efforts. Defendants lingered in limbo; little meaningful improvement could be found. Lawyers groused. The press grumbled. Discontent festered, needing only a catalytic event for it to erupt into rebellion.

Cullen Whitehurst, shielded by the power of his position, never heard any of the adverse comments. Tony Costello heard them all. But the more he heard, the more defensive he became, attributing the fault to everyone else.

"Hey, Tony, how ya been?"

Tony Costello quit worrying about his responsibility for a moment. The voice belonged to an old friend, Jake Selby, a pleasant, diminutive man who held a similar position to Tony's with one of the civil judges on the sixth floor of the courthouse. Tony and Jake had been close at one time; they had recently shared the common interest of sons on the same high school football team.

Jake shuffled up next to Tony and waved at a passing waiter. "Gimme a beer. He's buying." Jake pointed at Tony.

"Put it on my tab," Costello confirmed.

"How's little Anthony?"

"Doin' great," Tony responded laconically, glancing one last time in the direction of Cullen Whitehurst.

"Has he decided on a school yet?" Anthony Costello had made enough of a name for himself on the football field to draw the interest of several small colleges, but not quite enough to earn any solid offers yet.

"Looks like he might walk on at State," Tony answered. It's a shame, too, he thought. The kid's a helluva lot better than some of the ones they've signed.

"The kid's a helluva lot better than some of the one's they've signed," Jake announced, as if he had just read Tony's mind.

Tony laughed. "Tell the coaches that."

"You really want me to? I'll by God do it!" Jake said, his voice appropriately tinged with righteous indignation. Tony smiled and looked at his friend.

Jake gulped down the last dregs of the tawny liquid in his glass. "Gimme another," he belched. "You know, Tony, if it hadn't been for the last two quarters of that game against East ..." He droned on, vividly recounting in minute detail some lost moment when destiny hung in the balance, when fate intervened.

Across the room, Tony watched Cullen Whitehurst burst into laughter. Part of the drink the judge was holding sloshed out of its glass and onto his hand and sleeve. As the judge concentrated on brushing off the offending drops, the glass tilted precariously in the other direction, almost spilling out again. Tony Costello's mind was drawn away from his friend's words. The final "Don't you think so?" was all he heard.

"What?" he asked.

"I said ... oh, never mind," Jake muttered. "Where's your mind tonight, anyway, buddy?" Jake sounded irritated, disgusted. "You haven't heard a thing I said."

"Sure I have," Tony said, but he hadn't. For the past four hours he hadn't been able to relax for an instant. Hoping for the best, he had watched an endless parade of hypocritical well-wishers pay their respects to the judge, trying to get on the good side of this man they couldn't stand.

The two of them had arrived at half past seven, in separate cars. Costello had offered to drive the judge. He frequently did. But Judge Whitehurst had refused this time, insisting he wanted to be free to leave when he pleased, or stay as long as he liked, without inconveniencing his friend. Costello had followed in his own car, watching carefully. Although he had convinced himself that Judge Whitehurst was in control, he knew that the judge was drinking again. It was a discovery he had only recently made, and he hadn't yet decided what he should do about it. But he felt personally responsible for seeing to it that nothing bad happened.

The evening was turning into a nightmare. Cullen Whitehurst had accepted a drink from the first well-meaning barrister to offer one. From then on the night had been an unending series of loud jokes, backslapping, and insincere greetings. At dinner Judge Whitehurst merely continued on course, his language spiced with tasteless humor, to the chagrin of those around him. He was inattentive during the program and distractingly loud even during the Bar president's remarks. Dinner had finally come to a merciful conclusion. Now Costello stood in the dark-paneled bar and watched from a distance as his charge continued to poison himself.

Tony Costello was angry, and he was scared. He didn't know what to do. It had been a long time since he had seen Cullen Whitehurst like this. A very long time. Eight years. And yet here he was, right where he had left off, as if nothing had ever happened. This couldn't be. It wasn't possible. But it was happening, right before his eyes.

Costello looked at his watch. Nearly eleven-thirty. Dread it as he might, it was time to do something. He needed to bring an end to the evening, to get Judge Whitehurst home safely. Dammit, he thought, I wish he hadn't brought his car.

A hand touched his arm. He expected to see Jake again, but instead he looked down at the face of Barbara Patterson.

"Tony, can we talk for a minute?" she asked.

Tony Costello was taken aback by her familiarity. He hardly considered them to be friends, though she had spoken to him in court. He liked her as a lawyer in their court, and he remembered her from the other time, too, the painful time. It made her special.

He also liked the way she treated his judge. Unlike most of her colleagues, she never treated Cullen Whitehurst with the same plastic, hypocritical attitude that characterized most lawyers. He looked over at the judge, then back at Barbara, who was glancing nervously at the men and women around them.

"Of course," he replied.

"Can we go somewhere else, someplace quieter?"

Tony put his glass on a vacant table, took her arm, and led her across the crowded room. Pushing open a door, he ushered her into a service hallway that connected the ballroom to the kitchen. It was brightly lit and uninviting, and there was no place for them to sit, but it was deserted. They could talk privately.

Costello was curious. Very curious. "What do you want, Ms. Patterson?" he asked, deliberately using her last name. Keep your distance, he told himself. That's important. Keep your distance.

"I'm concerned about Judge Whitehurst." Barbara's words rushed out nervously and tumbled over one another. She gripped her hands tightly together. "I know you're more than just a court officer. You're his friend." She stopped for a moment and glanced down, avoiding his gaze. She didn't care to know his reaction. Not yet.

"What are you talking about?" Costello asked. "What do you want me to do?" He was more than just curious now. He felt his anger rising.

Barbara swallowed hard, then pressed on. It was too late to draw back now. "Surely you know what people are saying. Everyone thinks he's gone off the deep end."

Tony Costello's eyes widened. No one had ever spoken to him so bluntly. "Why are you telling me this?"

"Because I have to practice in your court."

"I don't see how this will make that any easier," Costello said.

For a moment Barbara said nothing. Then she continued hesitantly, "There's more to it than that. I care about Judge Whitehurst. You know that. Do I really have to explain?"

Barbara was beginning to regret what she had done. There was a cold, angry look in Costello's eyes.

"I've done the wrong thing. I'm sorry." She started to leave, but he took her arm and stared down at her.

"Ms. Patterson, I don't think you ought to be talking like this. There's nothing wrong with the judge. You people have got to leave him alone, to quit saying these things." Costello spit his words out one at a time. "Now, if you will please excuse me." He turned abruptly and headed back toward the bar.

Barbara stood in the cold light of the hallway and watched him walk away. She felt beaten, defeated, vulnerable. But at least she had tried. And she still cared.

Fumbling for a tissue, she headed for the front hall.

Back in the bar, Tony's eyes slowly adjusted to the dim light. He scanned the crowded room in search of Judge Whitehurst. The chair where the judge had been sitting was empty. Costello walked around the room to get a better view; his eyes jumped from group to group. Judge Whitehurst was nowhere to be seen. The first mild feeling of panic gripped him.

Costello left the bar and crossed the hall to the ballroom. It was nearly deserted. The lights in the crystal chandeliers had been turned up. White-coated waiters were folding the massive round tables; busboys were stacking chairs in metal racks. Two women were unpinning the white linen bunting and peeling it from the front of the long head table. There was no one else in the room.

Costello quickly left the ballroom and headed toward the front entrance. The crowd became thicker as he approached the check-room. He saw many familiar faces, but no Judge Whitehurst. He elbowed his way through the insistent crowd that had gathered around the checkroom counter, looking frantically from face to face, without success.

His feeling of panic was no longer mild.

Just inside the front door, other men and women milled about, impatiently waiting to be called when their cars had been brought around. Cullen Whitehurst was not there either.

"Have you seen Judge Whitehurst?" Tony asked, first one person then another.

One lawyer, somewhat miffed at being interrupted, gave bad news.

"He left. Bulled his way ahead of everybody, as usual." Costello bristled at the caustic remark. The lawyer turned back to his conversation. Costello rushed toward the leaded-glass front doors. Little brass bells on a large Christmas wreath tinkled sharply as he pulled one open. Outside, a doorman busily directed traffic as young men, hired for the occasion, hustled automobiles for the departing guests.

As he stepped out on the porch, Tony bumped hard against a woman. He turned to apologize; it was Barbara Patterson. She stared at him but didn't speak.

"Have you seen—"

"The judge has left," Barbara interjected.

Costello turned and caught sight of the familiar judicial license plate on the back of Judge Whitehurst's Lincoln Town Car as it started down the long drive. He watched in despair as the red taillights trailed off down the driveway. The headlights cut twin pathways through the falling snow.

"Oh, shit," Costello muttered audibly.

"I beg you pardon?" the doorman responded.

Costello's face reddened. "I'm sorry." Gathering his wits, he made a decision. "Look, I'm in a hurry. I need to catch Judge Whitehurst. If you will just give me my keys and tell me where my car is ..." He fumbled in his pocket for some change to give the doorman.

"Certainly, sir," the doorman replied, taking the tip. "One moment." Costello pulled his suit jacket together in the front to ward off the chill as the doorman fumbled in the cabinet where the keys were kept. There was no time to worry about his topcoat now; he would never get it quickly enough with that crowd ahead of him.

The doorman returned with the keys. "Space fourteen. Over there in the front lot." He pointed toward a parking lot hidden by hedges.

"I'll find it." Costello took the keys. "Thanks a lot." He stepped briskly down the granite stairs and out onto the driveway. He looked down the long drive. It was empty. Judge Whitehurst had turned out onto the highway. Then Tony glanced at his watch. It was eleven forty-five. He broke into a run and headed toward the parking lot.

CHAPTER

Five

From his place behind the counter, nestled into the corner by the only entrance, Randy Beckett could see all of the parking area as well as the entire interior of the small drive-in market. Fish-eye mirrors mounted near the ceiling enabled him to keep his eye on all three aisles at once. The store was designed to allow one person to run the checkout and still catch shoplifters in the act. During his two years of employment, Randy Beckett had never even come close to catching anyone in such an act. At the moment there wasn't even anyone in the store to be suspicious of. No one had come in for more than an hour, ever since the snow had started falling.

Randy looked out over the paved parking area, past the gas pumps, to the deserted pavement where State Highway 40 intersected County Road 8. They were equally empty. The shiny black surface of the road contrasted starkly with the whiteness everywhere else. A thin sheet of powdery snow covered the parking lot and grassy fields across the highway; everything seemed to glow with newly adorned whiteness. The snow had started falling earlier in the evening. Now, as midnight approached, the usually sparse traffic in this remote area was even lighter than usual. Anyone with any sense was staying indoors. The temperature was dropping. It was going to get worse.

Randy was lonely and bored. He looked up at the tawdry beer clock that hung over the coolers lining the back wall. He could barely see the hands as they made their way around its face. A picture of snowcapped mountains occupied the center of the plastic master-piece. He looked down at his watch to confirm the time. It was quarter till midnight.

This is the pits, he told himself as he slid off the stool. I'm going home. Nobody's coming here in the next fifteen minutes, and nobody will care.

Just then the telephone rang. He knew who it would be before he picked up the receiver.

Lynn Beckett called every evening at that hour. The conver-sation was always the same. She would ask him to come on home, and he would promise that he would. She would warn him to be careful, and he would feign surprise, saying he had forgotten all about using care, but thanks to her warning, now he would do so. Then they would laugh. Laughter was the hallmark of their lives together.

Lynn hated her husband's job. Convenience-market robberies were common, and every report of one on the news made her feel that much worse. But for Randy it was a godsend. The hours were late and long, but it enabled him to support his family and still have time to keep up with his studies. He was in his last year at City College. Many an evening during the last two years had been spent behind that counter, attending to the needs of an occasional cus-tomer and hitting the books between interruptions. It was the best setup he could have hoped for, at least when school was in session.

But on nights such as this, between semesters, with no custom-ers and no need to study, it was an exercise in boredom. He picked up the pay phone's receiver on the third ring.

"Luigi's Bar and Grille," he said in an affected Italian accent. "Luigi speaking." It was another old joke. Knowing it had to be her, he almost always answered in some fractured accent or used some phony name.

"That's not funny," Lynn answered. "Have you looked outside?"

"How could I miss it?"

"Come on home," Lynn pleaded. "It's getting slippery outside. The radio says everyone should stay in except in an emergency. They're expecting up to four inches."

Lynn was deathly afraid of driving in the snow. She wasn't very good at it and automatically assumed that no one else was, either. This was no time for a joke, so he resisted the temptation.

"Look, it's okay," he said, trying to comfort her. "I'm closing up right now. I'll be home in thirty minutes." No need to get her any more upset.

Pregnant now with their second child, she was more on edge than ever. He couldn't blame her. He would have been stir-crazy by now, trapped in that small apartment with a toddler. But that could all end in June!

"Be careful, you hear? Call a cab if you need to."

Why does she think a cabdriver can handle this snow any better than I can, he thought. Besides, who can afford such luxury?

"Look, honey, it's not even sticking on the streets yet." He glanced outside as he spoke. That was no longer true. In the last few minutes a thin white glaze had formed on the highway and the snow was coming down even harder. "Besides, that old truck of mine can plow through anything. I've got a couple of blocks in the back for traction. Don't worry."

"Okay, but take your time. I love you."

"I love you, too," Randy whispered into the receiver, as if there were someone near to eavesdrop. "I'll see you in a few minutes." He placed the receiver gently in its cradle and reached under the counter for his puffy jacket.

Randy and Lynn Beckett didn't want much out of life. A safe home, a decent job for Randy, a chance to enjoy each other—that was about it. They had met in high school and dated steadily until graduation, so caught up in a whirlwind of youthful passion that they had time for little else except each other.

Randy did want one thing. He wanted very badly to go to college. He knew education could break the cycle that his family had been stuck in for generations—mediocrity begetting mediocrity. But he had no money, and his grades weren't good enough to win him a scholarship. Yet he certainly wasn't ready to sell himself into slavery, which was what he thought of the job opportunities open to him.

Lynn had better grades but less motivation. None of the women in her family had ever been beyond high school, and she had never even considered breaking that pattern. Instead she pinned all of her hopes on Randy, whom she dearly loved, and in whom she saw the mysterious spark of success. If only he could be given a chance ...

Her hopes were temporarily shattered the day after graduation when Randy announced he had joined the navy. At the time she couldn't see it the way he did, as a means to an end. She saw only a broken dream. A week later, her heart full of uncertainty, they were married in a hastily arranged ceremony.

Lynn now saw the value of their years in the service. Armed with his experience, training, and benefits, Randy had placed himself back on the track that had been all but closed to him four years earlier. He enrolled in college. His family was growing, and thanks to the study time afforded by his night job at Simpson's 7-Eleven, he would graduate with honors in another six months. This was going to be a nice Christmas.

The freezing wind bit into Randy's cheeks as he slid across the parking lot toward the gas pumps. He closed and locked the rack that held the oilcans, then tried in vain to read the meters on the pumps. The brisk wind flipped up the papers on his clipboard; little flakes of snow landed on his glasses and quickly melted. It was nearly too dark to see, much less to write. With one gloved hand he wiped ice off the face of the pump and tried again. Finally successful, he locked the pumps and headed to his truck behind the store, walking carefully to keep from sliding on the snow-slicked surface.

His pickup started quickly, just as he had known it would. The truck was old and not much to look at, but with the skills he'd learned in the navy he kept it well. It ran like a top.

"Atta girl," he said, patting the dashboard as the engine groaned and snapped into action. He slipped the truck in gear, eased around to the front of the building, and climbed out of the cab, leaving the engine running to stay warm.

Closing up didn't take long. There was cash to count and drop in the safe, coolers to check, a floor to sweep, some lights to turn off. He was soon back in the truck, heading across Highway 40 and straight down County Road 8, toward home.

Only old-timers and country folk still called it County Road 8. For many years now its official name had been Cameron's Bridge

Road. What had started as a horse trail, a meandering pathway up and down hills, through meadows, and over creeks, now served as a perimeter road connecting two highways and bypassing the city.

The new name was originally coined by one of the local newspapers after Linville Cameron had used his considerable influence to have the city build a handsome bridge where the road crossed over Cane Creek. This bridge rendered the roadway passable in all seasons, opening the land for residential development and targeting Linville Cameron for criticism. That expensive bit of construction had benefited only one family—his.

Cameron's Bridge Road became one of the most desirable residential streets in that part of the state. Along the strip of hilly asphalt, with no white line and practically no shoulders, sat some of the most beautiful residences to be found anywhere. Set way back from the road and separated by rolling acres of pastureland, the fine old homes made the road a popular Sunday-afternoon drive.

But for most people, that was as close as they would ever get. Cameron's Bridge Road was restricted by unwritten law and rendered even more exclusive by economics. For the affluent who lived along this remote stretch of roadway, Cameron's Bridge Road was a quiet, secluded haven well worth the inconvenience of being so far from the rest of the world. To Randy Beckett, however, it was simply a convenient shortcut, one he used nightly.

As he drove along, both hands gripped the steering wheel. It was becoming more and more difficult to see. When he had started out, a few black patches had still peered out from beneath the thin blanket of snow. Now everything was covered; only the sharply inclined shoulders gave definition to the roadway. He rolled smoothly along the snow covered pavement, keeping a steady pace, listening to the rhythmic *slap-slap-slap* of his windshield wipers as they swept the flakes from his field of vision. Though nervous, he was at least warm and comfortable. He could just imagine what it would be like to be outside on a night such as this. Randy reached over and switched on his radio. The soft sound of music filled the darkened cab, serving as counterpoint to the rhythm of the wipers.

There was a strange, comforting peacefulness to the night. As it had been since it started, the snow was steady but not impassable; the kind of small flakes that sparkled in the reflected glow of headlights, the kind through which one could readily find one's way.

Most of the old estates were shrouded in darkness at this late hour. He could see some lights to his left, way up the hillside. He mused idly as he rode along, wondering what life must be like behind that fence, up that long driveway, inside that huge old home. He conjured up visions of a paneled den, a warm crackling fire, a man and a woman in soft chairs, feet propped up, reading. That'll be us someday, he thought. Soon he had glided on past. The lights disappeared, leaving him alone with his thoughts. He relaxed a bit. His confidence was returning; the snow seemed to be letting up a little.

"They'll never get their four inches at this rate," he said out loud. He glanced at his speedometer, then increased his speed slightly to be certain he didn't lose traction on the hill in front of him. It worked; the old truck moved smoothly up the incline. He eased back on the gas as the truck reached the unusually sharp crest, then crossed it. As he started downhill, his thoughts turned to home, to Lynn, to safety. At that exact instant he heard the first sputtering cough and felt the first slight lurch.

"Oh, shit," he whispered. But then the coughing stopped, and the soft purr of the motor continued.

Randy permitted himself a moment of self-deception. After all, no one runs out of gas. Not in real life. It just doesn't happen to decent, thinking people. So he assumed the best, as if ignoring the problem would make it go away.

"This ain't happening, people," he muttered. He looked for the first time at the gas gauge. He tapped on the glass with one finger, but the needle didn't move. It hung on to E like an old friend.

Soon he heard the second cough, louder than before, and felt another lurching of the engine, this one more pronounced. He knew what would happen next. It was inevitable. He let up on the gas pedal, as if to conserve every last drop, and waited for the low rumble of the engine to stop. In a moment the last cough came, then silence. The old truck continued down the hill, rolling along with the force of gravity.

"I'm not believing this," he muttered to himself as he struggled with the steering wheel. "I just left the gas station! Good grief!" He snapped off the radio so he could concentrate, then pressed the brake lightly to control his speed and let the old truck coast.

At the bottom of the long incline he guided the truck to the right as far as he dared until it leaned to the side at a precarious angle. He sat there in the stillness, listening to the wipers as they continued to slap out a mocking rhythm. He turned them off, too, then cut the ignition.

"DAMMIT, DAMMIT, DAMMIT!" he yelled at the top of his lungs, beating on the steering wheel with both fists. "How can you be so damn DUMB!" He lowered his head to the steering wheel and covered his eyes with his hands. Then, after a moment, he leaned back against the old vinyl seatback and smiled, uttering a sound that was half groan and half laughter.

"What the hell," he said out loud. "Might as well get moving."

He jumped out of the cab, zipped up his jacket, then pulled the collar up around his neck. He checked the back of the truck. Empty. No gas, no can. Just two useless concrete blocks, sitting all alone.

Leaning into the cab, he opened the glove compartment and rummaged around for the stocking cap and flashlight which he usually kept there. The light was there; the cap was not. His thumb flicked the switch on the flashlight, but nothing happened. He shook it, then beat the end against the heel of his hand, but still nothing happened. He unscrewed the back. One of the batteries was rusted; both were corroded. He threw the whole mess out into the field, heaving it as far as he could as if to punish the flashlight for letting him down. The effort gave him a strange satisfaction. He checked his watch by the dim light in the roof of the cab. He could just make out the time. Fourteen minutes past midnight.

Thoroughly disgusted with himself, Randy Beckett slammed the door of the old truck and set out on foot back up the long hill he had just coasted down. He would head back toward the only light he had seen in the area. It was all he knew to do.

Randy found the going rough. The roadway was covered with a thick layer of slippery snow, and the wind was cold. Snowflakes slapped against his face, stinging as they landed. His pace was slow. He felt beaten, discouraged, and unfairly burdened as he looked up the hill in front of him. He stopped for a moment and looked behind him. Still nothing but darkness. He took a deep breath, folded his arms across his chest, lowered his head to avoid the wind's cruel bite, and trudged on up the hill, one labored step at a time.

CHAPTER
Six

Cullen Whitehurst glanced down at the digital clock on the dashboard of his car; it was four minutes past midnight. That idle gesture, almost an afterthought, chiseled forever in his mind the precise instant when he missed the turnoff at Cameron's Bridge Road.

When he finally realized his mistake, he invented an excuse to make himself feel better. It was because the familiar lights of Simpson's 7-Eleven were not on. Simpson's was the landmark he always looked for as he traveled out State Highway 40 on his way home. Simpson's was the lighthouse, the welcoming candle, the beacon in the night. But not tonight. The truth, however, was that he had taken his eyes off the road to check the time.

He had come this way after midnight plenty of times. There were lots of landmarks, and after fifteen years he knew the area like the back of his hand. But events of the evening had dulled his perception to the point that none of the familiar landmarks had registered—at least not until he had rolled a good quarter mile past the intersection. Only then did it hit him; he had missed the turn.

"Shit," he muttered as he pressed down sharply on the brake pedal of his black Lincoln. The instant he did, he lost control of the car.

Cullen Whitehurst held on for dear life as the tires of the big Lincoln carved a crazy pattern of black streaks down the snow-covered hill. He jerked the steering wheel back and forth to compensate for the violent fishtailing of the giant automobile, but each effort, late and ill-conceived, only made matters worse. Finally he did the only thing he could do and quit struggling. The car took one last spin across the opposing lane and slid off the highway nose first, rolling down the shoulder that rose up on the other side of the drainage ditch, slamming its front end into the foot of an embankment.

For a moment Cullen Whitehurst sat in the plush seat of his car and listened to the rapid beating of his own heart. Time was suspended. He thought of nothing. His only emotion was overwhelming relief. In spite of the cold, beads of perspiration gathered across his forehead and at his temples. Finally his mind eased back into the real world, and the reality of his plight came into focus. He turned off the engine and reached for the door handle.

The cold, biting wind pierced the fabric of his suit. He stuffed his hands into his pockets and scrunched his shoulders together, then turned his back to the breeze. That was when he remembered leaving his topcoat and scarf at the Cambridge Club. Somehow the cold hadn't mattered then. Now, with his upper body soaked in panic-induced perspiration, the cold was terribly uncomfortable.

Whitehurst climbed up the incline and stepped onto the pavement. His right foot scooted forward on the slippery surface and he barely kept himself from falling. All he needed was a broken bone to add to his misery.

Heavy clouds blocked out any light the moon might have cast. There were no road lights and no nearby buildings. Yet because of the snow, he could see remarkably well. He looked back up the highway toward Simpson's.

The evidence of his slide was incredible. His tracks covered both sides of the highway for a hundred yards back. Looking at the crazy, irregular pattern, he felt again the panic that had gripped him while the heavy car was making all of those ruts.

His tracks were the only ones to be seen. Few cars traveled that route anymore, especially late at night. Beyond Cameron's Bridge Road the chance of someone's coming along was even more remote. Few people lived out that far; those who did were hardworking country folk, early to bed and early to rise. Cullen Whitehurst was very much alone, and very likely to remain so.

Way up the highway in the direction of town he saw the lights of a lone car coming his way. It was moving slowly, but coming steadily onward. He eased carefully over toward the center of the roadway and stood there in anticipation, waving his arms. His anticipation was short-lived. The car turned off the highway at least a quarter mile away. Whitehurst's heart sank.

Alone once more, he walked back toward his disabled vehicle to survey his predicament. The Lincoln bridged the drainage ditch, its front tires hidden in the snow-encrusted grass of the hill on the other side. The front end seemed relatively undamaged. The front wheels appeared to be firmly entrenched in the mire; the rear wheels, at least, were touching the shoulder of the road. His trunk stuck precariously out into the right-of-way. In spite of the lack of traffic, the danger was obvious. With what little judgment he had left, Judge Whitehurst determined that the car must be moved. He got back in and restarted the engine. It quickly roared to life.

Throwing the car into reverse and pressing on the accelerator, he heard the whine of his rear tires and the sound of gravel being thrown against the underside of the car, but the big, bulky automobile remained where it was, front end nose-down, like a huge black metal cow munching on the icy grass of the embankment. He put the gearshift into drive and tried again, but that was even more futile. He opened the car door and leaned out. There was an icy rut where the rear wheels had spun helplessly. He was getting no traction at all.

Slamming the gearshift alternately into reverse and drive, he violently depressed the accelerator each time, as if he might coerce the big car into action by sheer force of will. The tires whined and smoked; gravel and mud flew everywhere. Then, his anger thus vented, he eased up on the accelerator and noticed the tiniest movement as the rear end of the car started to follow the path of least resistance, sliding sideways down the inclined shoulder of the road toward the ditch.

"Oh, great," Whitehurst said as the slide picked up momentum, pulling the nose away from the opposing embankment. The rear wheels crunched into the snowy grass as they left the gravel shoulder and nestled into the drainage ditch. Finally the Lincoln came to rest, fully in the ditch, parallel to the highway, its front end facing back up the hill toward Simpson's.

Whitehurst studied this new state of affairs for a moment. Then he had his only good idea of the evening. Forward progress up this snowy incline would be impossible. But reverse? Down the hill? It was certainly worth a try. Perhaps he could get up enough speed to vault the big car up the shoulder and onto the roadway.

Here's mud in your eye, he thought. And everywhere else, too.

He slipped the gearshift into reverse. But this time he didn't press on the accelerator. He didn't want to make any new ruts, just encourage the car to roll backward. With one hand on the wheel, he twisted his body around to look through the rear window.

He hoped for the best. The best came. The car began to move backward, ever so slightly.

As the car began to roll, Whitehurst eased his foot down on the accelerator, hoping he could avoid another skid. Tall dry grass scraped against the sides of the car as it lumbered backward down the incline, still squarely situated with its wheels on either side of the drainage ditch. The ground was rough; the big car lurched and rattled as it gathered speed. Rocks and roadside debris slapped against the underside as the downhill rate increased.

Whitehurst could see the bottom of the hill coming fast. It was time to do something quickly or miss his chance.

He pressed down hard on the accelerator, at the same time jerking the steering wheel to one side in an effort to aim the car toward the road. Wrong way! He had forgotten he was going backward; the rear of the car headed up the embankment instead! He quickly reversed the steering wheel. The car sailed back down the embankment, picked up badly needed speed, and hit the inclined shoulder. Squarely in its path was a speed limit sign that Whitehurst had failed to see. He never flinched. The sign disappeared from view with the crunch of metal on metal as the big car hurtled up onto the highway.

Whitehurst took his foot off of the gas and struggled with the steering wheel as the car skidded once again on the slick pavement. Tapping the brake lightly, he came to a stop at the bottom of the hill, facing in the right direction.

Whitehurst landed back in the seat and breathed a deep sigh of relief. He opened the car door and stepped out to survey the damage. The car was a mess, but nothing seemed seriously wrong. His front lights were caked with mud. He wiped at the lenses with his bare hands, nearly freezing his fingers in the process. He soon quit and stuffed his hands back into his pockets. It didn't matter; the snow made seeing easy enough.

He squatted down at the back of the car. Judging from the noise, he was afraid the speed sign had torn up the underside of the Lincoln, but he couldn't tell much in the darkness. Nothing was dripping from the gas tank or oil pan. Apparently he had been lucky.

He climbed back into the car, slipped it into drive, and slowly let up on the brake pedal. The car rolled forward effortlessly, as if nothing at all had happened. As he passed the spot where he had left the road, he glanced over at the mess his car had made.

"I'm glad to be out of there," he mumbled.

This time he knew where the turnoff was, and he slowed down well in advance. Getting safely onto Cameron's Bridge Road was the last serious obstacle. Though hilly, the road was fairly straight and easy to negotiate in the snow. If he could make that turn, he would be home free with only five smooth miles to go.

At the intersection he came almost to a complete stop, then eased around the corner at a snail's pace. No problem. He aimed the big car down the country road that led to home. As his confidence returned, he picked up speed. The orange needle on his speedometer eased past twenty, climbed to thirty, and slowly continued on beyond.

Whitehurst glanced again at the digital clock on his dashboard: 12:14 A.M. The whole incident had taken only ten minutes. Astounding! It had seemed like an eternity to him.

CHAPTER
Seven

Although the slow, struggling walk up the long hill actually took Randy Beckett only a few minutes, it seemed much longer. His legs ached from the strain as he turned his feet first inward, then outward, in a futile effort to gain some traction. He had seen skiers climb up slopes herringbone fashion, but in his slick-bottomed sneakers all he accomplished was to make his legs even more weary.

Randy looked down at his wet shoes. They were the worst possible choice. The cold dampness had soaked through to his thick socks and stiffened his toes, making walking miserable. But then, he hadn't really made a choice. He hadn't anticipated snow; his hunting boots were back home on the floor of the closet.

"Boy, I wish I had those boots now," Randy mumbled.

Back behind him, down the long steep hill, his footprints cut a staggered path in the snow, tracking his wandering from side to side as he searched desperately for traction.

He had tried both shoulders, but to no avail. The roadway dropped off sharply at the edge, and beyond that his tentative exploration had revealed only thick, icy grass and mushy ground. Slow as it was, the pavement offered greater promise, so he had finally settled himself at the center of the roadway and simply did the best he could, one step at a time.

He slipped several times, even ending up seated on the snowy surface once. But he quickly pulled himself up before the moisture had time to soak through. He brushed himself off and stoically returned to the task of finding help. But now his face was stinging, his feet and hands numb with cold, his spirits lagging. He had made a mess of things.

A few yards from the top he stopped and looked from side to side. To his right was a dark board fence, its creosoted planks offering stark contrast to the white field beyond. Little ridges of snow were perched along the top of each board; tiny peaked caps of white fluff adorned the fence posts that stood at dependable eight-foot intervals. The geometric precision of the pattern was fascinating; the bleakness of the landscape beyond was depressing. A home was visible far beyond the fence, but no lights bade him welcome, no promise of aid brought him comfort. On the other side of the road the scene was no more encouraging. A long stretch of hedgerow bordered the roadway. Snow collected on the hedge in an irregular pattern. The vista beyond was bleak—the black outline of another sleeping house.

He thought about waking its occupants up, possibly banging on the door until someone came. But it was a long, snowy walk up to that house, and what if no one were home? He stood in the center of the road and stared at the outline of the rambling structure as seconds slipped past. He couldn't decide, so he weighed the possibilities again. No, he thought, it's not worth the risk. I know about the other place, the one where I saw the lights. I know someone is home there.

He made his decision and started up the hill once more.

The quiet majesty of the scene seemed mocking, arrogant, as if the wealthy neighborhood had intentionally darkened itself to reject his unwelcome intrusion and force him to find help elsewhere. He focused his anger at the nameless, faceless people who hid in warm safety within these plank-fenced fortresses, self-righteously ignoring his plight.

"Get up, goddammit," he screamed into the wind. "I need help. Where the hell is everybody?"

This outburst was uncharacteristic of Randy. It was also a waste of good energy. His words were whisked away by an unfeeling wind.

Actually, he had made the better decision, and he spent the next few minutes reminding himself of that fact. Fighting his way up one of those hills with no sure hope of reward seemed a foolish choice, but neither of his choices presented much promise. But he couldn't be all that far from the lights he had seen earlier, could he? Just over the top of this hill? Surely he would be there in a moment.

He stopped to rest, straightening his spine and stretching his arms upward to relieve the ache in his back. He eased up onto his toes and craned his neck. All he could see was the crest of the hill rising up in front of him. Though his feet and hands were freezing, his body was uncommonly warm from the exertion. He returned to struggling up the hill.

The hill seemed steeper, almost precarious, as he approached its crest.

Cameron's Bridge Road had been laid out long before engineers had learned such niceties as cuts and fills. The old wagon path had simply been widened and paved; it still hugged the rolling hillsides faithfully. The hilltop Randy was approaching was the highest peak of the ten-mile stretch. For three generations teenaged drivers had played chicken here on Roller Coaster Hill. Driven fast enough, it gave the sensation of levitation as one mounted the sharp crest and then dove sharply down the other side. The sudden crest made passage hazardous under ideal conditions. Tonight was hardly ideal.

Only a few feet from the top, painfully close to success, Randy stepped unwittingly into a pothole hidden under the snow. His right foot slid out from under him as his left foot sank into the slush. He hit the cold ground with both hands and his face, then came up spitting fresh snow out of his mouth. Falling flat on his face was all Randy needed. The final humiliation. In frustration he stuck his face back into the snow, spread-eagled himself on the white surface, and screamed. He kicked at the unyielding ground until his already-hurting toes could take no more.

Rolling over in the snow, Randy started to laugh. Cold and miserable as he was, he simply lay there and laughed, his anger yielding to the ridiculousness of his situation. He was taken back in time to the days of his youth, when he and his friends would throw themselves down onto the new-fallen snow and make snow angels by swinging their arms and legs. For a moment he quit worrying about the cold or the wetness of the ground or the aching in his legs or the hopelessness of his plight.

Finally he pulled himself up by the strength of his arms and sat in the middle of the roadway, his back to the crest of the hill. He closed his eyes and breathed deeply, having worn himself out with all of his effort. Then he began to laugh out loud.

His own laughter was the last sound Randy ever heard.

The heavy metal bumper slammed into the back of his head, dividing his scalp, splitting his skull, sending bone, blood, and brain fragments splattering obscenely into the soft white blanket of snow, wrenching his neck forward, flattening his body.

He never saw the lights reflecting off of the snowflakes, heralding the approach of the car from the opposite direction, over the hill. He never saw the dark underside of the car as it crested the hill, then ripped at his clothing and beat at his body, twisting and turning his dying form, slamming him repeatedly against the hard pavement, dragging him down the hill as his arms and legs cut random pathways in the frosty surface.

He never heard the sound of the engine or smelled the exhaust fumes as the tail pipe passed by his blood-soaked face. He never saw the red taillights that briefly bathed the scene in their macabre glow as the huge vehicle lumbered on, leaving his battered body in a tangled heap in the center of the roadway, a remnant of the vibrant young man it had been only seconds before.

Randy Beckett was spared all of the pain, all of the fear, all of the agony and anger that would have been his had the bumper not been so heavy and sharp at the edge, had the first blow not been so swift and sure. Instead, he was killed instantly. He never knew what hit him.

CHAPTER
Eight

Cullen Whitehurst didn't know what he had hit, but he knew that he had hit something big.

After turning his car onto the familiar stretch of Cameron's Bridge Road, his confidence began to return in earnest. As he glided down the straight road, the seconds ticking away, he congratulated himself on how well he had handled the mishap, and how little real damage he had incurred. He took a mental inventory as he rode along, to make himself feel better and quiet the hammering of his heart.

It could have been worse. Far worse. The car could have been dented. He could have been hurt. Or he could have been so firmly stuck in the ditch as to require him to call for help, his condition thus exposed to public scrutiny. But none of that had happened. He'd dodged another of life's bullets, and now he was feeling pretty good again.

Cullen Whitehurst slowly let his guard drift downward. The

adrenaline stopped flowing. The mental fog that had lifted when the car first started its slide now began to settle back in. He turned on the car radio; soft music filled the air. He loosened his tie. The roadway slipped by in front of him as he peered through the gaps formed by the rhythmic motion of the windshield wipers. *Slap-slap, slap-slap, slap-slap* . . . The sound of the wipers was mesmerizing; the scene was really quite enchanting. He always enjoyed the first snow. He, too, was taken back in time to his childhood days. The memories were delicious and comforting.

Lost in his reverie, he didn't notice the speedometer as the needle crept upward. He was glad to be moving right along, perhaps even unconsciously willing more speed. His thoughts were on home, safety, finally bringing an end to this adventure.

Neither did he pay any special heed to Roller Coaster Hill as it approached. He had mounted it safely thousands of times over the years. Its special dangers on this snowy evening were the farthest thing from his mind.

Where was his mind? Where was his awareness? Perhaps it was the radio. The soft music ended and a raucous commercial began just as the front end of his Lincoln crested Roller Coaster Hill. He looked down toward the dial and leaned over, reaching a finger out to change stations.

His eyes darted back to the road just as he heard and felt the loud thump. The car clearly had struck something. He felt a series of thuds through the floorboard as the object, whatever it was, bumped along under the chassis. He could tell it was something large. He saw its shadowy form in the rearview mirror. But his eyes snapped forward in a flood of panic as he realized his car was hurtling down the hill.

"Goddammit," he roared. His heart raced; his burly hands gripped the steering wheel; his mind groped desperately for a way to handle this new emergency. No answer came. No idea surfaced. All he could do was hang on for the ride.

As it turned out, that was the best thing to do. By some miracle the big car never veered from its straight-ahead path. Its wheels never skidded; there was no struggle for control. The path of least resistance was the only safe path available, straight down the hill.

Near the bottom of the hill, where the road finally hit a level stretch, Whitehurst eased the steering wheel ever so slightly to the right, pulling the car away from the center of the road. He pressed lightly on the brakes. The car finally came to a stop, its lights aimed at an old pickup truck that was parked on the shoulder.

"What in the hell was that?" he breathed, as he leaned against the steering wheel and cradled his head in his arms.

Possibilities quickly ran through his mind: Was it a dog? A cow? Should he go back up the hill and see? Maybe it had run away.

Not likely, he thought, remembering the motionless hulk he had seen in his rearview mirror. It wasn't big enough to be a cow, certainly not a horse. Must have been a dog. He rattled off the possibilities, ignoring those that were unpleasant.

He turned and looked up the hill through his back window. What if there was some danger? Whatever it was, it wasn't moving. What if he didn't go back, and there was something he could have done? Or should have done? If someone found out that he hadn't even tried . . .

That last thought carried the day. He slipped the car into reverse and started backing the big Lincoln slowly up the hill, doing his best to stay on the road.

His tires made a crunching sound as they cut new pathways in the snowy veneer. He made it almost two thirds of the way back up before the incline sharpened distinctly and he started to fishtail. He pulled off the road as far as he was able and turned off the engine. Having no other choice, he got out of the car and started walking the rest of the way up the hill, toward the dark, ominous, motionless lump in the roadway near the peak.

The walk was difficult, the road slippery, but he trudged upward, drawn by curiosity despite his fearful dread of what he might find. He was cold and wet, but he drove himself on. Like Randy Beckett earlier, he found progress hard to achieve and took what he could get a step at a time.

He had reached the object in the road and had stared down at it for several seconds before his mind accepted the horrible reality of what it was. His heart leapt to his throat. His blood ran cold. The worst possibility, the one he had refused to even consider, was true. It was a person. Mangled, twisted, distorted, almost unrecognizable, but unmistakable. A person.

"My God," he whispered as he reached down toward Randy Beckett's crumpled body.

He picked up one of Randy's wrists and struggled to find a pulse. Nothing. He pulled Randy's shoulders around so that his face turned upward. Blood matted the young man's hair. His eyes were wide open, but they were totally unresponsive. Rivulets of thick blood trailed down from the sides of his mouth and ran out of his ears. Cullen leaned close to Randy's mouth and nose. He heard nothing and felt nothing. No breath, no sign of life. He let go of the shoulder he was holding. The lifeless head fell back to the pavement, striking with a thud.

"My God," Whitehurst whispered to himself again. "What have I done?"

He stood up for a moment and looked around, as if to see if he was being watched. He no longer felt cold or wet; he was conscious of nothing except the hammering of his own heart as it raced out of control. He was numb with shock. None of this seemed real. It couldn't be real.

He dropped to his knees next to the young man's body and began yelling at the motionless form.

"Are you all right? Can you hear me?" He shouted at the top of his voice, knowing—but not admitting—that his words were fall-ing on unhearing ears. By now his shock was giving way to panic. Almost without realizing what he was doing, he grabbed the young man's shoulders and began to shake them. He was grasping at straws, hoping against hope.

"Speak to me, damn you, speak to me," he screamed. "Don't die. Hang on, please, hang on. I'll get help. Just hang on." Whitehurst was sobbing uncontrollably. He let go of the young man's shoulders and raised himself upright, still on his knees. He turned one way then another, searching for something to do that would change things.

But it was too late. There was nothing to do, nowhere to go. He did the only thing left, the only thing he was capable of at that moment. He screamed. In the middle of the roadway, still on his knees, he screamed. Not from will, but from reaction. He couldn't help himself. His emotions exploded in one piercing cry. Then he yielded to racking sobs that gripped his body and shook him like a rag doll.

"What will I do? What will I do?" he moaned, his thoughts now focused entirely on himself. He could picture nothing but the sudden ruination of all that he had worked for all his life.

Then it struck him. There was one thing he could do, only one solution, but would it work? It had to. And he had to hurry, too, if his plan was to succeed.

Quickly he stood up and took hold of the young man's ankles. Straining like a mule harnessed to its load, he pulled with all of his strength, digging his heels against the pavement. Slowly the body began to move.

One torturous step at a time, he began to drag the lifeless remains of Randy Beckett back up the hill, toward the crest, toward the spot where the young man had crossed paths with death. Randy's arms trailed along behind him. The back of his head plowed a fresh path in the snow as Whitehurst pulled him nearer and nearer to the summit. Then, just a few feet from the top, Whitehurst's heart lurched. The thick snow above him was bathed in the lights of a vehicle climbing up on the other side of the hill.

"Dammit," he cursed as he dropped Randy's feet. "Too soon! Too soon! I'm not ready!"

With a sudden burst of adrenaline he called on a reserve of strength he didn't know he had. He pulled the body into the center of the roadway, then he leapt to one side and threw himself in the ditch beside the road, pressing his body flat to the ground just as a car crested the hill.

Randy Beckett's body was in exactly the right position. One wheel caught his chest and tumbled him over; a rear wheel followed suit, pummeling the young man's head and shoulders. Whitehurst peered up from his position in the ditch. He watched as the car's brake light flashed on. It began to spin sideways. Snow flew up from the pavement as the car careened down the hill, wiping away all traces of the drama that had gone on just a few moments earlier.

The car skidded along sideways for an instant, then spun halfway around and settled against the embankment on Whitehurst's side of the road, not fifty yards away, its lights facing up the hill, pointing diagonally across the highway.

Whitehurst froze, petrified with the fear that he might be seen. But he needn't have worried. The driver of the car wasn't thinking about another person's intruding on the grisly scene. He had only one thing on his mind as he leapt out of his car and scrambled up the hill, slipping and sliding as he ran, half-crazed with his own fear.

"Holy shit," the driver shouted as he leaned over the crumpled body, not twenty feet from Whitehurst's trembling form.

He pressed his face into the snowy grass. It's going to work! Whitehurst thought. By God, it's going to work.

The driver leaned over the body for what seemed an eternity. Whitehurst couldn't resist. He raised his head again, just enough to see the unknown driver pulling Randy Beckett's body toward the opposite shoulder of the road.

My God, he thought. What if he had dragged him over this way?

Whitehurst lost sight of the driver for a moment as he disappeared down the inclined shoulder. Then he saw the man rush back onto the pavement, several feet downhill from where he had dragged the body. He was leaving! He was headed back down the hill! This was perfect!

Whitehurst crouched low to the ground and crawled up the shadowy embankment. Briers tore at the rich fabric of his suit; gravel dug into his knees. None of that mattered now. He had one chance to get out of this. There was no turning back. He knew he was risking detection if there was anyone else in the car, but he had to take the chance.

At the top of the embankment Whitehurst dove into the thick hedgerow and forced himself on through; its prickly branches scratched at the skin of his face and hands. Safely on the other side of the hedge, he stayed in a low crouch and ran down the hill as quickly as possible. He had to get there before it was too late!

By the time he reached the stranger's car, the driver was already inside, struggling to get the vehicle back onto the road.

Whitehurst watched in rapt fascination as the car lurched backward down the hill, then rolled up onto the roadway. The driver slammed on his brakes; the front end spun around once again. The maneuver worked perfectly. This time when the spin ended, the car was facing downhill. After a moment's hesitation the car began to inch forward.

Timing was everything! He would have only an instant! He jerked a pen out of his shirt pocket, then fumbled with his other hand in the pocket of his jacket. Thank God! His fingers closed around a small scrap of paper.

The car began to move faster now. No time to wait! He would have to take a chance!

He burst through the hedgerow, still crouching, and ran down the embankment toward the roadway, his gaze fixed on the retreating license plate. A smile played on his lips as he scratched out the numbers across the paper.

As the hit-and-run driver started up the next hill, Whitehurst stood straight up and began running full speed along the edge of the road, down toward his own waiting automobile.

Near the bottom of the hill, his right foot came down on the edge of the pavement. He lurched sideways and hit the ground with a thud.

"Dammit," he cried out, wincing with pain. He pulled himself to his knees and groped around in the darkness, panic setting in again. He felt like screaming.

There it was, faceup on the snow, numbers clearly showing. He picked it up carefully, wiped off one hand, then smoothed it out to be certain that the numbers still showed. As best as he could tell, they did.

"I sure as hell hope so," he muttered as he got to his feet and started down the hill again, slower this time. He had to go on. If the next part of his plan was to work, he couldn't afford to lose any more time.

CHAPTER
Nine

The Honorable Judge Whitehurst managed the short drive to the front gate of his home without further incident, in spite of his extreme agitation. His heart was racing and his hands were shaking like pine needles in the winter wind.

He slowed down long before approaching the gate itself and turned off his lights, a reflex action in keeping with his cloak-and-dagger mood. He needn't have bothered; no one was coming from either direction.

What he was trying to accomplish was to get into his house without awakening his wife. That was a vital part of his plan. The long driveway was straight as a stick, climbing slowly from the roadway and heading straight for the old white brick house. He knew his car lights would have shone right into the upstairs bedroom window.

Driving blind, he guided the car between the massive stone pillars on either side of the entrance to the property. He pressed gingerly on the accelerator, just enough to keep the heavy car moving steadily up the inclined driveway, which was well enough defined in spite of the snow. The engine groaned as he searched for the right balance of power and silence. In the stillness of the snowy evening, he was astounded at the sound his tires made on the loose gravel that lay beneath the thin covering of snow. Each snap and crunch seemed capable of waking the dead. He pulled his car slightly to the side, letting the left wheels roll on the grass next to the driveway.

Much better, he thought.

As he pulled closer to the house, he saw nothing but darkness in the upstairs windows. Tension increased steadily as he closed the distance between himself and the house. He was almost safe, almost home free.

The driveway leveled off and divided about forty yards from the front door. One branch looped to the right, to a parking area in front of the front doors; the other cut to the left and headed for the side of the house, where a small portico sheltered passengers entering the huge home through the side entrance. Once on level ground, Whitehurst slowed to the barest crawl and veered left. This would be the safest and quickest way to enter.

At last he pulled the car safely up under the portico, pressed lightly on the brakes, and quit rolling. He turned off the ignition and quickly slipped out of the car, pressing the door closed until he heard a click. Then he tiptoed through the gravel to the entrance and let himself in. Safely inside, he leaned against the wall and collected his thoughts. Despite his being out in the cold for so long, beads of perspiration still tracked down his cheeks.

Is she awake? he thought. Has she heard me?

He kept his body as still as he could and listened to the pounding of his heart. All else was quiet except for the steady tick of the grandfather clock in the entrance hall. The silence was reassuring and welcome.

Whitehurst leaned down and slipped off his shoes. Stepping as lightly as he could, he made his way down the hall to the door of his study. Every creak of the old wooden floor sounded as loud and clear as an alarm, but still no one stirred. Finally he reached the door to his private sanctuary, turned the handle with great care, then pushed open the heavy door.

The room was dark. Whitehurst didn't need any light; he

knew this room by heart. He walked on in, closed the door behind him, and headed directly to the cluttered desk. Seated in his leather desk chair, he fumbled through the top drawer a moment, eventually coming up with what he was looking for. A book of matches. He closed the drawer, then reached across the desk to find his address book. Thank heavens, it was right where he expected it to be.

Holding a lit match above the book, he thumbed through the pages until he found what he was looking for. His finger slid quickly down the list of numbers, coming to a stop about halfway down.

OSBORNE, AL—724-4618

"Seven two four four six one eight," he repeated to himself, staring at the number. "Seven two four four six one eight." Satisfied that he had engraved the number on his brain, he blew out the match, closed the address book, and reached for the telephone.

"Shit," he muttered. He wouldn't be able to see the tiny buttons of the phone.

"Seven two four four six one eight," he repeated again, afraid that he would forget. He lit another match and lifted the receiver from its cradle. The push buttons lit up brightly. He laughed and blew out the match.

"Seven. Two. Four. Four. Six. One. Eight." He repeated the numbers in cadence as he pressed the tiny buttons, then listened intently to the connections being made, then the familiar tinny sound of a distant phone ringing.

"God, let him be there," he whispered as the ringing continued. Three, four, five; finally *click,* and the ringing stopped. Silence for a moment, then a familiar voice at the other end.

"Hello." The voice sounded surprisingly alert considering the hour. Unmistakably the voice of Police Captain Al Osborne.

Whitehurst cupped his hand around the receiver. He tightened the muscles in his throat, twisted his mouth into a grotesque grimace, and lowered his tone to a gravelly whisper. He wanted desperately not to be recognized.

"Listen carefully," he began, forming each word slowly and deliberately so that he could not possibly be misunderstood. "I'm only going to say this one time."

As he spoke, Whitehurst reached into his coat pocket with his free hand. His fingers retrieved the small scrap of paper and pressed it open against the smooth top of the desk. He tilted the phone toward the paper so the light from the dial lit up the crumpled surface. He could read the numbers easily.

"Hit and run on County Road Eight." Whitehurst labored over each word, fearful that one mistake could blow his cover. "You will find the subject if you check out this number: two eight seven four seven. Repeat, two eight seven four seven."

"Who is this?" Al Osborne asked.

"You have what you need," Whitehurst growled into the phone. "Two eight seven four seven." He couldn't resist the temptation to give the number one last time. He placed the receiver gently back on its cradle, stuffed the note back into his pocket, and leaned back into the soft leather of his chair.

"Touchdown," he said softly. Then he reached into the bottom drawer of his desk, pulled away some papers, and felt the cool glass surface of a bottle.

At the other end of the line, Al Osborne was wide-awake. He cradled the phone against his ear while making notes on the pad he always kept on the writing table in his bedroom.

"Who was it this time?" Teresa Osborne asked her husband from across the room. She lifted her groggy head from the pillow and leaned up on one elbow so that she could see the alarm clock. "Good grief, it's almost one A.M.," she moaned. "What's going on tonight? I wish people would leave you alone."

"Wait a minute," her husband snapped as he finished scratching out the number. Then he pressed the button on the phone, dialed quickly, and looked over at his wife as the phone rang in his ear. "I've got to follow up on this."

"Follow up on what?" his wife asked, just as the ringing stopped.

"Metro police, dispatcher's office." The voice on the other end was crisp and efficient.

"This is Captain Al Osborne. Who's speaking?"

"Sergeant Morgan, sir. Willis Morgan."

"Morgan, have you had a report of any trouble on Cameron's Bridge Road?"

"Yes, sir," came the reply. "We had a report about ten minutes ago. Passing motorist reported a body, possible hit and run, about four miles east of Highway Forty. Appeared to be dead, but we dispatched an ambulance along with a squad car, just in case. Both should be arriving right about now. I can get you the exact time of the call if you hang on for a second."

"No, I don't need that. Who did you send?"

"Car seventy-three was the closest, sir. Taylor and Crumby. They were a few miles away, but like I say, they ought to be on the scene by now. They haven't checked in, though. Should be hearing something any minute."

"Call them for me, Sergeant. Tell them to secure the area. Tell them I'm on my way." Osborne was standing now and headed toward his closet, the phone pressed to his ear, the cord stretched to the limit. "Tell them not to touch anything."

"Will do, Captain. Anything else?"

"You better send another car over, Morgan. I think we're going to need some help. Send someone from downtown—whoever's there. Ask them to bring some blank search warrants and arrest warrants. We may need them."

"Ten-four. I'll get right on it."

"One last thing," Osborne said as he hastily tucked his shirt under the waistband of his trousers and zipped them up. "Run a check on this license number: two eight seven four seven. I'll be in my car in ten minutes. Call me as soon as you get a make on the owner."

"Yes, sir."

Al Osborne placed the receiver back on its cradle and picked up his service revolver from the top of the dresser. Teresa Osborne sat up in bed. She looked dejected.

"You're not on duty. Why can't someone else handle it? You promised me." Her irritation was obvious; she made no attempt to hide it. "This isn't fair."

"I got the tip. If we need a warrant, I'll have to be there to get it. Besides, I'm already awake. I couldn't rest until I find out what's going on. You know that."

"Mister Dedicated," Teresa muttered under her breath. "Public servant number one."

"I don't need that," Osborne told her, glaring at his wife.

"I don't need this either," Teresa moaned. She flopped back down on the bed, buried her face in the sheet, and pulled her pillow over her head.

Osborne looked down at his wife, her long, slender form outlined by the quilt. She was a beautiful woman, much younger-looking than her fifty-one years. She had put up with a lot during his three decades on the force. He felt a twinge of guilt. He really could have sent someone else. He didn't even know who the caller was. But the warhorse in him would never die. Like an old dalmatian, when the fire bell rang, he was ready to go.

"I won't be long." It was the same old lie he always used. He would be on this thing until the end and he knew it. So did his wife.

"Don't wake me," Teresa responded, her voice laced with sarcasm. She didn't look up.

Al Osborne stuffed his arms into his coat sleeves and pulled the collar up around his neck. He stared at his reflection in the mirror, dragged a brush through his tousled mass of graying hair, then gave up. He didn't look all that bad. And who would care in the middle of the night?

He leaned down, planted a kiss on the back of his wife's neck, switched off the bedside lamp, and headed for his waiting car.

Cullen Whitehurst snapped the waistband of his pajamas. Then he fumbled with the top, searching for the arm holes in the dark.

It had taken him forever to get up the stairs, treating each step as though it were the only thing standing between himself and safety. Gently easing his foot down on the carpeted tread, he would pause, then follow with a gradual shift in body weight until he had managed to navigate his way up. Once upstairs, he had made his way across the oversize bedroom to the dressing area. His clothes now lay in a heap on the floor, but he would worry about that later.

Pajamas on, he crept across the bedroom toward the king-size bed. Ever so gently he lifted the covers and slipped in, first one leg and then the other. He shifted one pillow up under his head, pulled the cover around his shoulders, and lay motionless on his side, his eyes wide open.

He breathed as lightly as possible, staying in one position for what seemed an eternity. There was a disquieting lack of movement from his wife's side of the bed. He tentatively slid one hand forward.

The sheet was cool. The hand kept going. There was no one there, only a pillow and the empty covers. He was alone.

He heard a click across the room, then blinked reflexively at the sudden bright light. As his eyes adjusted, his gaze shifted to the chair where his wife was sitting, fully dressed, staring at him.

CHAPTER

Ten

Cullen Whitehurst stared back at his wife. She was seated in the easy chair she used each evening to read or knit or just to think. She had a good deal to think about these days. Seeing her suddenly like that resurrected old memories; the whole scene was painfully reminiscent of that Sunday morning eight years ago. Déjà vu slapped him squarely in the face; the feeling made him sick.

Her hands were folded in her lap. Her eyes riveted on his, the muscles in her neck strained with tension, her lips drawn tightly together—she was the picture of repressed anger.

His mind raced as he searched for alternatives. What did she know? What had she seen? Did he dare ask? A cold chill ran through his body.

The silence continued. It seemed like an eternity. Whitehurst sat still and forced himself to meet Margaret's gaze without flinching. He knew the best thing to do was to act calm, to meet strength with strength, to act as if nothing were wrong. He reached around behind his back and propped the disordered pillows against the headboard, patting and pushing at them until they were just right. That gave him a moment to think—and an excuse not to return his wife's steady gaze. Finally, pillows in place, he leaned back against the fluffy mass and crossed his arms in front of himself.

He was beginning to feel intensely nauseated. Oh, God, not now, he thought. The whole room seemed to be tilting at a precarious angle. He shouldn't have had that last drink, he told himself.

The only sound in the room was the steady ticking of a clock. Margaret said nothing.

"What are you doing up?" he finally said, in as positive a tone as he could manage.

She still said nothing. Her eyes never left his face.

Guilty until proven innocent, he thought.

A few more seconds passed before she finally spoke. "Where have you been?"

"You know where I've been. I've been to the Bar banquet. You know that. I told you where I was going. That's where I've been, to the Cambridge Club. Exactly where I said I'd be."

"You left there long ago."

His heart skipped a beat. "How do you know when I left?"

"Tony Costello called, looking for you. He said you left the banquet without telling him, and he was worried because of the snow."

"When was that?" A defensive question, but he was irritated. Why would Costello call and involve Margaret?

"A little while ago. I don't know exactly. I didn't look at the clock. He sounded funny, sort of panicked. He scared me."

"What did you tell him?"

"I lied to him, of course. I covered for you. I told him you were already home, that you were in the shower. I even bluffed by offering to get you, but he said no. I knew he would say that. I'm getting good at this."

"Why did you do that? Why did you feel it necessary to lie for me? Why couldn't you just tell the truth?"

"I didn't know the truth, thanks to you. Besides, I was scared. I didn't think it through. I just said it."

Margaret took a cigarette from a package on the table beside her. She tapped it lightly on her wrist, then lit it, taking a long drag and letting the smoke seep slowly out. She leaned back in the chair, closed her eyes, and sighed.

"When did you start that?" he demanded. He was shocked; she had quit smoking years ago.

"None of your damn business," she answered tersely, not opening her eyes. "If you were ever home, you'd know more about me." She laughed, but not because anything was funny. "You'd probably be shocked at some of the things you would learn."

"That's unnecessary," he shot back. "Listen, you know what your doctor would say about your smoking."

Her head snapped up straight; her eyes opened wide. "Who are you to talk to me about health habits? I know what you've been up to, so I don't want any bullshit from you about my body."

"What do you mean by that?" Cullen Whitehurst recoiled at his wife's sudden aggressiveness. He hoped his voice didn't give away his sense of panic. He wished to hell he could clear his head. If the room would just quit spinning!

"Never mind that now. Don't change the subject. Where have you been?"

"I told you. I went to the Bar banquet."

"You left there at eleven forty-five, goddammit." She was leaning forward now, talking loudly, nearly screaming. "It's almost two. Where the hell have you been?"

Cullen Whitehurst said nothing. It was as though his brain had stopped functioning. He turned away from her and tried to look disgusted. Margaret leaned back into her chair.

"All right," she said, breaking the silence, "I'll make the questions easier. What were you doing coming up the driveway with your lights off?"

Every nerve in his body leapt to attention. He groped for an idea. For a few agonizing seconds nothing came, then it struck him. The truth! Of course! Not the whole truth, but enough to get her off his back.

"The fact is, I had an accident on the way home. I slid off the road in the snow, into an embankment. Nobody came along, and I finally managed to free the car. It took forever. That's why my clothes are messed up."

Margaret took another drag on the cigarette. "Why didn't you call me?" Her voice was softer now.

"There was no place to call from." He was regaining his confidence. He wheeled his legs around to the side of the bed and started to stand, but instantly thought better of the idea as the floor began to spin. Gotta go slow, he thought.

"How did it happen?"

"If you must know, I was going too fast. I wanted to get home before the snow got worse, so I was hurrying. When I put on my brakes to turn off of Highway Forty, I went into a spin. It was a stupid mistake. That's all."

Honest confession. Take the blame. Humility. That's it! His fertile brain was finally in gear, conniving a defense. He tried once more to stand; it worked! He was doing great! He walked over to the chair across the table from his wife and sat down.

"That still doesn't explain the fact that your lights were off, nor does it explain how slowly you were coming up the drive."

"What is this, the third degree? Why do you need an explanation? Do you distrust me that much? Am I going to spend the rest of my life justifying my every move? My God, you're driving me crazy with questions!"

The best defense was a good offense. It was working! He could hear her tone softening, could almost see an apology creeping into her expression. He pressed on.

"Besides, if you check, you'll find that both of the front lights were busted out when I hit the embankment. That's why I was coming up without lights on." She wasn't the only one who could bluff. "You would have crept too if you couldn't see more than a few feet ahead of you." He made a mental note to take care of the front lights as soon as her harangue was over. "If you weren't so damned suspicious, so anxious to find fault, you probably would have figured that out for yourself."

Margaret was silent for a moment. She lowered her head, stared at her nervously folded hands, then spoke almost in a whisper.

"I almost called the police."

"I'm sorry you were worried. I really am." Soften things now. Change your approach. She's falling for it. "I thought you were asleep. I even stayed downstairs until I calmed down so that I wouldn't wake you up. If I had known you were up here conjuring up all kinds of crimes on my part, I would have come on up."

Margaret Whitehurst slowly raised her head and looked over at her husband. Tears welled up in her reddened eyes.

"Cullen, I'm worried."

"Worried about what?" His voice took on a warm, solicitous tone.

"About you. About me. About our life together."

Oh, God, here we go, he thought.

"We need to talk. We haven't talked in a long time." Another line he had heard before. It raised the hackles on the back of his neck every time he heard it.

"There's no room for talk when one person is so suspicious of the other that she won't take time to listen."

"I don't just want to talk about you," she said. "I want you to help me, too. I need you."

He said nothing.

"I'm worried about you, Cullen. I'm worried sick. You're changing again. You're impossible to deal with. You snap my head off when I try to help; you're mean and belligerent; you're impossible to reach."

"I can't take this now, Margaret. I really can't." He got up from the chair and walked back to the bed. It was the first truthful thing he had said so far. He flopped on the edge of the bed, let his shoulders sag, and stared down at the floor. "I'm tired, I've been through a frightening, harrowing experience, and I'm totally drained. This is no time for a confrontation."

"That's the problem. Every time I try to talk to you, you consider it a confrontation, an attack. Why are you so defensive? What are you afraid of?"

"I'll tell you what I'm afraid of," he answered, his voice getting louder with each word. "I'm afraid of a neurotic woman who has nothing better to do all day long than to sit around thinking of reasons to be dissatisfied. I'm afraid of a woman who thinks that we have had a meaningful conversation when she has spent the whole time picking me to pieces. I'm afraid of a woman who lies in wait and ambushes me when I am at my weakest, after a long, hard day, and keeps me up half the night. That's what I am afraid of." He stalked over to the big double window that faced the broad lawn and the long, straight drive. He stared out into the darkness.

Margaret's hands began to tremble as she forced her courage to rise. "Cullen, are you drinking again?"

For an instant he froze, but he quickly recovered. "Come on, Margaret." He turned to face his wife. He looked directly into her pleading eyes and knew he had to answer her gently. "I wouldn't do that to you or to me. Surely you know that."

She wanted to know that. She wanted to trust him.

"I'm so afraid," she said quietly. "You've been acting so much like you did back then. I've been worried sick." She got up from her chair and walked over to where he was standing. He held out his arms; she eased her body up against his and pressed her cheek to his waiting shoulder.

Whitehurst carefully turned his head away to keep his breath from his wife's face as he spoke. "We've been through all that once. That was enough." His arms closed around her back; he rubbed her shoulders gently.

Margaret nestled her face into the crook of his neck. She closed her eyes and felt his warmth. She wanted to believe him. God knows she wanted to believe him more than anything.

She pulled her head back and looked at her husband through moist eyes. "I love you," she said.

Now tears were welling in his eyes too. They stood there for a moment, locked in an embrace, each warmed by the other's touch. Neither of them noticed the faint crunch of gravel or saw the car in the driveway until it had almost reached the front porch.

CHAPTER
Eleven

Cullen and Margaret Whitehurst both stiffened as they watched the plain black automobile wheel around the circular drive and come to a stop in front of the huge old home that Margaret had inherited from her father many years earlier.

The driver's door opened. A man got out. He was wearing a dark topcoat and a hat that blocked any possible view of his face. He walked straight toward the main door of the house, almost directly below the master bedroom. In a matter of seconds the doorbell rang, followed immediately by the pounding of the brass knocker.

"Who the hell is that?" Judge Whitehurst whispered.

"I'll go see."

"No. I'll go. You wait here. Could be some nut. Might be dangerous." Judge Whitehurst started toward the bedroom door, but Margaret gripped his arm and pulled him back.

"Don't be ridiculous," she said. "You forget, I'm here by myself all the time. It's a little late to start being my protector, don't you think?"

"Does every little thing I do call for sarcasm?"

Margaret stopped and glared at him, the mood broken. She resisted the urge to respond caustically as she walked toward the door.

"Get dressed," she snapped as she stepped out into the darkened hall. "You look like a fool with your pajama top inside out."

Cullen Whitehurst looked down at his shirtfront. He had donned his pajamas in the dark, with his mind in a fog. He suddenly felt as silly as he looked.

He walked over to the dressing room, glanced at the disheveled pile of clothing he had discarded a few moments earlier, grabbed a baggy sweater and pair of slacks from the closet shelf, slipped them on as quickly as possible, stuffed his bare feet into his slippers, and hurried downstairs. He heard voices as he reached the landing.

The front hall light was ablaze, but the hall was empty. Lights were on in his study. The door was closed. He pushed it open, then stopped dead in his tracks and stared at Al Osborne.

He knows, the judge thought, his expression frozen by fear. Margaret stared at her husband. Her eyes were also wide with shock.

"I'm sorry to disturb you like this, Judge Whitehurst," Osborne said, his voice calm and businesslike. "There's been a hit and run on your road about two miles from here. A young man has been killed."

Judge Whitehurst struggled to keep his features fixed. "I'm sorry, Al. I was in bed. You'll have to give me a moment. I'm really not in focus yet. Here, have a seat."

"I can't stay but a minute, Judge." Osborne took a seat on the visitor's chair next to the judge's desk.

"You can dispense with the title, Al. We've been friends long enough for that. Would you care for a cup of coffee? We can whip some up in no time. Margaret?" He glanced at his wife. She was leaning against the bookcase that lined the wall opposite the desk, staring at the two men. She didn't respond to her husband's suggestion. Her silence was unsettling. The judge turned back to Captain Osborne.

"No, really, I don't have time," Osborne answered. "Thanks anyway." Margaret Whitehurst sat down on the sofa.

"Tell me what happened." Judge Whitehurst settled back in his leather desk chair. He felt more in control of the situation now, shifting into his judicial demeanor almost without thinking. "I thought you'd been sentenced to a desk. How did you happen to get called out in the middle of the night?"

"I'm not sure, to tell you the truth. Dispatch didn't call me. Bob Taylor and Porter Crumby from Patrol Division are officially working this one. But I got called and went over to the scene. It was sad. Young kid, about twenty-five, I'd say. Lying on the side of the road about two miles west of here, maybe five minutes from the main highway."

"What a shame. Pretty clearly a hit and run?" Whitehurst queried.

"Not much doubt. It happened near the crest of that sharp hill in front of the Barkhoff place. You know, the one the kids call Roller Coaster, the one they drive so crazy on. That could be what happened here, though I can't imagine even the wildest punk taking chances on that hill in this weather."

Captain Osborne glanced out of the large window behind Judge Whitehurst's chair. Snow still came down at a steady pace.

"Have you identified the victim?" the judge inquired. "And have you found out what he was doing out walking on a night like this?"

"His name is Beckett. Randall Beckett. Plenty of identification on him. We found his truck down at the bottom of the hill, out of gas. He must have been looking for help when he got hit." Osborne shifted in his seat as he saw that grisly scene all over again. "Poor kid. Seeing him out there, his head cut to pieces, his body all twisted—it's enough to make you sick. I'll never get used to that part of it."

Judge Whitehurst swallowed hard. He hadn't looked that closely. There hadn't been time. He didn't want to hear any more. But he had no choice.

"Any family?" Margaret asked.

"We're checking on that. Crumby is on his way to the house right now. There were pictures in his wallet. A pretty young girl, undoubtedly his wife, a little baby; I'm afraid it's gonna be tough. I don't envy Crumby. I offered to do it, but he said no. I don't think he's ever done this kind of thing before, though. It's gonna be even harder than he thinks."

"Any clues?" Whitehurst was dreading the answer, but he needed to know; he struggled to do what would seem natural under the circumstances.

"Nothing at the scene. The boy was a mess. Looked as though the back of his head had been split open with an ax. I don't know what part of the car hit him, but it knocked the hell out of him, that's for sure. Knocked him into the drainage ditch. Probably died instantly, though that's just a guess. Not much blood at the scene."

Whitehurst was suddenly gripped with nausea as he recalled the horrible thud. His eyes closed, his mind focused on the steel bumper of his car, sitting in the driveway only a few feet from where they now sat. He imagined it tearing at the young man's scalp, cutting through his skull, slamming into the soft tissue of his brain, destroying years of feeling, knowledge, and memory, snuffing out his life.

"Apparently the boy was dragged around a good bit," Osborne continued, not realizing that the judge wasn't hearing a word. "There were tracks in the snow all over the place, a real crazy pattern that doesn't make much sense. But most of the slide marks have been covered with new snow, so it's tough to pinpoint the exact area of impact, or the size of the car that hit him—if it was a car—or even the direction, though it's pretty clear the boy had to be walking up the hill away from his abandoned truck."

"What do you mean, 'if it was a car'?" Judge Whitehurst asked.

"Nothing really. Just speculation. Of course it had to be some kind of car or truck. But I'm not sure a car's bumper could split a man's head open like that," the veteran officer replied. "It was such a clean, straight cut. Usually when a person is hit by a car, the impact is at mid-body. In order for a bumper to do what I saw, he would have had to be almost on the ground at the time of impact. If it weren't for the tip, and the presence of the Beckett boy's truck, I might suspect he'd been dumped there, or moved from one place to the other. But I guess not."

"Then you've had a tip?" Whitehurst asked.

"Yes, that's why I came over. I had a call from an informer. It came almost before the boy's body had cooled down. We have a suspect, and I need a warrant. Two warrants. One for his arrest, and one that will allow me to search his place and impound whatever he was driving." Captain Osborne reached into a vinyl folder and pulled out some forms, which he handed across to the judge. "I realize this is an ungodly hour, but I thought we needed to move on this right away. Hope you don't mind."

"Of course not." The judge took the forms and placed them on the surface of his desk. "I figured you must need something like that. Tell me what you've learned."

"I got the call around an hour ago. The caller told me about the hit and run and gave me a license number. Said if I checked out that number, I'd have an owner; it belongs to a fellow who lives in the Green Springs area."

"Whew," Judge Whitehurst whispered reflexively. "That's pretty fancy territory. Not what you would expect."

"Sure isn't. We contacted a squad car in the area and sent them by. Place is all shut down and dark, and the vehicle in question is sitting in the drive. They're parked out front now, watching to be sure no one comes or goes, or touches that car."

"Who is it?"

"Hang on to your seat, Judge. You aren't gonna believe this. The subject we are looking at is young Martin Post."

"Good God," Judge Whitehurst muttered, staring at Al Osborne. The veteran officer was right; the judge couldn't believe his ears.

"I know what you're thinking, Judge. I was surprised, too. But it checked out. The car is one of those four-wheel-drive jobs, which explains why it was out in the snow, I suppose. Registered to Martin Baxter Post, Jr. And that's not all. I pulled his record. I couldn't remember the details, but I remembered the controversy. Sure enough, there it was. Two prior DUI arrests, all dismissed for lack of prosecution because the officers didn't show up."

"At daddy's request?" Whitehurst asked.

"You figure it out. Anyway, the judge just smiled and threw the cases out, and young Post walked out scot-free, thumbing his nose at the world. A really classy guy, that one. You'd of thought he was some punk teenager instead of a supposedly highbrow fellow already in his twenties."

"Nothing was even pinned down about that, as I recall." The judge stared out the window as he spoke. "There was one hell of a stink about it—letters to the editor, petitions, the works. There was a lot of talk about the old man paying somebody off, but nothing was ever proved. I'm glad I wasn't on the bench when those cases came through. The judge took a lot of flack on that, as if he could make the prosecutors change their minds." He turned a warning look on the captain. "You had better dot your *i*'s and cross your *t*'s on this one. The old man will come after you with guns blazing."

"I know. That's another reason I came out here instead of going downtown to the night judge. I knew you wouldn't kowtow to the old man, and I knew you'd insist on being absolutely certain before you gave me the warrant. It's no secret that the flap over the Post boy had a lot to do with your decision to work on the new DUI law. The irony of this whole thing hasn't escaped me. It won't escape the press, either."

"It sure won't. That whole episode smelled to high heaven, and I said so. There's no love lost between old Martin Post and me. You're right, I want to be certain. Now tell me everything."

"It was an informer, Judge. Called me at home. Gave me the license number." Osborne thumbed through a small pad he took from his pocket. "Here it is, two eight seven four seven. He told me that was what I would need, then hung up."

"Who was it?" The judge already knew what would come next. He had heard this story many times before.

"I can't tell you. But it was a reliable source. I'll swear to that. It was a person I've dealt with before, one I know to be trustworthy. One who's given me solid information in the past. I'll vouch for his credibility, but I cannot reveal his identity without placing him in danger of life or limb."

All the right words. Everything neatly in place. Everything necessary to allow the judge to issue a warrant on the basis of an anonymous tip. Judge Whitehurst was astounded by the ease with which Osborne glibly uttered the required litany, none of which was true. How easy. How convenient. He wondered how many times he had issued warrants before with no more basis in fact than existed tonight. He was glad he didn't know.

"You know you may be required to reveal your source at a later date, don't you?"

"Yes, Judge. I know." Of course he knew. But by then, with any luck at all there would be enough independent evidence to sustain a conviction without the so-called fruit from the poisoned tree.

Cullen Whitehurst looked down at the forms. They were already neatly filled in. All it would take was the stroke of a pen. The wave of guilt he felt was quickly drowned in a flood of self-preservation as he inscribed his name and title with a flourish. Then he handed the papers over to the waiting officer, who had already risen from his chair and slipped his arms back into the sleeves of his topcoat.

"Good night, Al," the judge said as the three of them walked out into the hallway. "I hope you can make this stick."

"Thanks, Judge. Sorry to interrupt your sleep. Sorry, Mrs. White-hurst," he called to Margaret, who had already started up the stairway. She didn't answer; she didn't even turn around.

Cullen Whitehurst stood at one of the narrow sidelights that flanked the large front door. He watched as Al Osborne got back into his car and rolled down the barely visible drive.

Incredible, he thought as he watched the red taillights diminish in the distance. Martin Baxter Post, Jr. Playboy. Ne'er-do-well. Bum. And his father a power broker that half the town hated. It was absolutely perfect. A smile crept across his face as Osborne's car reached the end of the drive and turned onto the road.

Upstairs in the master suite, Margaret Whitehurst was numb, operating on sheer will. She stared with sad eyes at the pile of crumpled clothing that her husband had thrown on the dressing room floor. With a sigh she began draping some garments over the back of the small chair in front of her vanity, tossing others into the hamper. She picked up her husband's soiled jacket and rummaged through his pockets, piling their contents onto the vanity. Keys, change, wallet, a handkerchief, and a scrap of paper. She started to throw the paper away, but opened it to see what it was lest she toss away some important reminder.

Margaret Whitehurst looked in disbelief at the familiar numbers on the note.

A chill crawled down her spine. Subconsciously she knew what it was, but her conscious mind refused to make sense of it. She couldn't understand what it was doing in his pocket.

Margaret failed to hear her husband until he was directly behind her. But he was intent on getting into bed without starting another confrontation. He walked on past and noticed nothing as she hastily stuffed the small piece of paper into her own pocket.

CHAPTER
Twelve

T he most frightening thing in the world, when you're waiting for a loved one's safe return, is to wake up to a knock on the door in the middle of the night.

Lynn Beckett had drifted off to sleep, stretched out on the sofa in the living room of the modest duplex she shared with her husband and their son. She was wearing a flannel nightgown; her arms were folded across her chest, nestled in the space between her breasts and the swollen abdomen that carried their next child. The living room lights were off; the only illumination came from the range hood light she had left on in the kitchen.

Lynn was tiptoeing along the outer edge of slumber, drifting in and out of consciousness while waiting for the sound of her husband's key as he let himself in through the kitchen door. She would hear that scraping sound, soft though it was. Even in sleep she was tuned into the familiar sounds of her husband and her child.

By the time Randy reached the living room she would be awake, arms outstretched, waiting for his embrace. It was a nightly routine for the two of them, as he returned from his long, lonely job at the market. But for now she was asleep. Her mind was elsewhere, lost in the pleasure of a dream, one in which she and Randy were already enjoying the future for which they were both struggling so hard.

She would never forget that dream. It was to be her last pleasant dream for a long time.

From the driver's seat of his squad car, Porter Crumby couldn't see the kitchen light. He couldn't see any light at all. The flowered draperies Lynn had made were tightly closed. Randy always insisted she keep the draperies pulled when she was home alone, which was often.

Crumby was dreading what he was about to do. He wished he could find the place and get on with it, but he couldn't tell which of the darkened look-alike buildings was the one he wanted. Some of the doors had numbers, but not all.

Getting out of the car, he switched on his flashlight and shone it on the clipboard he carried. Flakes of fresh snow gathered on the paper as he scanned his notes, looking once more for the address, thinking that perhaps he had misread the number. No, he was right; it was 3723-A.

He looked intently at one of the numberless front doors. The building next door was clearly marked—3721—the A unit on the left and the B unit on the right. This had to be it.

Crumby mounted the snowy steps with care. He pulled open the storm door, slipped off his leather glove, took a deep breath, then rapped his bare knuckles sharply against the painted door. Once, twice, a third time, then a fourth. As he knocked, he could hear the hollow sound reverberating inside the tiny home. In a moment a light turned on. He waited patiently while snowflakes fluttered down and landed on his cap and the shoulders of his raincoat.

Lynn heard each knock, from the first to the last. She was already awake before they started; the creaking of the hinges as the storm door opened had yanked her away from her dream. By the time Crumby's hand made first contact with the door, her eyes were already opened wide. Between the first and second rapping her head jerked upward, and a chilling sense of panic set in. She instinctively knew that something had gone wrong. Even before the third knock she was sitting upright on the sofa; by the fourth her intuition had delivered its dreaded message to her heart. Something was definitely wrong. Where was Randy? Something bad had happened at the market. She just knew it.

Lynn reached for the lamp switch and turned it on. Her heart was beating at a rapid clip. She felt an urge to sob but held back. She started toward the door, then went instead to the front window, pulling the draperies slightly apart in the middle. She could see a car parked across the street, directly in front of her home, its emergency lights flashing. A police car. Her heart beat even faster as she switched on the outside light. An officer was standing on her stoop. She bit her lip hard to keep from losing control; tears welled up in her eyes.

Lynn ran back to the bedroom, snatched her robe off the hook on the closet door, and hastily stuffed her arms into its sleeves. As she came back out into the hallway, she glanced over into the other bedroom where little Randy lay sleeping, his tousled blond curls peeking out from beneath the covers. Tiny beads of perspiration were gathered at his temples. Lynn pulled the blanket down and folded it at his feet.

"Please, God, please ..." she whispered. It was all she could think of to say as she left Randy's room and walked quickly toward the front door, hoping against hope.

"Mrs. Randall Beckett?" The officer removed his hat out of respect in spite of the falling snow.

"Yes, I'm Mrs. Beckett."

"I'm Officer Crumby of the Metro county police."

Lynn realized she was shivering from the cold air. "Why don't you step inside."

Porter Crumby walked into the small living room. He looked idly around, taking in the scene, killing time, avoiding Lynn Beckett's eyes, delaying the inevitable. The glass storm door closed behind them.

Lynn gestured toward the sofa, then folded her arms and hugged herself, trying not to tremble.

Officer Crumby didn't move. His hands hung loosely by his sides; water still dripped from his cap.

"There's been an accident, ma'am. Your husband has been struck by a car."

"How bad is it?"

He looked down at the hat he held in his hands, then lifted his eyes toward the frightened face of the young woman. "I'm afraid he's dead, ma'am."

No one was asleep in the Post home on Wellington Road when the first knock came. The commotion out front had already awakened everyone by the time Al Osborne brought the heavy brass knocker sharply down against its plate.

Martin Post scurried down the stairs, hastily tied the sash of his velour robe, then opened the heavy front door as he switched on the porch light. He glared into the face of Captain Osborne, then looked past the veteran officer to the scene in his front yard. Three squad cars were lined up in the driveway, followed by a large van marked "Mobile Laboratory." A spotlight from the top of the van shone on the jeep his son had left parked in the drive; several officers milled around it, as if ready to pounce at a given signal. Two other officers stood on the porch behind Captain Osborne. Flashing blue lights bathed the scene in an eerie, intermittent light.

"What in the hell is going on?" Martin Post growled.

"I'm Captain Osborne of the Metro police. I want to talk with Baxter Post." Osborne had his identification out in front of him. "Is he here?"

"What do you want to talk to him about? And what are all those men doing in my yard?" Martin Post glared at the officer. "You had better know what you are up to, Osborne. If this is some grotesque mistake on your part, you'll never hear the end of it."

"There's no mistake, Mr. Post," Osborne told him, somewhat surprised that Martin Post had caught his name. "You'll be making one if you hinder this investigation, however. Now, where is your son?"

"Baxter isn't here," Post growled. "What are you investigating? I demand an answer."

"There's been a hit and run on Cameron's Bridge Road. I have a search warrant, Mr. Post. Don't get in my way." Captain Osborne stepped inside the front hall and looked around at the lavishly furnished interior of the Post home. As he spoke, he reached inside his breast pocket, pulled out a folded sheet of paper, and started to open it up.

"Let me see that," Post barked, snatching the paper out of Osborne's hand. He snapped the document open with a flick of one wrist while his other hand pulled down his reading glasses from their perch on top of his head.

"It's a good warrant," Osborne snapped back. "Good as gold. And while you're at it, read this one too." The officer handed a second folded document to the flustered patriarch of the Post family. "It's an order allowing me to search and impound that jeep out front." Captain Osborne stepped back out onto the porch. "Okay, fellas, have at it," he called out. Several men closed in on the vehicle.

"Now, Mr. Post," Osborne said as he returned to face the bewildered old man, "do you want to cooperate, or shall I just tell my men to come on in and turn this place upside down?"

"Baxter's not here," Martin Post stammered. "I told you that. I don't know where he is."

"Look, Mr. Post, my patience is wearing thin. That's your son's jeep out there. If he were gone, it would be gone too. Now, I am going to give you five minutes. Then you're going to tell me where he is, or I'm going to take you downtown and charge you with obstructing justice. It's your choice."

Martin Post stared indignantly at this officer who had dared to intrude upon his family's privacy.

"You'll live to regret this," he whispered between tightly clenched teeth. "You'll rue the day you came in here and talked to me like that, giving me an ultimatum! I'll show you what an ultimatum is!" He wheeled around and walked toward the small telephone table at the rear of the entrance hall.

"That's all right, Dad," Baxter Post said softly as he came down the staircase. "You don't have to call anybody." He was fully dressed. His mother stood on the landing behind him, clutching a robe around her body, her forehead deeply furrowed.

"Goddammit, boy, why didn't you stay upstairs like I told you to," Martin Post hissed at his son.

Al Osborne met the young man at the bottom of the stairs. "Are you Martin Baxter Post, Jr.?"

"Yes, I am." His voice held not a trace of arrogance or cockiness. He thrust his wrists out in front of him in an awkward gesture, then let them drop as Captain Osborne pulled a small plastic card from his pocket.

"Mr. Post, you are under investigation for suspicion of vehicular homicide, leaving the scene, hit and run. I want to ask you some questions. You don't have to answer them. You have a right to remain silent. If you choose to make a statement, anything you say can and will be used against you in a court of law."

"We know all that," Martin Post said as he pushed himself in between his son and the officer. "Baxter, what is this all about? Vehicular homicide? My God, boy, what is this about? Arlene, get Jason McCarthy on the line. His number is in the Rolodex on my desk. Quickly!" He glared at his wife. She didn't move.

Baxter Post stepped around his father and continued to look straight at Captain Osborne. His expression never changed.

"Why are you reading me my rights if I'm not under arrest?"

"Because if my men find what I think they will find, you are going to be under arrest soon enough." Then Osborne looked back down at the plastic card and continued, "You have a right to counsel—"

"Damn right he does, and we're getting one, too," Martin Post barked, training his angry eyes first on his son, then on the officer.

"I've got one," Baxter said calmly. "Barbara Patterson."

"Who the hell is that?" Martin Post said, pulling his son aside. Then he lowered his voice to a whisper. "Look, boy, if you need a lawyer, I'll arrange it, you understand? I'm not having any unknown handling my family's affairs. You understand that?" Martin Post's finger thumped against his son's chest. "Now, you keep your god-damned mouth shut and let me handle this."

Baxter Post looked at his father, then turned back toward Al Osborne. "I've got a lawyer. Barbara Patterson. I called her before I came downstairs. She's on her way over. She told me not to say anything until she got here."

Martin Post's eyes widened and his jaw dropped open. "I don't believe this," he finally said.

Captain Osborne pointed toward the living room sofa. "All right, son. Just have a seat and we'll wait until she gets here. We have plenty to do. My lab people are going to take a sample of your blood. We can do that in here, or you can step out to the van. I don't care which."

"What about my lawyer?" the young man asked.

"We've got a right to take a blood sample whether you say anything or not. You are a prime suspect. That's the law."

Arlene Post stepped down into the hallway. "Is all of this really necessary?" Her eyes were red, but her voice was calm and her words deliberate. "Whatever has happened, my son isn't a criminal.

Surely you know that." She brushed back a wisp of hair, then folded her arms tightly across her chest. "Please tell us what this is about."

"There's been a hit and run on Cameron's Bridge Road, Mrs. Post. A young man was killed." Baxter closed his eyes and took a deep breath as the officer continued. "We received a tip that your son was involved."

"From whom?" Mrs. Post asked, looking at her son.

"I can't say, ma'am."

"Typical government bullshit," Martin Post interjected. "Storm troopers take over your home in the middle of the night, but they won't tell you who your accuser is." He turned to his wife. "Arlene, please stay out of this. Let me handle it."

"Mrs. Post," Osborne went on, "I have a search warrant. I'm going to have to search this house, and especially your son's room. I know this is difficult, and I don't want to make it any worse than it has to be. If you want to cooperate, tell me now."

Arlene Post swallowed hard. "Come with me." She turned and started back up the stairs.

Al Osborne motioned for the two other officers to follow her. A white-coated technician brought in a small tray holding several bottles, some gauze, and a syringe. He followed Baxter to the couch. Martin Post retreated once more to the telephone. This time he began thumbing through the phone book.

Al Osborne stepped back out onto the porch and took a deep breath, filling his lungs with the cold, clear air. It was going to be a long, long night. He stuffed his hands in his coat pockets, then walked over to the jeep, where several men with flashlights worked feverishly.

"Anything yet?" he asked one of them.

"So far we've found a nearly empty pocket flask under the front seat, with what appears to be gin or vodka in it, and some material fragments hanging on to the underside of the front bumper. We called for a wrecker and some jacks so we can lift this thing up and get under it. I'm afraid if we tow it, we'll lose whatever's there."

"I've found something else," another technician called. He came to Osborne's side, holding up a small plastic bag. "I scraped this off the bumper."

"Looks like mud," Osborne said, peering into the pouch.

"More than that. Mixed in with that mud is hair. Can't tell for sure yet, but I'd just about bet it's human hair."

Al Osborne closed his eyes as the image of Randy Beckett, lying twisted and mangled on the cold pavement, flashed across his mind.

"Tell your men to keep at it," he said to the technician. "I've got another job to do." He pulled the plastic card out of his pocket again, reached around behind himself and unfastened the handcuffs that were clipped to his belt loop, took one last breath of fresh air, and headed back into the Post home.

CHAPTER
Thirteen

It was the next morning, well after dawn, before Barbara Patterson was finally able to spend any time alone with her new client.

She and Baxter Post had been friends for the better part of nine years. They had attended the state university together, until he had left at the end of his freshman year. His departure from the bustling school had been no surprise. It was his presence in the first place that had caused a lifting of eyebrows all over campus.

Baxter Post was born and bred within a few miles of the family's present home. After an uneventful trip through the lower grades, he attended Winfield Academy, an exclusive boys' school located on the southern edge of town, on a campus that would put some colleges to shame. It was where all the sons of the city's elite received their college preparation, starting them on their way toward filling their fathers' shoes. It was the only place for a young man such as Baxter to be.

Young Baxter Post fit the pattern perfectly. Scion of a wealthy family, possessed of natural charm and good looks, brought up in the "right" way amongst all the "right" people, he was the ideal Winfield student, save for one damning characteristic. He hated himself, and he hated what his father expected him to be; what the old man *demanded* that he be.

He attended Winfield just as he was supposed to do, but he was determined to fail.

Baxter saw more of the administrative suite than he did of the classroom. His boyish grin and manly good looks carried him only so far. As the years rolled by, his teachers tired of his arrogance, his absenteeism, and his lack of effort. Finally, during the spring of his senior year, he got what he wanted, though he never would have admitted it to be his goal. He was expelled.

Over the next two months it was Martin Post's face that was seen regularly in the administrative suite of Winfield Academy, rather than that of his son. Endless meetings were held. Voices were raised behind closed doors. Teachers were shuffled in and out, their faces reflecting concern as they entered, flushed with anger as they left. Martin Post, frustrated, embarrassed, and fast running out of ideas, finally played his trump in the waning days of the school term.

On the third day of June, Martin Baxter Post, Jr., walked across the platform at Winfield Academy's ninety-fifth commencement and received his diploma, to the delight of his parents and the undisguised disgust of his classmates.

On the fifth day of June, the raucous sound of bulldozers filled the campus as work commenced on the new science building that the headmaster had wanted for so long, the very science center that, as it turned out, would eventually be named for that headmaster. On the tenth day of June, the school office received in the mail the diplomas of all six graduating members of the school's Honor Council. It was a matter of conscience, the letter said. Within a short time, thirty-seven other diplomas followed.

His tainted degree safely tucked away in a drawer, Baxter Post enrolled the following autumn at the state university, settling in on the mammoth main campus located in a bucolic setting two hours' drive from the city. There was no need for his father's manipulation to gain him admittance. No new buildings mysteriously appeared;

no new scholarships were established. All state residents who grad-
uated from high school were automatically accepted at State, and
Baxter Post was, after all, a graduate.

The natural result of State's open-enrollment policy was the
need to quickly cull from this mass of humanity all those students
who really shouldn't have been there. Like a huge herd of cattle,
seven-thousand-plus freshmen were rounded up on a daily basis
and marched in and out of cavernous lecture halls and endless
laboratories, along an academic obstacle course designed to be
survived only by the fittest. By the end of the first semester the
cream had started to rise to the top; by the end of the second
semester there was little left except the cream. Barbara Patterson,
recent graduate of Central High, was one of those who went onward and upward. Baxter Post, recent pseudograduate of exclusive
Winfield Academy, fell by the wayside, a victim of the numbers
game.

Barbara Patterson and Baxter Post met at registration that first
semester, thrown together by the happenstance of alphabet. Though
opposites in many ways, they both needed someone to turn to during
a time of upheaval, and a friendship quickly developed.

There's no telling where it might have led had Baxter Post's
college career not been cut short. Yet even though they spent little
time together after that first year, a bond had formed that survived
the separation. There was a kinship between them that bridged the
gap regardless of how far apart they drifted.

Actually, only Baxter Post drifted. Barbara Patterson marched.
During the years that followed, she marched through college, then
through law school, then on to immediate success in her career.
Baxter Post, meanwhile, drifted through a series of meaningless
jobs and continued to live off the largess of his father. It was his
way of getting back at the old man for trying to make him into
something he wasn't, something he never could be. But the "old
man" never quit trying, and never quit hoping. Ne'er-do-well that
Baxter was, at least he had never been in serious trouble. Well,
nothing so serious that his father couldn't get him out of it. Not
until now.

Barbara Patterson had been in bed asleep when Baxter called
in the middle of the night. He was obviously in deep trouble and
scared to death. It had taken her little time to shake out the cobwebs
and get dressed.

She had arrived at the Post home on Wellington Road just as a handcuffed Baxter was being led out the front door.

"I was afraid you wouldn't get here in time," Baxter said when he saw her approach.

"I'm Barbara Patterson, Baxter's lawyer," she said to the policeman who had a grip on Baxter's arm. "May I speak privately with my client?"

The officer looked over at Al Osborne, who nodded his assent.

Martin Post followed Barbara and his son back into the house and into the den.

"All right, now that you're here, do something," Martin Post demanded. "Put a stop to this charade."

"What do you mean?"

"Make them take off those cuffs. Have him released to my custody."

"That's impossible," she said. "He's charged with DUI, among other things. Under the law they have to hold him for a minimum of twelve hours, to let whatever he's had wear off."

"Bullshit," Post snapped. "Nothing is impossible if you know how to get it done."

Barbara bristled. Her muscles tensed. She could see trouble coming. Big trouble.

She walked over to the doorway where the officer was waiting. "You can take him now."

Martin Post's eyebrows arched. He was incredulous. "What the hell ..."

"Baxter, you go on downtown. They're going to put you in the tank for tonight. We can't stop that. Don't worry, you'll be okay. I'll come first thing in the morning. We can talk then."

The officer took an incredulous Baxter Post by the arm and led him out. Martin Post stared in disbelief, his jaw slack.

Barbara stuffed her hands in the pockets of her jacket and curled her fingers into tightly clenched fists. "Good night, Mr. Post." She followed her client out of the room, then walked briskly to her waiting car and left.

Several hours later, after Baxter had endured all the various procedures required to make him officially a prisoner of the state, he and his lawyer finally had an opportunity to talk.

There seemed little to say at first. Barbara stood behind one of the two vinyl-covered chairs in the spartan room. Baxter sat in the other. A gray metal table stood between the chairs, forming a neutral zone. They both looked haggard and worn out. It had been a long, long night.

"I don't know where to begin," Baxter said.

"I'm the one who's supposed to know what questions to ask. But right now I'm fresh out."

They looked at each other. Barbara stood up and paced nervously around the little room. Her glance moved from bare wall to bare wall. There was absolutely nothing to look at.

"I'm sorry about last night," she said.

"It wasn't what I expected. It wasn't what I wanted either."

"You have a right to be pissed," Barbara admitted. "Go ahead, let me have it."

"I don't want to do that. I need you as a friend, not as an enemy."

"I don't know who I was protecting, you or me. Maybe both of us. As soon as your father started taking over, my blood pressure jumped up. I backed off quickly before I did something I would regret later."

She looked at her client. He didn't respond, just stared back at her.

"Okay, you were caught in the middle. I'm sorry."

Still no response.

"You want me out?" she finally said. "Now's the time to say so."

"No." That was all he said, and he said it flatly, revealing neither emotion nor conviction. Barbara pulled the chair out from the table and sat down, arranging her papers in front of her.

"Is he always like that?"

"I'm afraid so," Baxter said, softening somewhat.

"At least now I know what he expects. Anyway, we have more important things to talk about."

"It looks bad, doesn't it?" he asked.

"Pretty rough. I've talked to Captain Osborne. Thank God he's on your case. At least he'll shoot straight with you and not try to be a smartass. But what he tells me is grim. Real grim. They have your license number, and that's not all. They have a ton of physical evidence that they think is going to check out. Blood samples, material, hair, the works. Then there's the blood test. If that shows you were under the influence, you're going to be in this up to your neck."

"How did they get my license number? Who the hell gave it to them?"

Barbara dragged her chair around the small table until it was next to his. She sat down facing him and looked him steadily in the eyes as she spoke, looking for some faint glimmer of recollection, anything that might help.

"I don't know how they got it, but they did," she said. "Obviously, you weren't the only one out there."

"Of course not. There was another car."

"What?"

"There was another car. I remember now. There was the boy's truck, and a car."

"What kind of car?"

"I don't know. I can't remember."

"Describe it."

"Big and dark. That's all I remember."

"Try harder."

"I *am* trying, dammit," Baxter cried out, frustrated with himself. "I guess it didn't register with me. I was in shock, scared shitless. But I can see it, on the right as I rolled downhill. It was facing the truck."

Barbara continued to study her client carefully as he searched through the farthest reaches of his conscious mind.

"Full sized. Kind of squared off and dark."

Barbara waited a few seconds, but nothing else was forthcoming. "We'll come back to this later," she said. "Keep thinking about it. For now, we've got other problems."

"Like what?"

"Like what the blood test is going to show. Give it to me straight. All of it."

"I had a few beers. Just a few."

"How many?"

"Three. Four at the most."

"The straight of it, Baxter," Barbara said, glaring at him. "You were there for hours. Nobody's gonna buy that."

"That's it. I'm telling you, that's it."

"Blood tests don't lie."

"Neither do I, dammit! You know me better than that." He crossed his arms and tipped his chair back, propping his feet against the edge of the table. "The *last* thing I'm going to do is lie to *you*."

There was nothing but silence in the small room as lawyer and client looked at each other.

"Why don't you believe me?"

"You're missing the point, Baxter. What I believe doesn't matter. I've got to know the honest-to-God truth. There's no room for belief in this business."

"Well, there's no way for you to know. But *I* know. I wasn't drunk. Not in the least." When he pulled his feet down from the table, the chair pitched forward and landed on its front legs with a clunk that echoed off the bare walls. "I wasn't feeling it. That much I know. All I'd had was beer. I swear it. I wasn't counting. I couldn't say how much. Who the hell counts, anyway?"

"Drugs?"

"None. I don't do drugs."

"Pot?"

"Not for several days. I was clean."

"Why did you leave the scene?"

"I was scared shitless."

"I can understand that," she said. "I've checked your record. Two prior DUIs, both of which were miraculously disposed of, leaving no marks on your record. One involved an accident where a girl was injured. What happened to those cases?"

"Ask my father. Ask his high-priced lawyers."

"It's you they're going to be asking in court."

"I honestly don't know. He said it would be taken care of, and it was. I didn't worry about it. He took care of the girl too. I never asked. He wasn't doing it for me anyway. He couldn't care less about me. It was his own precious reputation he was protecting. I just let him do it. It was the least he could do for his only son and heir. I didn't sweat it."

"Well, now it's time to sweat. That kind of thing on your record is like a time bomb. It's going to blow up all over you."

Baxter rose from his chair and walked to the one small window set in the institutional-green wall. He stared through the dusty glass at the street below, the street that ran between the municipal jail building where the two of them sat now, and the municipal court-house, where his future would ultimately be decided.

"There's one question that you haven't asked me yet." He still stared out the window.

"What's that?"

"You haven't asked me if I killed that guy. Don't you think that's important?"

Barbara's face flushed.

"Did you?"

"I hit him. I know that. But he never was there. I mean, I never saw him in front of me, you know? I was looking. I wasn't drunk. I knew what was going on. I was being careful. It was a mess out on that road. The only way to drive was to go slow and look straight ahead. If he had been standing in front of my car, there is no way I would have missed him. I'm telling you the truth. He wasn't there."

"What *did* you see?"

"Nothing. That's the point. I came over the hill, the same hill I've topped a hundred times. I came over it and felt this terrible bump. I almost didn't stop, but then I thought, what if I had hit somebody's dog or something, and someone saw me?"

"So you stopped?"

"Yeah, I stopped. I guess my conscience got to me, whatever is left of it. I cared. So I stopped. It didn't take me long because I wasn't going fast. I slid some, but I stopped. When I saw what I had hit ..."

Baxter walked back to the chair and sat down facing Barbara. He took her hands in his. Tears were gathering in his eyes.

"Barbara, you've got to help me. I didn't do this. That's why I called you. My father's lawyers wouldn't care whether I did it or not. They would just look for somebody to pay off. But that's not what I need. I need someone who believes me. I need a friend. You've got to find out what happened. I don't know how that guy got there. I don't know who else was out there. I know I hit the guy, and I know I panicked and left the scene, but I swear to God he was never in front of my car. Never. It just didn't happen."

Barbara Patterson leaned forward and threw her arms around Baxter. She held him close as he surrendered to the sweet release of racking sobs.

"Can you help me?" Baxter pleaded.

"Of course I'll try. I'll try my best. I promise you that."

Baxter Post pulled away. He held his face in his hand for a while, then rubbed at his weary eyes while his friend and counselor allowed him all of the time he needed. Finally he felt composed.

"Where do we begin," he asked, looking at Barbara through still-red eyes. "What do we do first?"

"I guess the first thing we need to do is to face up to our most serious problem."

"What's that?"

"If you didn't kill Randy Beckett, who did?"

CHAPTER
Fourteen

Later that evening, Barbara smelled the pungent aroma of Chinese food as she climbed the stairs toward the entrance to her second-floor apartment. She could feel the warmth seeping through the paper bag pressed against her chest. She leaned back against the wall next to her apartment door and considered the options. She could put the sack down and unlock the door, she could fumble for her key while holding the sack, or she could just wait for Bernie to park the car and come take care of things himself. She chose the latter. He wouldn't be but a minute. She closed her eyes and took a deep whiff.

She opened her eyes again as soon as she heard the door open at the bottom of the stairs.

"Come on," she called out. "This stuff's getting cold." She smiled as Bernie bounced up the stairs toward her.

"I thought you'd have had the table set and the wine uncorked by now," he said as he approached. "Whatcha waiting for?"

"My key is in here," Barbara said, extending one arm out toward him. He opened the dangling purse and fumbled around until he found a key chain. "It's the big one." She watched him flip through the keys until he had the right one. "That's it."

"You know, of course, that if you'd given me a key to this place like I asked you to, we'd be in by now."

"I can handle the wait," Barbara said with a smile as she walked into the dark apartment. "If I gave you a key, I'd have to sleep with a club at my side." She kicked the door shut behind her.

"A relationship clearly based on trust," he mused as he threw his jacket on the couch.

"We have no relationship," Barbara quickly interjected. "Just a mutual love for Chinese food." Barbara put the still-warm sack on the counter in the small kitchen.

"That's better than nothing, I suppose. After all, the way to a woman's bedroom is through her stomach."

"Set the table, dreamer," Barbara said with a laugh as she slipped out of his grasp. Just then the phone rang. Bernie was closest.

"Shall I?" he asked, reaching for the receiver.

"Let the machine do it." She held up her hand as the second ring was interrupted by a click, and then by the raspy sound of a tape scraping over the surface of a frequently used playback head.

"Hi, this is Barbara Patterson," the voice blared out. "I'm not available right this minute . . ." She adjusted the volume downward as they both listened to the rest of the message.

"I know it by heart, I've heard it so often," Bernie said as the message ended.

"Shhh." Barbara held one finger to her pursed lips.

The beep blared out.

"This is Martin Post," the gruff voice barked out of the tiny speaker. "Call me. I've left my number several times already." The last sentence was punctuated by the sharp report of a receiver's being slammed down.

"Mr. Congeniality," Bernie Fine muttered as Barbara turned the volume on the answering machine all the way down. "Is he always that pleasant?"

"I've only known him for twenty-four hours. But if that's any indication . . ."

* * *

Bernie Fine pushed away his plate and leaned back in his chair. The plate had been empty for some time.

"This is as quiet as I have ever seen you be." As he spoke, Barbara's head snapped almost imperceptibly, as if she were awakening from a trance.

"I've only got one thing on my mind," she said, "and I can't talk to you about that. You're the enemy."

"The opposition, not the enemy," Bernie suggested. "Besides, my chances of getting assigned this case are nil. The district attorney will handle this one himself, I'll bet."

"You're still the enemy. A very sweet enemy, but the enemy nonetheless." Barbara stood and began to gather dishes.

"Have you made a mistake?" Bernie asked, reaching for his own plate. He followed Barbara into the kitchen. "I mean, do you really want to put yourself through all of this? Is it worth it?"

"I guess I won't know until it's over. That's the trouble. You can never regret anything in advance. Not until it's way too late to do anything about it."

"But you can read the handwriting on the wall. Especially when it's written in bold red letters. And you can smell the stink, too."

Barbara put the dishes in the sink and turned the faucet on. The water ran down over the plates, washing off the last remains of a pleasant meal.

"There are some luxuries a lawyer doesn't have," Barbara said. "Like picking and choosing clients. You get what comes your way, and you help people when they are in trouble. Trouble stinks. Trouble hurts. It's part of the program. If you don't have the stomach for it, you do something else."

She smiled at her friend.

"Besides, I'm tough enough," she continued. "You should know, of all people. I've fought you off for more than a year, and you're as obnoxious as any client I ever had. Maybe more obnoxious than most."

Bernie returned the smile and slipped his arms around her. "Yeah, but I'm melting you down. I can see it in your eyes." Barbara pushed gently at him with her hands, but not too hard. She let him kiss her on the neck and then on the cheek. Then she slipped her arms up around his neck and rested her face against his shoulder, yielding to the insistence of her own need to be held. Behind her, on the counter, the answering machine silently accepted another irate message.

Barbara Patterson successfully avoided contact with Martin Post for another twelve hours after that.

Following her initial introduction at his home in the middle of a very difficult night, she had intentionally avoided him. Her desk was littered with call slips demanding that she get back to him or his secretary or one of his many legal representatives. She had truthfully been too busy to answer his calls, or to deal with him at all. The hours between Baxter's arrest and his preliminary hearing, which was due to begin in less than an hour, had been crammed with activity.

The sudden, untimely death of Randy Beckett had become a media event in the area. For the past two days it had dominated the airwaves and been spread all over town by the city's two daily newspapers. Few citizens of the community had failed to see the gut-wrenching pictures of Randy and Lynn Beckett and their son.

Every small triumph of Randy's young life, every example of his integrity and diligence, of his kindness and concern, was ferreted out by reporters and magnified in the media. By the time the press had finished its job, Randy and Lynn Beckett were a model couple exemplifying all that was good in American society.

The involvement of the Post family had likewise been a journalistic bonanza, providing endless opportunities for editorial comment, both on and off the editorial pages. Martin Post had his admirers, but they were badly outnumbered, particularly among the city's press corps. And Baxter Post had even less support in the Fourth Estate. He was fair game for every crusading reporter in search of a story.

In the public mind, Baxter Post became the ultimate overindulged rich kid, a product of society's excesses, whose very freedom on the night of the accident was the result of his father's ability to pull strings and cover tracks. And there was no shortage of examples to cite, including the two DUI charges that had been mysteriously disposed of to Baxter's advantage.

The comparisons between Randy Beckett and Baxter Post were classic in their simplicity, and in their naïveté. According to the press, the world had lost an exemplary young citizen, one destined to make a real contribution. What it had retained, also according to the press, was something not worth saving.

It was in the midst of this volatile atmosphere that Barbara Patterson tried to carry on her simple existence. Her efforts were fruitless. All she could think about was escorting her illustrious client into court to stand before the bar of justice for his preliminary hearing.

At eight o'clock, Barbara walked through the halls of the court-house, followed by several reporters and photographers. She carried under one arm a copy of the morning newspaper. Her other hand held a leather folder containing her file on the case, plus a single sheet of paper she had just been given. The front-page story in the paper was the funeral of Randall Allen Beckett, including photos and endless descriptions of his grieving widow and other family members. On the single sheet in her folder, a much smaller group of words delivered even more bad news to Baxter Post.

The gallery of the Seventh Circuit Court was nearly filled, mostly by reporters and photographers, even though the hearing was not scheduled to start for an hour. Ignoring them, Barbara tossed her newspaper into one of the leather chairs pulled up to the defense table and headed straight to the doorway next to the judge's bench. In the hallway beyond, a uniformed officer motioned toward the jury deliberation room, where her client was being held until time for court to begin. She nodded her thanks and pushed open the opaque-glass door, then stopped dead in her tracks. Baxter Post was not alone.

Seated next to him at the end of the long table was Martin Post. Veteran criminal lawyer Jason McCarthy was standing behind them.

"Why haven't you returned my calls?" Martin Post demanded.

Barbara stared at him, but didn't respond.

"Why is my son still in jail? Why haven't you arranged for bond? You know full well I can afford any bond the court might set. Why haven't you done anything about it?"

Barbara bought time by closing the door gently behind her, then looked at her client. Baxter avoided her gaze, said nothing, and simply stared down at his folded hands.

Jason McCarthy felt sorry for his colleague at the bar. "Barbara, I know this is uncomfortable for you—" he began, but was imme-diately interrupted by Martin Post.

"Her comfort is irrelevant, dammit."

McCarthy clasped his hands behind his back and bit his tongue. His expression never changed.

Post turned his attention back to Barbara. "Baxter says you haven't been to see him in twenty-four hours, and haven't told him what to do in court this morning. Why not?"

Barbara placed her folder on the table and gripped the back of a chair with both hands, squeezing it tightly as she fought to control her anger.

"I have no intention of explaining my actions to you, Mr. Post," she said evenly. "Now, I'll thank you to leave. I have work to do, and you are in the way. Kindly take Mr. McCarthy with you." She looked up at the older lawyer. He was clearly uncomfortable.

"You have *nothing* to do, young lady," Post growled with all the charm of a pit bull snapping at an intruder. "You are fired. You are off this case, as of now."

Barbara pulled out the chair she was gripping and sat down. She paused for a moment to assess her choices. At this point she had little to lose.

"Mr. Post, unless you wish to be referred to as 'old man,' kindly do not refer to me as 'young lady.' I have a name. Show me the courtesy of using it, and I will do the same for you."

Martin Post's jaw dropped. Jason McCarthy smiled, then quickly forced a somber expression back into place. Seconds ticked away.

"All right, *Ms.* Patterson," Post finally said. "You are fired."

"Thank you for your apology, Mr. Post. Now on that point, let me remind you of one thing. You can't fire me. You didn't hire me. Baxter did."

"I'm paying you, young lady—I mean, Ms. Patterson. As far as I'm concerned, that makes me your boss."

"I'll spare you the details of what you can do with your money, Mr. Post," Barbara retorted. She was in control now and was enjoying the feeling. "I repeat: Baxter called me, he hired me, and if I'm to be fired, it will have to come from his lips." She turned toward the younger man. "What will it be?"

Again the seconds ticked away in awkward silence.

"Barbara, I don't know," Baxter said, rubbing his hands nervously. He glanced at his father, then back at his lawyer. "I don't know what to do. Mr. McCarthy here tells me one thing, you tell me another—I'm just confused."

"Baxter," she said sternly, "we're coming up to the wall. Rapidly. A decision has to be made. I just picked up a copy of the toxicologist's report from the district attorney's office. It's not good. You registered point-fourteen almost two hours after the accident. That's drunk. Under the influence as a matter of law. That hurts us bad. You're going to have to make some hard choices. Your lawyer, whoever it is, can advise you, but the choices are yours. And the first choice you've got to make is a lawyer. Right now."

Baxter's lips parted but he didn't speak. He let his head fall forward and stared silently at his folded hands. Barbara pulled her chair closer to his and took his hands in hers, ignoring the other two men in the room.

"Baxter," she pleaded, "listen to me. All I want is what's best for you. Forget about my feelings for a minute; they don't matter. Forget about your father, too. He's not the one who'll have to pay the price. Nobody else matters but you. Whatever you decide, whether it's me, McCarthy, or someone else, you've got to stand by that decision and accept its consequences. You can't keep passing the buck. You can't let others run your life." Her voice rose in volume as she finished. "Dammit, Baxter, at some point in your life you have got to grow up. Let it be now!"

The room was silent. Everyone stared at the anguished young man.

Baxter Post finally pulled his hands from Barbara's grip and slowly rose to his feet. He walked to the glass door that led out into the hallway, gripped the handle, then turned back toward the table.

"Dad, Mr. McCarthy, my lawyer and I have work to do. If you will please excuse us ..."

To Barbara's surprise, the two older men said nothing. They slowly began to gather up their belongings.

"Mr. Post," Barbara said as he rose to leave, "I think you deserve an answer to the question you asked when I first walked in here. It was my decision to leave your son in jail, and I accept responsibility for it. It was my belief—and it still is—that with public opinion riding so high, and public scrutiny so detailed, it was better for Baxter to remain in jail and appear to be as contrite as possible. So I chose not to ask for bond. When bond is set at the preliminary hearing—which I'm sure will happen—I will decide then whether or not to pay it."

"Thank you, Barbara," Jason McCarthy said. Martin Post said

nothing. His thin lips remained tightly drawn as he followed Mc-Carthy out into the hallway. Baxter pushed the door closed behind them.

"Terrific," Barbara said. "Now let's get to work. Your preliminary hearing is in less than an hour. We don't have very much time."

CHAPTER
Fifteen

"All right. That's enough. Let's clear the courtroom. No more pictures, please. Clear the courtroom."

The deep voice of Tony Costello boomed out over the din created by the shuffling and maneuvering of photographers, and the clicking and whirling of their cameras. By agreement, the working press was allowed five minutes to take pictures of Baxter Post, his family, and the family of the deceased. Five minutes had long since passed, however, and the confusion continued.

"Ladies and gentlemen, please! Let's clear the courtroom!" Costello cried out even louder this time. Still no success. He stepped up to the judge's bench, picked up the heavy walnut gavel, and brought it down on its strike plate with a resounding crack. The loud report bounced off the paneled walls of the courtroom like a gunshot. The noise stopped immediately. All heads turned toward the bench.

"Thank you, ladies and gentlemen," Costello said quietly, almost sarcastically. "Now, if you will please put away your cameras and take your seats ..."

Like a wave broken against the shore, the crowd drew back to their gallery seats, leaving only the lawyers and their clients at the counsel tables.

Al Osborne sat alone at the prosecution table. Barbara Patterson and Baxter Post sat at the defense table, facing the jury box. A small lectern rested at the point where the two tables joined at right angles. A court reporter was in his place in front of the judge's bench. The jury box was empty. Other than Tony Costello, who was occupying his customary spot next to the bench, no one else was inside the rail that day. The other officers who had participated in the investigation of Randy Beckett's death were seated in the front row of the gallery, as were Lynn Beckett, Martin and Arlene Post, and Jason McCarthy.

At the last possible moment Assistant District Attorney Bernard Fine entered through the main doorway, strode past the railing and then past the defense table, finally ending up at the empty place next to Al Osborne. He tossed his file folder on the table but remained standing behind the chair he would soon occupy. He glanced at Barbara Patterson and cocked one eyebrow; she stared back but didn't respond.

The crowd finally under control, and everyone finally in place, Tony Costello stood to his full height, straightened an errant flap on the pocket of his jacket, and watched the door next to the bench until he saw it move ever so slightly, signifying the judge's readiness.

"All rise," Costello bellowed out. Everyone else stood up. Judge Cullen Whitehurst stepped through the door, ascended the steps, and took his place. He stood at attention, just below the great seal of the state that was carved into the paneling above the bench. A young woman followed him, carrying a folder and a leather-bound book. She crossed in front of the bench and stopped at a small table to the judge's right, well within his reach.

"Open court, Mr. Costello," the judge said, gazing out at the assemblage.

"Oyez, oyez, oyez, this honorable Seventh Circuit Court is now open, pursuant to adjournment. All persons having business before this court draw nigh, give attention, and ye shall be heard."

Costello and the judge bowed their heads. Those in the know

followed suit; everyone else stared dumbly at the veteran court officer as he continued.

"God save this state, the United States, and this honorable court," he said. Then he lifted his head. "Be seated, please."

Judge Whitehurst shuffled the papers on the bench in front of him. Then he turned toward the young woman at his right.

"Miss Hamilton, call the docket," he said.

Nikki Hamilton opened the leather-bound volume and read from it. She tried without success to sound serious and dignified. With her lifting, singsong voice, this simply wasn't possible.

"Case number eight five four one three eight, *State* versus *Martin Baxter Post, Jr.*, preliminary hearing. Charges in this case are vehicular homicide, in violation of Criminal Code Chapter one oh two, Section eight eight five point six; leaving the scene of an accident, in violation of Criminal Code Chapter one oh two, Section eight four six point five; and driving while under the influence of alcohol, narcotics, or legend drugs, in violation of Criminal Code Chapter one oh two, Section nine one oh point oh."

"Who represents the state?" the judge asked.

Bernie Fine rose quickly to his feet. "Bernard A. Fine, assistant district attorney."

"And the defendant?"

"Barbara F. Patterson of the State Bar, Your Honor." Barbara stood in place, waiting for the judge's next words. Having been through this procedure many times, she knew what to expect.

"Is your client ready to plead?" the judge asked.

"Your Honor, we are ready to enter a plea to the charges, but before doing so, I have some motions to take up with the court. May I do that now?"

"Go ahead."

Barbara Patterson gathered up some of the folders and books in front of her and walked to the lectern. She spread out her papers, then pulled down the gooseneck microphone to a more comfortable height.

"Your Honor," she started out, "on behalf of the defendant, Baxter Post, and in the interest of justice, we respectfully request that Your Honor recuse himself from this case and petition the Supreme Court to assign another judge to this matter at the earliest possible moment."

A low murmur of surprise rumbled through the courtroom.

Judge Whitehurst brought everyone back to attention with a quick rap of his gavel. "What's the basis for your motion?"

"Your Honor, we respectfully suggest that it will not be possible for you to hear this case without being subject to the influence of certain outside considerations."

"Such as?" Judge Whitehurst leaned back in his black leather chair, frowning as he spoke.

"Your Honor, this tragic accident took place in your neighborhood, indeed on the very road where you live. Surely this would give the court a special interest in resolving the matter in such a way as to produce a good feeling among those persons with whom the court regularly associates—"

Judge Whitehurst leaned forward. "Are you suggesting that I might be inclined to bend the rules or stretch justice a little too far to make myself a neighborhood hero?"

"Not exactly, Your Honor, but—"

"That's absurd," he said. "What else do you have?"

Barbara Patterson glanced down at her notes. "One moment, Your Honor," she said, buying time. Her mind was reeling from the judge's rebuke.

"Your Honor signed the arrest warrant, and also the search warrants. The warrants were issued on the basis of an informer's tip, as I understand it. The identity of that informer would have to be known to you at the time you signed them, or else you would have to have such confidence in the person who sought the warrants—which in this case was Captain Osborne—that you would be willing to issue them on the basis of his word. Now in either case, having either this special confidence or inside information would lead to the conclusion that you are not starting from a position of complete neutrality—"

Judge Whitehurst raised his hand and stopped Ms. Patterson in midsentence. "Apart from your suggestion that I am not starting out neutral, do you have any authority for your suggestion that those were my only choices at the time the warrants were issued?"

"No, Your Honor. It's just a matter of common sense."

"Well, are you questioning my integrity, or that of Captain Osborne?"

"No, Your Honor."

"Motion denied. Your suggestion is simply not correct. I have absolutely no preconceived notion about this matter at all. I issued the warrants in good faith, but presumed nothing. Now, is that it?"

"There's one more point. On the authority of *State* versus *Thurman*, which is cited in Volume Six of the *Midwestern Reporter*, Series Two, we feel that the court's public pronouncements on the drunk-driving law recently enacted in this state place this court in the position of being an advocate for the rigid enforcement of that law. Futhermore, this case will be subjected to an unusual amount of public scrutiny, because of the people involved and especially because it is the first major prosecution under the law that you lobbied heavily to pass. We feel that this would make it difficult for the court—"

Judge Whitehurst interrupted again. "I am familiar with *State* versus *Thurman*. It has no application here. If you had read it carefully, you would know that. I suggest you do so when you return to your office."

Barbara Patterson's face reddened as the judge continued.

"Futhermore, I'll not apologize to you or to anyone else for my position with regard to Governor Foreman's drunk-driving law. I advocated it, I supported it, and I intend to enforce it. I'm no different from any other citizen in this respect; I cannot and will not tolerate the continued use of our streets and roadways by persons who let themselves succumb to the influence of alcohol."

Everyone in the courtroom—at least everyone who had ever been there before—knew that once Judge Whitehurst started in on one of his speeches there was no stopping him until he was through. Certainly Barbara Patterson knew it. She stood at the lectern, looked down at her notes, and waited as patiently as she knew how.

"Frankly," the judge continued, "I get tired of defendants trying to shop around until they find a judge who is so neutral as to be ineffective. I doubt seriously if you could find a judge in this state who feels any differently than I do about this issue. You certainly couldn't find one who could do a better job. Motion denied. Anything else?"

The rest of Barbara Patterson's preliminary motions were routine. She recited them in turn, stating her authority and arguments as crisply as possible. The judge dealt with them in an equally routine manner. A change of venue was denied. A motion to quash the search warrant was discussed at some length, but as she had expected, it was also denied. A pretrial gag rule was not granted either, but certain routine restrictions were placed on the press, restrictions that sounded good but that in truth would do little or nothing to stem the flow of publicity the case would generate. Finally, the time came to enter a plea.

"Your Honor, Baxter Post pleads not guilty to all these charges. We decline to waive a preliminary hearing."

Barbara Patterson made her announcement in a straightforward, undramatic manner. Now the issues were joined. It was up to the state to put on enough evidence to convince the court to bind the case over to the grand jury.

Bernie Fine rose to begin his presentation, and arrived at the lectern just as Barbara finished gathering her notes and papers.

"Nice job," he said, smiling, keeping his voice so quiet that no one else would be able to hear. "You thought up some good ones."

Barbara turned toward the assistant DA, her eyes flashing anger. "Did you know about this last night?" Her voice wasn't quiet at all.

Bernie's smile disappeared. "No, I swear—"

"General Fine, are you ready to proceed?" It was the judge. Bernie turned toward the bench, then back to Barbara, who was still glaring at him. Finally she turned on her heels and left him standing there alone. He quickly composed himself; he had no other choice.

"Yes, Your Honor," he announced. "The state calls Police Captain Al Osborne."

"Captain Osborne!" Tony Costello barked loudly.

Al Osborne began with an antiseptic recital of the call he had received in the middle of the night and what he did in response to that call. Unlike the warm, robust persona he usually exhibited, on the witness stand he was cold, mechanical, and lifeless. His presentation wasn't helped at all by the distracted, obviously preoccupied demeanor of the prosecutor.

"We proceeded to the subject's home and staked the place out. The vehicle in question was in the driveway, in plain view. The license number matched the number I had received from the informant. We placed men around the perimeter of the property and instructed them to maintain surveillance. Then I proceeded to obtain search warrants and an arrest warrant for the subject."

People were never "people" to the police, at least not on the witness stand. They were "subjects." Cars were never "cars," they were "vehicles." Through the years the police in this city, as in most others, had developed a stilted, artificial manner of speaking that obscured all traces of personal involvement and instantly identified them as officers of the law.

"At the residence, which is located on, um . . ." Captain Osborne rummaged through the notes he held in his hand, then continued, "Well, I don't have the number, but it's the Martin Post residence on Wellington Road in the Green Springs community. Anyway, we entered the premises . . ."

Never a "home" or a "store" or a "market." Always the "residence" or the "premises."

". . . and presented the occupants . . ."

Barbara thought she could practically recite the testimony along with him as she jotted down notes on her legal pad.

". . . with copies of our warrants. Martin Baxter Post, Jr., the subject under investigation, was present and identified himself. We read him his Miranda rights. He declined to make any statement and advised us that he had already called a lawyer, whom he identified as Ms. Barbara Patterson." Captain Osborne nodded toward the defense table. "We asked no more questions."

He had called a lawyer before the police arrived. That didn't look good, and Barbara knew it.

"We took a blood sample," Osborne continued, "and proceeded to search the vehicle. We found fragments of material on the underside of the vehicle, which, upon visual inspection, appeared to be the same color and kind as the sweater worn by the deceased. We found other substances there that could not be readily identified, but appeared to include human hair. They are being analyzed as quickly as possible. There was an empty vodka bottle under the front seat. Based upon what we had, we proceeded to serve our arrest warrant and carried the subject downtown and booked him as a suspect on charges of vehicular homicide, hit and run, and DUI."

Captain Osborne then related the brief history of the investigation, including the match between the material fibers from the jeep and the sweater Randy Beckett had been wearing. He then presented the toxicologist's report, showing Baxter Post's blood alcohol level at .14, and finally related in somber detail Lynn Beckett's identification of her husband's body in the early hours of the morning.

Much of what he said was hearsay and would never have been admissible at a trial, but technical objections seldom met with success in the informal atmosphere of a preliminary hearing. Barbara decided not to incur more of the judge's wrath by objecting. She also decided not to ask any questions about the identity of the informer. She knew what the judge would do with that, and she didn't want to start out looking like a loser. When it came her turn to ask questions on cross-examination, she went straight to the points she deemed most important.

"Captain Osborne," she began as she approached the podium, "from whom did you obtain an arrest warrant for Baxter Post?"

Osborne looked puzzled. She knew full well who had issued the warrant. He wondered why she would ask. Nevertheless, he answered.

"From Judge Whitehurst."

"And the search warrants?"

"Also from Judge Whitehurst," he said, squirming in his seat.

"And the information you gave to Judge Whitehurst was based on a call from an informer whose identity you cannot reveal. This is correct, isn't it?"

"Yes, it is."

Barbara put down her notes, stepped to the side of the lectern, and faced the witness.

"Tell me, Captain Osborne, as specifically as you can, what the information was that your informant gave you."

Bernie Fine considered objecting but decided not to. He positioned himself on the edge of his chair, however, ready to spring forward if the questioning wandered any further into unacceptable areas.

"I was told that there had been a hit and run on County Road Eight, and I was given a license number. The implication was clear that the vehicle with that license number was involved in the hit and run."

"You ran that license number through Central Records and came up with the name Martin Baxter Post, Jr., is that correct?"

"Yes, that's right, and the make and model of the vehicle as well."

"I take it then, Captain Osborne, that this information was all passed along to the judge. Was there anything else that you told him, anything at all?"

"No, there was nothing else." The look on the officer's face revealed his curiosity about where all of this was leading.

Barbara retrieved a book from the table and opened it on the lectern. She turned one or two pages, then looked at the officer.

"Captain Osborne, are you familiar with all of the provisions of the state code with regard to search and arrest warrants?"

"Well ..." Osborne hesitated.

"Are you, or are you not?" Barbara demanded.

"I couldn't quote them, but yes, I am familiar with them."

"You know then, Captain, that all search warrants, and all arrest warrants, must be based upon sworn allegations, facts given to the issuing judge under oath?"

Osborne hesitated again.

"Would you like to see the statute?" Barbara asked, holding up the leather-bound book.

"No, I don't need to see it. I know that's right."

Barbara put down her book and walked slowly around the defense table, then approached the witness stand, her eyes fixed on Osborne. She moved silently along the front of the empty jury box like a sleek cat stalking a cornered mouse. She stopped right in front of Osborne and spoke almost in a conversational tone.

"It is true, isn't it Captain Osborne, that when you knocked on Judge Whitehurst's door, in the middle of the night, armed with all of this information, you had no idea whether it was Baxter Post who was driving that jeep on that evening or not. As far as you knew, it could have been someone else. That is the truth, isn't it?"

"Yes, that's the truth," Osborne answered, tugging nervously at the knot in his dark blue tie.

"And it is equally true that when you left Judge Whitehurst's house that evening, you had in your possession not only search warrants for the Post home and Baxter Post's jeep, but also an arrest warrant for Baxter Post himself. You had both of those in hand, didn't you?"

"Uh ... yes ... of course," Osborne stammered.

It was a cardinal rule. Barbara Patterson knew it. Never ask a hostile expert a question unless you know the answer. What you know can't hurt you, but what you don't know can kill you. Al Osborne was an expert, a veteran officer, and by now he was definitely hostile toward his interrogator. Yet every rule had its exception. Barbara knew that, too. She thought over the possibilities for the barest instant, then turned toward Judge Whitehurst and looked straight at the elderly jurist while speaking to the witness, as if to emphasize her concern.

"Captain Osborne," she asked, "how did you manage to get the judge to sign an arrest warrant for Baxter Post when you have admitted here in court that at the time you presented yourself at the judge's house, seeking that warrant, you couldn't in good conscience swear that he was even *at* the scene of the crime, let alone that he committed it?"

CHAPTER

Sixteen

J udge Whitehurst slammed down his gavel and exploded to his feet. "Court will be in recess for ten minutes," he barked, scowling at Barbara Patterson. His face was flushed; wide-open eyes gave him the look of a madman.

"I want to see counsel in chambers immediately," he demanded.

"All rise," Tony Costello called out as the judge stormed down the steps and jerked open the door to his private office, all the while pulling at the snaps of his robe. "Court is in recess," Costello concluded before following the judge into his chamber.

Barbara and Bernie Fine hustled through the door on the other side of the bench and out into the small hall. With his hand on the knob of Lorene Crosby's door, Bernie glanced back at his worried colleague.

"I'll give you credit for guts," he said. "No sense, but lots of guts."

Lorene Crosby stared in surprise as the two of them walked

past her desk without speaking. At that instant Tony Costello opened the door to the judge's office.

Whitehurst was standing behind his desk, his robe lying in a heap on the credenza behind him, his tie loose, his collar unbuttoned, his sleeves rolled up. He didn't offer anyone a seat. Barbara and Bernie stood at attention in front of him like children called before the school principal.

Tony picked up the crumpled robe, carried it over to the coatrack near the door, and hung it up. Then he stood and watched as Judge Whitehurst began to address Barbara Patterson.

"Ms. Patterson," the judge began, "I shall make every effort to restrain myself. Unless you have some explanation that has totally escaped my grasp, you have just accused me, in public, of judicial malfeasance. Am I correct?"

"No, Your Honor," Barbara replied, wishing she had more time to think. "My questions were directed at Captain Osborne. My concern was over what *he* did, not what you might have done. Obviously he didn't know whether or not Baxter Post was driving that car. I don't know what he might have said to you. That's what I was trying to find out."

"Of course you know what he said to me," the judge continued. "He told me exactly what he knew. You weren't raising any question about him, and you know it. The clear implication of your question was that I issued that warrant without grounds. It was as much a slap in the face as if you had walked up to the bench and personally attacked me."

"That was not my intent," Barbara insisted. She was holding on for dear life, trying not to let her emotions get the best of her.

"Let me tell you something, young lady," Whitehurst grumbled. "I'm not going to excuse myself from this case, and I'm not going to be badgered off of it, either. And I'm certainly not going to be subjected to the insults of a young upstart like yourself. You may think I'm the meanest son of a bitch who ever pounded a gavel, but like it or not, I'm the son of a bitch who is going to sit on this case. Now you had better get used to that idea, and learn to conduct yourself with civility in my courtroom, do you understand?"

Barbara swallowed hard. "Yes, Your Honor."

"Do you have anything to add, General Fine?"

"No, Your Honor."

"Good. Now the two of you get out of here and let's get back to work."

Bernie Fine headed toward the doorway that lead to safety, but Barbara stood where she was. Judge Whitehurst stared at her.

"Well?" he demanded.

"There are two things you need to know, Judge," she began in a deliberate voice. "First, I meant no disrespect. I apologize if you thought so. I have always had a high regard for you. You know that. And I still do. I'm just doing the best I can for my client under extremely difficult circumstances. If you wish, I will repeat that apology out there, for the record."

"Thank you," Judge Whitehurst said in a voice totally devoid of feeling.

"Second, I want you to know that when court resumes, I shall have no choice but to move to quash that warrant. It was issued without proper foundation, and I cannot in good conscience fail to raise that issue, no matter whom it hurts."

Judge Whitehurst leaned forward, his hands on his desk, and drew himself as close as possible to her face.

"And I, no doubt to your considerable surprise, will deny your motion. Furthermore, I intend to bring this matter to the attention of the Bar Association when this case is concluded. You will not stand in my courtroom, or in my office, and accuse me of deliberate misconduct and get away with it. Do I make myself clear?"

"Yes, Your Honor."

"Good." He drew back from her face. "Now get out of here."

Barbara turned and followed Bernie Fine out the door, her ears burning with embarrassment and anger. She avoided looking at Lorene Crosby, who stared at them both with curiosity, unsure what all the shouting had been about.

As the door of the judge's office closed behind them, Tony Costello watched in dismay as his longtime friend pulled a bottle from the desk drawer, uncapped it, and put it to his lips. Just before downing a shot, Whitehurst glowered at Costello. Tony got the message. He left.

* * *

"What was that about?" Baxter asked.

"I'll tell you later," Barbara answered. There was no point upsetting him until she saw how things played out. "But I've decided that I want you to make bond. I want you out of there."

Baxter smiled. "Fine by me. But why?"

"All rise," Tony Costello barked as he walked through the door. Like everyone else, Barbara and Baxter quickly stood.

"Because I don't want to give that old fart the satisfaction of knowing you're in jail," she whispered. Baxter knew exactly whom she was talking about.

The hearing continued for another two hours. True to her word, Barbara made a terse motion for the record to quash the warrant with which Baxter Post had been plucked from the safety of his parents' home. She made a direct request with no argument, and no detail, fully realizing she was playing with fire. To her surprise, Judge Whitehurst's response was equally matter-of-fact. He simply denied it without fanfare or explanation, then instructed Mr. Fine to continue. Several spectators looked at each other in bewilderment, wondering what that was all about.

For his part, Bernie Fine was chagrined over the events of the morning. Barbara was obviously angry with him for even being there. That was disquieting enough. Then her line of questioning had caught him flat-footed and ill-prepared. He would have a tough time explaining to his boss, the District Attorney, why he hadn't anticipated questions about the arrest warrant and properly prepared his witness. It seemed so obvious, now that she had brought it out. How in the world *did* Al Osborne get that warrant? To have failed to notice such a glaring weakness in the testimony of his most important witness was something he dreaded having to explain.

Not wanting to take any more chances, he scrapped his plan to use only Captain Osborne. He called each of his witnesses to the stand, doing everything he could to protect the record—and to protect his own hide from the wrath of his superior.

Judge Whitehurst bound the case of *State* v. *Baxter Post* over to the grand jury on all three counts. Barbara asked that bond be set, expecting to have to address that issue at length. She didn't. Whitehurst set bond at one hundred thousand dollars, slapped down his gavel, and retreated to the safety of his private chambers, leaving Tony Costello to adjourn court.

A few minutes later, when Barbara finally emerged from the courtroom, Bernie Fine was waiting.

"Have you got a minute?" he asked.

"Not right now. Later."

"We need to talk," he insisted.

"Bernie, I've got a tough evening ahead."

"I'll call you," he insisted.

"Sure," she said curtly, brushing past him, headed for the clerk's office to begin arranging for her client's bond. He watched her until she disappeared behind the frosted-glass doors.

Later that evening all conversation ceased in the den of the Post home as a familiar theme began to play. A fatigued Barbara Patterson, surrounded by the Post family, turned her attention to the TV screen, where a woman's face appeared. Well-coiffed, well-scrubbed, antiseptic. An all-American face.

"Good evening, and welcome to Channel Three's Evening News. I'm Ann Taylor . . ."

The camera switched to her male counterpart. Equally well-coiffed. Equally antiseptic. Somewhat older, though, with just the right touch of gray at the temples.

". . . and I'm Barry Smith. In the news tonight, Judge Cullen Whitehurst bound over to the grand jury the case of Baxter Post, son of wealthy industrialist Martin Post, who is charged in the vehicular slaying three nights ago of young Randy Beckett, father of two, a student at Community College. Channel Three's David Crane was on the scene in the Seventh Circuit Court this morning, and he files this report. David . . ."

Now another face flashed on the screen. A younger fellow this time. He was no stranger to the group gathered around the television set. He had hounded all four of them for the past three days. The camera moved in for a close-up.

"Thank you, Barry. One of the most highly publicized hit-and-run cases in the history of this city began in the courtroom of Judge Cullen Whitehurst today, as the district attorney's office presented its case against the alleged slayer of Randall Allen Beckett, father of a small child, who was brutally run down on Cameron's Bridge Road earlier this week."

The picture switched to a file tape they had seen over and over for the past three days. In a grisly replay, police cars once again gathered on Cameron's Bridge Road, their blue lights flashing; the sheet-shrouded body of Randy Beckett was once again being wheeled into an ambulance. Instantly the scene changed and the events of the morning began anew. There on the screen was Baxter Post, being led into court by two deputies.

"The suspect in this tragic slaying, Baxter Post, appeared in court today and pled not guilty to all charges. The lengthy hearing included a heated private exchange between the judge and Post's lawyer, Barbara Patterson, when she moved to have the judge's original warrants quashed because of supposed irregularities. . . ."

How had they learned about that, Barbara wondered. It had all taken place in chambers.

"But the judge refused her request without comment and bound the charges over to the grand jury. After the hearing . . ."

Barbara watched as the cameras focused on her earlier exchange outside the courtroom with Bernie Fine, then followed her down the hallway to the clerk's office, reporters shouting questions, none of which could she hear any better now than she could earlier in the day.

"Ms. Patterson had no comment about either the case or her run-in with Judge Whitehurst. But Lynn Beckett, wife of the victim, was more outspoken in her views."

The four of them looked on in stunned silence as Lynn Beckett's anguished face appeared on the screen.

Except for distant shots taken at the funeral, this was their first chance to contemplate the reality of what had happened. All of their thoughts and energies had been directed toward Baxter and his problems. Randy Beckett was only a name, not a real person. Not yet. Now, all of a sudden, here was the face of a woman whose life had been ruined. Here she was, in their home, talking to them as if intending the words for no one else, anguish etched in her face, tears welling in her eyes. None of them had expected to see this, but nobody could turn away as she answered the reporter's question.

"All I want is justice. That's all that's left for me now. Nothing can bring Randy back. It's too late for that. I'm glad this case is in Judge Whitehurst's court. I know he will do what's right for us, and for Randy."

Lynn Beckett turned and walked away from the camera. The

picture suddenly shrank to a glowing spot of light in the center of the screen as Martin Post pressed the remote control in his hand. Tears were rolling down his wife's cheeks; Baxter stared down at his folded hands.

"What's next?" Martin Post asked quietly.

"We'll talk tomorrow," Barbara answered as she rose from her chair. "I know you'd all like to be alone tonight. This day has really taken its toll. And we all have a lot to think about."

As the family walked Barbara to the front hall, she elaborated. "Our biggest decision right now is whether to make a deal with the state or fight this out. In the long run that's Baxter's decision. After all, he tells us he doesn't think he killed Randy Beckett."

"Don't take this wrong," Arlene Post said with a quick, worried look at her son. "I don't mean to throw cold water on your effort. But even if it's true, you're going to have a tough time convincing a jury."

"I know, believe me, I know," Barbara said.

"Do you have any ideas?" Martin Post asked.

"Not yet. Not really. But something about all this doesn't make sense. The state's case is too pat, too easy. There's something here somewhere. Now all I have to do is find it."

Martin Post said nothing. He wanted very badly for her to be right, for there to be some shred of hope in all of this.

"Anyway, we'll talk tomorrow." She started out the door.

"I do want to say one thing before you leave," Martin Post said, touching Barbara's arm. "I owe you an apology. I was rude the other night. I hope you'll understand what I was going through and forgive me."

"Of course. I understand."

"I'm glad you didn't let me push you around," he continued. "You did one hell of a job today. You've got guts. I was proud to have you representing my son."

"Thank you," she said, feeling halfway decent for the first time that day. "I appreciate that. And I needed to hear it. We have all the problems we need without fighting each other."

Barbara turned up her collar and walked out onto the porch. The bitter wind stung her face as she made her way to her car. Her smile disappeared as she thought of the enormity of the task ahead of her, and of the unbelievable odds that Baxter Post faced.

* * *

That same thought haunted her hours later as she tossed and
turned in the double bed that nearly filled her modest bedroom. She
sat up in bed for what seemed like the hundredth time, turned and
fluffed the pillows, adjusted the covers, then flopped back against
the fluffy mass, determined to try again.

Within minutes the phone intruded once more on her privacy.

The machine will answer it, she thought.

The ringing stopped abruptly as the tape started rolling, beginning its monotonous message one more time. The volume was turned
off, but Barbara recited the litany in her mind, just as if she were
hearing it.

"Hi, this is Barbara Patterson," she mimicked in a barely
audible voice. "I'm not available right this minute ..." She reached
for the extension phone on her bedside table. "What the hell,"
she mumbled as she grasped the receiver in the dark. "Can't sleep
anyway."

"Hello," she said, just as the message played itself out. "Wait a
minute," she added before the caller had time to answer. "Let the
tape run out." She listened to the beep, then the scratching of the
tape machine, and finally the signal that the end of the message had
come. "Now go on," she said. By this time she had pulled the phone
over to the bed and wedged the receiver between her pillow and
her ear. Her eyes were closed.

"Thanks for answering," Bernie said.

"Self-defense. I want to get some sleep eventually."

"I take it you've listened to my messages."

"The earlier ones."

"Then you already know I'm sorry. Listen, I had no idea they
would toss that one my way. The DA called me in first thing this
morning and laid it in my lap. What did you expect me to do?"

"Why didn't he take it himself?"

"Beats me."

"No, it doesn't," Barbara said with disgust. "I'll bet Martin Post
had something to do with it. You know that as well as I do."

"Anyway, I got it. I had no choice. I couldn't turn it down. I
didn't even want to."

"I know that, Bernie. It's just that—"

"Can we talk tomorrow?"

"We can talk when the case is over," Barbara answered. "Not until then. And until this is over, nothing more."

"Are you sure that's what you want?"

"That's what you've forced me into. I have no choice."

The conversation continued for several minutes longer, but nothing changed after that.

CHAPTER
Seventeen

The whole week was a blur as far as Lynn Beckett was concerned. There was no place to hide. Her most intimate moments of grief and sorrow were played out in public, thanks to the prying eyes and ears of the press.

Being in the house was difficult for Lynn. In some ways it was the hardest part. Every piece of furniture, every picture, every curtain ...

He had carried her across this threshold; they had made love on the bare mattress even before the frame had been assembled. Then they had sat cross-legged on the floor, among the unpacked boxes, and munched cold pizza. The first meal. Dinner at home. Their home.

Room by room, staying up until the wee hours, they had slapped on the paint, ending their evenings with soiled shirts and smudged faces, their tired bodies entwined on the threadbare couch, too worn out to move. Finally that odious job had been finished, and one by one the little touches had been added. A bit of wallpaper, a picture here and there, a throw rug, some pillows scattered about. They were more than just things, they were small reflections of two personalities, two sets of taste and style being merged into one through the process of shared experience, with love as the catalyst. Slowly it had taken shape. Slowly it had come around. She had adored it all. Every bit.

Their last project had been little Randall's room. She and Randy had declined the tests that would have robbed them of the surprise, but they had painted the room blue in hopes of a boy.

Randy had wanted a boy; not so much a boy, really, but a namesake. Randall Allen Beckett, Jr.—the name had been selected practically at the moment of conception. Lynn had been all for it. She loved Randy and wanted his name to live on. Back then the whole idea had sounded so abstract, so far away. Now she thanked God for that name.

The pain of familiar surroundings.

Everywhere she turned, Randy was there. Every piece of clothing had a story of its own. His personal effects clutched at her heart as she packed them away. His tools, his lawn mower, the little list of things he was going to do the next Saturday, his records, his favorite coffee mug—it was endless. There was nowhere to hide, no way to avoid his presence.

"Don't move too fast. Don't do anything you will regret later." She listened to her friend and nodded agreement. But once alone, she had to do something. Doing nothing was driving her crazy.

Advice was plentiful, but neither friends nor family knew enough to advise her well. No one could possibly know. Each human relationship is unique. When the relationship ends, no matter how that happens, the loosened cords come unraveled. Each person must organize the shattered pieces as best he can. Each pattern is different; each set of priorities is intensely personal. There is no formula. Lynn learned that from the start. No formula, only pain, then numbness, followed by the slow-dawning of reality.

Daddy and Mama Beckett came, suffered, cried, and left.

Lynn's mother came, too. She was the most help of all. But it wasn't easy. Lynn was no longer a child. They tried, but each soon felt the need to be alone. It wasn't working. It couldn't ever work

again, not like it had before. So her mother finally packed and prepared to go back home, leaving Lynn to do the only thing left—to
take care of herself.

Lynn signaled well in advance of the exit. The morning sun lit
up the landscape as cars zipped past her on the left; busy, preoccupied drivers headed for their day's activities, unaware of the identity of the woman they were passing, oblivious to the sadness in her
heart.

She guided the little Toyota down the exit ramp. Patches of
dirty snow still piled up along the edges of the pavement where the
plows had dumped them a week ago, disheveled, dirty remnants of
the early winter storm that had played such a significant part in her
life. A week of sunshine had melted away almost all traces of that
white blanket. For most people it had been at best a lark; at worst
an unexpected inconvenience. For most it was just a memory; the
warming rays of the sun had long since brought relief. It would be
a much longer time before sunshine warmed Lynn's heart again.

"I think it's the next left," Lynn's mother said, peering ahead.
"You'll need to get into the middle lane so you can turn."

Still the mom, Lynn thought, still in charge. Still giving me
directions. But she didn't say anything.

Lynn glanced in her rearview mirror, then slipped across two
empty lanes and eased into the center turn lane.

"As many times as I've been to this airport, you'd think I would
know it by heart," she said. "Only I was never driving ..."

A sob choked off her words. Her face suddenly turned red; tears
rushed upward as if a small dam had just burst somewhere in her
heart.

"I'm sorry," she said, barely able to get the words out. She
struggled to control her emotions as she guided the car down Airport
Road. Finally the terrible tightness in her throat subsided. Her mother
touched her arm, but said nothing.

"That's the way it happens," Lynn said. "I'll be going along just
fine, and all of a sudden I'll think of him ..."

Her lower lip quivered. The dam burst again, almost before the
last wave had subsided. In the backseat, strapped in his chair, young
Randy stared aimlessly out of the window, unaware of what was
taking place around him.

"I really wonder." Lynn stopped in midsentence, testing to see
if she was going to be able to finish. "How long it will be ..." She

continued after a pause, her voice cracking, "Before I get control of my emotions."

She smiled at her mother through a reddened face and tear-streaked cheeks.

"Have you got everything you need at home?" her mother asked, changing the subject.

"I think so. There's a ton of food there. I won't have to cook for a week. Daddy Beckett helped me with the insurance forms before he left. I have an appointment next week at the social security office. I've got a little money saved up. I'm going to be able to get by for a while. After that, I'll just see."

They rode along in silence past the familiar lineup of fast food restaurants and shopping centers that desecrated both sides of Airport Road.

"Daddy Beckett was so funny," Lynn said. "So cute. He had the car checked out, he fiddled with the heater to be sure it was ready for winter, he stocked me up on firewood, he checked all the locks—even the windows. And that tree, that ridiculous tree ..."

"That was sweet," her mother said, thinking of the drooping, bedraggled cedar tree back in the living room, so carefully and lovingly decorated.

"He wanted to be sure Christmas was in the house for his grandson," Lynn said. "That was thoughtful. I would never have been able to do that." She wiped at her eyes. "Heck, he got more done in three days than Randy and I would have accomplished in a month. There just never seemed to be enough time ..."

It came again. Lynn's face twisted into a grimace; tears rolled down her cheeks. Her mother began to sob. Each tried to hide it from the other, but their shoulders started to rock in unison. As each realized that the other had started up, they laughed out loud.

Lynn approached the old terminal building, eased over to the right, and fell into line with the other cars.

"You know what I'm going to do?" she said.

"What?"

"I'm going to go somewhere. I'm going to find me some place where I can be alone, and just scream and cry and rant and rave until I am totally worn out."

"I don't blame you," her mother said.

"I've got to get all of this out. I feel like everything is bottled up inside of me. I'm headed for an explosion. It keeps coming out a piece at a time. Every time something happens to remind me of Randy, it starts all over again."

The car came to a stop at the airport entrance.

"How long is it going to take, Mama? How long is it going to take? I'm not sure how much of this I can stand."

Those were her words, but that wasn't the question she wanted to ask. She really wanted to know something far more specific, far more painful.

"How long did it take you to feel better when Daddy died?" she asked. Did you *ever* feel good again? she thought to herself.

Only three years had passed since her father had died. Three years. It had been bad enough for Lynn; at least she had her husband and their son. Her mother had faced it alone. She was still facing it alone, and yet she had found the strength to come here, to be available.

If her mother had told her the truth, if she had explained to her that it was just as bad now as it ever had been, if she had admitted that three long, lonely years had failed to dull the pain of her loss, it would have been more than Lynn could stand. If her mother had lied, had told her that the emptiness goes away in time, Lynn would have known this wasn't true. So she left the question unanswered.

"I'm embarrassed," her mother said, managing a small laugh. She took out a small compact and studied her flushed face in the tiny mirror. "I look a sight. Everyone will know I've been crying."

Lynn pulled the car over to the sidewalk. Two uniformed men were checking luggage.

"Lynn, are you sure you don't want me to stay? You know I can make arrangements."

Lynn sniffed, took out a Kleenex, and wiped at her eyes first, then her nose.

"I'll be fine. Really I will. Besides, I've got to face this sometime. It won't help to put it off. I want to get it over with. When you come back, maybe I'll be able to enjoy you more. But I've got to get this period behind me."

The older woman paused, then hugged her daughter, holding the embrace for a moment. Then she slid back across the seat, opened the back door, and handed her valise to the waiting porter. She kissed her curly-headed grandchild, then walked away from the car.

Lynn pulled away from the curb as quickly as possible. She

didn't look back, fearing what might happen. Lynn's mother watched the outline of her grandson's little round head in the back window, getting smaller and smaller by the second.

"It never stops, my child," she whispered as the Toyota pulled into traffic, out of sight. "It never stops."

Lynn drove as fast as she dared. Tears were running down her cheeks. She groped in her purse for a Kleenex as the car slipped on past the fast food signs, car rental lots, and other odd businesses that clustered near the airport. Finally she turned onto the interstate.

By the time she reached the exit leading home, she had begun formulating a plan. That's what she needed. A plan. But first there was something else to take care of.

She drove on past the familiar corner that would have taken her home, staying instead on the main road. The buildings on the right gave way to a long stone wall. Beyond the wall a grassy hillside rose gently upward, the smoothness of the slope broken only by a few huge trees and the macabre pattern of headstones, all sizes and shapes, that marked the resting places of those who were buried in this pastoral setting.

She knew the way, even though she hadn't been back since the funeral. She stopped her car at the bottom of a hill; a hundred feet up the slope she could see a large maple tree. That's why she had chosen the site. Randy loved the color of maple leaves in the fall. Its branches were bare now, but in the spring its beautiful leaves would hover over his grave.

Around his grave, withered flowers still clung to their metal frames. Beneath the flowers she could see the fresh soil that covered her husband.

"You wait here, I'll only be a moment," she whispered to little Randy, checking to be certain that he was securely strapped.

The walk didn't take long. Soon she was standing next to his grave, staring down at the patchy surface.

Someone else had been there. At one end of the mound of dirt, where the headstone would soon stand, a bare place had been cleared. In the middle of that space was a single rose, its crimson flower stretching out from a tender stem.

Lynn picked up the rose and turned it in her hands. It was still fresh. She knelt on the cold, unyielding ground and stared at the dark mound of soil.

"Dear Lord . . ." she whispered, but then stopped.

"Why should I pray?" she said out loud. "Where were you when we needed you? Why did you let this happen? Are you even there at all?"

She turned her eyes toward the sky, her hands clasped like a child's ready for its nightly prayer. So vulnerable. So trusting.

"Why did you do this to us?" she asked her invisible God as tears once again started pouring from her eyes. "Don't you care about us?" Her voice was louder now. Her face twisted into a grimace; her body yielded to uncontrollable sobs. "Don't you care at all?"

All of her anger and resentment poured out in a rush, and she dumped it all onto the grave of her husband. Her anguished cries disappeared into the cold wind; her tears fell onto frozen ground.

Finally her shoulders stopped shaking and her crying ended. She didn't quit, it just stopped on its own, as if there wasn't anything left to come out.

Slowly she lifted herself up and brushed off her knees, picking at several small flakes of frozen dirt that still clung to her hose. The rose was still in her hand. As she walked back down the hill toward her car, she snapped the stem in two and tossed it aside into a patch of dead grass.

CHAPTER
Eighteen

B arbara stared aimlessly out of the window behind the receptionist's desk. Huge flakes of snow drifted downward from
heavy gray skies. It was the first snowfall of the new year; the
first since the surprise storm of early December.

"Did you have a nice holiday?" The receptionist smiled broadly.

"Yes, thank you." Barbara was in no mood for small talk.

"Me, too," the receptionist continued. "I'm sorry to see it end.
I love Christmas. We had the nicest time . . ."

The phone interrupted the receptionist's chatter.

Saved by the buzzer, Barbara thought. Thank God.

It was almost nine-thirty. Her appointment was for ten o'clock,
and she had come even earlier so as not to keep Bernie waiting.
She shifted in the hard wooden chair and picked up a tattered, out-
of-date magazine.

The district attorney's office was on the first floor of the massive
courthouse building, far removed from the various courts and

clerks' offices on the fourth and fifth floors. People wandered in and out as Barbara sat and waited. Some stared, others ignored her. Barbara thumbed through the pages, not really caring what was on them.

The reception area was furnished with typical governmental frugality. Or was it just bad taste? The walls were institutional green. Wooden chairs lined both sides of the room. The floor was a gray-speckled tile that looked a great deal like some kind of pressed lunch meat. The few random pictures adorning the walls were of poor quality and were even more poorly framed. The only pleasant-looking thing in the room was the receptionist; in any other surroundings she might not have looked so good.

"Did you have any trouble driving in this morning?" the receptionist asked, trying once again to strike up some form of conversation.

Barbara groaned inwardly, but smiled and replied, "Not really. Did you?" Barbara tossed the ball back to the young woman, hoping she would keep it for a while.

"Oh, my, yes. I slid all over the place. Cars were off the road. It was terrible. I hope they let us leave early." She glanced out the window. "It's going to be a mess at rush hour."

"It sure is." Barbara stared down at her magazine, trying to appear occupied. Her eyes wandered over the words on the page that was open in her lap. Something about breast feeding. She flipped the magazine over and looked at the cover. *Family Circle.* Oh, great, she thought. Just what I need.

"Boning up on your mothering skills, honey?" the man standing next to her asked. "I had no idea."

Barbara looked up with a start. Bernie Fine was staring at her. She tossed the magazine down.

"I've been sitting here long enough to conceive and give birth," she said, gathering up her briefcase and shoulder bag.

"Come on back. I'm sorry you had to wait." He held open the door that led into the office area. Barbara didn't smile as she walked past.

"I hope little Miss Sunshine didn't drive you up the wall," Bernie said as they headed down the long, dimly lit hall. "Sometimes she can be a bit much."

"She was okay. Quite nice, really," Barbara lied.

"This place is incredible," Barbara muttered. They had reached the end of one hallway and turned into another. It was lined on both sides with identical doors, bustling with activity.

"A monument to man's inability to get along in peace with his fellow man. I'll tell you something, Barbara. When this society of ours dies, it won't be because of nuclear war or outside aggression. It will be smothered to death by the weight of its own misdeeds. Our enemies need only sit back and watch."

"That's pretty heavy."

"This is a heavy job." Bernie pushed open the door to his office and motioned for her to enter. "This place will sour you quickly. All you see, all day long, is the dregs of society. They march in, take what little punishment we can get the court to give them, then march back out to do it again. It's a revolving door. That's all it is."

He took Barbara's coat, hung it on a hook fastened to the back of his door, then sat down in the swivel chair behind his cluttered desk. Barbara took the only other chair. Bernie Fine's office was just as sparsely furnished and tastelessly decorated as the reception area.

"Anyway, you didn't come here to listen to my standard speech on the ills of our society."

"I came here about Baxter Post."

"That's what I was afraid of." Bernie leaned forward, shifting the weight of his shoulders down onto his elbows. "Listen, Barbara. When are we going to get a chance to talk about each other? About you and me. You can't run from that subject forever, you know."

"I'm not running from it." Barbara's voice was laced with irritation. "I'm just smart enough to keep my social life and my business life completely separate."

Bernie looked at her, but didn't say anything.

"Be realistic, for Pete's sake," she added. "Don't you see? This is the biggest case I have ever had. The biggest I may *ever* have. It's a career-maker. Up front, big publicity, lots of press—I can't blow it. How do you think it would look if some snooping reporter decided you and I were some kind of an item? My God, if anyone ever found out that you were at my apartment the night before you got this assignment, what do you think would happen?"

"I'm not worried."

"You should be. This case could be every bit as big for you as it is for me. Don't you see that? It really doesn't matter who wins or loses. The public doesn't care. All they remember are the names."

"So it's damn the relationship and full speed ahead. Is that it?"

"Don't do this to me, Bernie. I'm right, and you know it."

Bernie swiveled his chair around so that he wouldn't have to face Barbara. He studied his diploma and his certificates for a moment. "You've got this all out of balance," he finally said.

"Balance is easy when you don't have any choices to make," Barbara snapped. "I didn't ask for this case. Neither did you. I hope you didn't, anyway. But we have it. It's a different ball game now."

"I didn't ask to care about you either, but I do. That hasn't changed."

"I care about you, too, Bernie. I really do." Barbara stiffened as she spoke. "I don't know what kind of track we were on, but I've stepped off for a while. I have to. I have no choice."

Bernie turned back toward her. "You may come back to an empty train, Barbara."

"I hope not."

He pulled his chair up closer to the desk and pulled the Baxter Post file off one of the stacks that cluttered its surface.

"Okay, you win. We'll do it your way. All business. What's on your mind?" He flipped open the file and began riffling through its contents.

"A whole lot. For openers, what's the rush? The grand jury wasn't even supposed to be in session during the last half of December. You have cases backed up that are much older than this one. Important cases. I haven't had time to do anything to get ready, and I get a notice in the mail! No call, no courtesy, nothing. My client has been indicted, and the case is set for trial in four weeks. What in the world gives?"

"There is a principle involved. We've just gone through another bloody holiday season, with more alcohol-related accidents than ever before. We didn't call the grand jury back just for this one. There were several other matters. We might have done it, though, even if this had been the only one. This is the first 'high visibility' case under the new DUI law. The DA has told us to use your client as an example. I'm just doing what I'm told."

Barbara's heart sank. "Were you also told to keep all of this a secret from defense counsel?"

"I should have called you. I got busy and forgot."

"Is this fair?" Immediately she regretted the question.

"What has fairness got to do with it?" Bernie leaned forward and looked straight at this woman who was now his adversary. "You can't have it both ways. Business is business. Besides, what kind of fair shake did Randy Beckett get? What kind of advance notice did Baxter Post send him, telling him about the time of his death? What kind of advance preparation was he allowed? Hell, this case is open-and-shut, and you know it. All we are concerned about now is how much time your client will get."

"I don't think Baxter Post is guilty."

Bernie Fine rose from his chair and walked around to the front of his desk. He folded his arms and stood in front of Barbara, leaning back against the dark wood.

"Look, Barbara, I don't mean to be sarcastic, but the only thing we don't have in this case is a Polaroid picture of Baxter Post hovering over Randy Beckett's body, slobbering. We've got everything else. We have him drinking at a bar for hours that evening. We have his driving record and his lack of responsibility. We have Randy Beckett's skin and samples of his clothing taken off the underside of Baxter's car. We have a license number from an eyewitness."

"Skin?" Barbara asked, her brows arching suddenly.

"Yes, skin. And that's not all. Hair samples, too. Positive ID. They were small; it took some time to make a match. The report just came in this morning. You haven't been furnished a copy yet. There hasn't been time. I'll give you one."

Bernie pulled an official-looking document out of the file and handed it to Barbara. She stared at it.

"That's evidence you can't use," she said, "unless you want to be reversed on appeal."

"You're dreaming, honey," Bernie snapped. "Judge Whitehurst has already told you what he thinks about the warrant. You wouldn't dare bring that one up again."

"I have no choice. That warrant was a sham, and you know it. All of the evidence you found after that is inadmissable."

"Desperate prattling from a desperate lawyer," Bernie said, returning to his chair. His voice was laced with sarcasm.

"Suppose you get all of that in. Suppose you manage to convince the jury that Baxter Post killed Randy Beckett. Suppose he's convicted. What good would it do to convict an innocent man?"

Bernie Fine's response was much more deliberate, much more measured than she had anticipated.

"You wouldn't say something like that just to hear yourself talk.

Why do you think he's innocent? Shoot straight with me. Is this just a gut feeling, or do you have something?"

"Baxter Post is a scoundrel, there's no question about that. A real loser, with a bad record. Yet when you get to know him, you realize that he's not really a bad person. Most of his scrapes have been minor; what complicates things is how his father has tried to cover them up. That's hurt Baxter far more than it's helped him."

"That doesn't carry much weight in court, now, does it?"

"No, but I believe what he says, and he tells me he's not a killer."

"My God, how does he explain the license number? The cloth and skin fragments? How does he explain that?"

Barbara was treading on thin ice; she didn't want to make an admission that she might regret later.

"Baxter Post doesn't deny being at the scene. He doesn't deny hitting Randy Beckett's body. But he wasn't drunk. He was aware of what he was doing, and paying attention. When he topped the hill, he saw nothing. He felt a thud. He ran over Randy's body, but it had to be there already, in the road. That's the only way it could have happened."

"You believe that?" Bernie smiled.

"He believes it. How can I deny the truth of what he believes? Besides, it fits in with the evidence. Your report says there wasn't any blood on the bumper, even though there was skin. It points that out. So why wasn't there any blood?"

Bernie took another look at the report. He had missed that detail. Then he tossed it back down.

"So what? Are you telling me that this young kid, a college student for God's sake, a father-to-be for God's sake, was somehow wiped out by an assassin and dumped on this highway to be run over? You want me to back off on that basis? Just because there's no bucket of blood? Doesn't that strike you as being a bit much to ask for?"

Barbara refused to be baited. She got up from her chair, stood in front of the assistant DA's desk, and looked him in the eye as she spoke.

"Has it occurred to you to wonder about the informer? *He* was out there. He phoned in Baxter Post's license number. Why didn't he wait for the police? Why didn't he stay at the scene with the body?"

"Okay, good question. I'll give you credit for that one. Maybe he didn't want to be involved. That's not so unusual these days. Maybe he thought that the best thing to do was to go somewhere and phone, instead of staying on the road. Maybe the boy was already dead and there was nothing he could do."

"There is no way he could have seen the license number and not be there when the body was still warm," Barbara countered. "And why didn't he come back later to see if everything was okay?"

"Maybe he was afraid that he might become a suspect himself. Have you thought of that? Maybe he was just plain scared."

"Bernie, don't you have any interest in finding the real killer of Randy Beckett?"

Bernie didn't answer.

"Have you checked the houses out there to see where this mysterious caller used the phone? The nearest pay phone is five miles away at the market where Randy Beckett worked. The market was closed; the phone was locked up. There aren't any others anywhere near that area, except in homes. Have you checked?"

"No." Bernie rubbed his chin with one hand.

"Use your common sense. This case has been in every newspaper for weeks. It dominates the television. If anybody knew anything about a mysterious visitor in the middle of the night asking to use the phone, both of us would know it by now. And any decent human being who had happened by would have attended to the needs of Randy Beckett first. He would have written down the license number to give to the police later, but he would have taken care of that boy first. And if he *did* decide to go call the police, if he really had thought that there was nothing he could do for Randy, he would have headed for the closest house, whether there were lights on or not. No matter how I cut this, I can't accept the proposition that your Good Samaritan informer just ran off and left that body bleeding to death in the middle of that road. It just doesn't make sense."

Bernie leaned back in his swivel chair. "Okay, you have raised an interesting point. I don't have an answer. I probably never will. But that doesn't change the facts. Your boy is still nailed to the wall."

Barbara didn't say anything. She kept looking at Bernie.

"So what do you want from me?" he finally asked.

"Two things. First, I want to know what the medical examiner had to say about the time of death."

"File a motion. You know how it's done."

"Don't play games with me. Let's at least shoot straight with each other."

"It won't help you. Death was definitely caused by complications from blunt trauma. No indication that the boy had been killed and moved. Time of death can only be fixed within a twenty-minute stretch. What's number two?"

"I want to talk to the informer."

"You're crazy. For that one you'd definitely need a court order, and Whitehurst would laugh you out of court."

"Not if you joined in the request," Barbara suggested.

"Now I *know* you are off your rocker," he shot back, springing up out of his seat. "Look, I'm in a tough spot. Real tough. The fact that you weren't notified was no accident. It was intentional. I was told not to make any contact with you. My marching orders are to give you absolutely nothing, and to throw your client so far into the can that he'll never see the light of day again.

"There's one thing you can count on, Barbara"—Bernie poked his finger at her for emphasis—"one other thing besides death and taxes. Cullen Whitehurst is going to ride this horse to glory. It's *his* DUI law, *his* governor, *his* neighborhood, and *his* chance to show how tough he is. You had better be ready. I'm your opponent, but I'll probably be the only friend you'll have in the courtroom."

Barbara sat back down in her chair. "You've talked to Judge Whitehurst?"

"No. He didn't have to say anything. We all know the score, and so do you."

Barbara picked up her briefcase and purse from beside her chair. Bernie retrieved her coat and scarf; she declined his help in putting them on. The two of them stood at the door to his tiny office.

"Would I be wasting my time to ask what you would give for a guilty plea?" she asked.

"Right now we have no offers to make. We've been told to go to court. If you have something to propose, of course I'll listen, but that's it. No promises. And I can't give you much hope that we could sell any deal to Whitehurst, either. Frankly, I think we'd both be wasting our time."

"When you said all business, you weren't kidding, were you?"

"Let me ask you a question," Bernie said. "Are you going to put Baxter on the stand?"

"I don't know," Barbara mused. "I really don't know."

CHAPTER

Nineteen

"What in the hell is going on here," Martin Post said, almost screaming as he waved the newspaper in Barbara Patterson's face.

"What do you mean?" Barbara asked, slipping out of her coat and tossing it over the back of one of the plush upholstered chairs in the den of the Post home.

"Listen, young lady, you know full well what I'm talking about. I sure as hell didn't expect to pick up the evening paper and learn that my son had been indicted. You're supposed to be keeping up with those things. You're supposed to know what's going on. Why didn't you let us know?"

"Because I didn't know either. I only got notice of the indictment this morning."

Martin Post stood toe-to-toe with Barbara, his eyes riveted to her.

"Why the hell *didn't* you know? That's what I'm paying you for.

You're supposed to be the goddamn expert, and the district attorney is making you look like an incompetent ass."

Arlene Post stared up at the two of them from the sofa where she was seated. Barbara looked over at her, hoping for some protection from the angry man.

"Look, Mr. Post, if you called me over here tonight to chew me out, that's fine. Go ahead. But let me know when you are through. I've got more important things to do."

Martin Post bristled. He walked over to his writing table that was nestled into the bay window overlooking a broad expanse of lawn. He tossed the newspaper on the table and plopped down into a chair. He drummed his fingers as he stared out into the darkness, watching snowflakes, brightly illuminated by the eave lights, settle gently onto the shrubbery and grass outside. Barbara stood in the center of the room feeling awkward, watching intently.

"I can understand your feelings," she said softly. "I should have called you. They are doing this on purpose. I went to the assistant district attorney this morning and learned how badly they want a conviction. After that I spent the day in the library, trying to see if there was anything we could use to our advantage. It never occurred to me that the press would pick this up so quickly."

"It should have," the old man snapped.

"I'll grant you that."

"Furthermore, you should never have been in that spot. You should have camped out on their doorstep if necessary. It's *your job* to demand to know what is going on. You shouldn't be waiting on a goddamned call. You should be bugging them to death. You should be the first to know."

"I'll grant you that, too, but there's nothing I can do about it now."

Martin Post lowered his head and slowly rubbed his tired eyes with one hand.

"May I sit down?" Barbara finally asked. Martin motioned toward a chair without looking up. Barbara took a seat near the table and continued to watch while he stared out of the window.

"Where's Baxter?" she asked.

"He's over at that rat hole he calls an apartment." Then Martin Post shifted his gaze from the snowy landscape and stared at the young lawyer. "Does he know about this?"

"Not yet," she replied. "I tried to call him all day. There's been no answer. Frankly, I assumed he would be over here. I guess I should have asked."

"Seems like this day has been a series of 'should have's for you, doesn't it?"

"I'll go there after I leave here. We have a great deal to do. Trial is just four weeks away."

"Four weeks!" Martin Post groaned. "My God! What are they trying to do? As if I didn't know. The district attorney would do anything he could to embarrass me." He reached for a small pad and pencil and began scribbling furiously. "He's not going to get away with this. Who is the prosecutor? What court is it in?"

"General Fine is the prosecutor. The case is still in Cullen White-hurst's court."

"What do you plan to do now?" he asked when he had finished his note. "What's next?"

"I plan to get this case ready for trial, that's what. What would you expect me to do?"

"Have you talked to the DA about a deal?"

"The state has no interest in a deal of any kind. The state wants a trial. That order came from the top man himself."

"There's always room to deal," Martin Post barked. "It's just a matter of knowing the right person, making the right contact, finding the right spot to start pushing."

"Your son isn't guilty. He won't plead guilty to something he didn't do."

"You believe that?"

"Of course I believe it. If I didn't believe it, I wouldn't be representing him."

"You and Baxter need to grow up," he barked. "This is the real world, not a Pepsi commercial. The state has Baxter by the balls, and you know it. Your only chance to get him out of this is to make a deal. That's what you'll do."

"Are you telling me that you don't believe your own son?"

"What I believe doesn't make a damn bit of difference. This is no time for idealistic bullshit. Truth only wins in the movies. In the real world, power and money come out on top. Baxter will never understand that. I would have thought you had learned it long ago. How the hell have you survived?"

Barbara was seething. She didn't answer his question. She couldn't.

There was nothing she could say that would make any difference anyway.

"I'll make some calls in the morning," Martin Post continued. "You do nothing until you hear from me. I know where the bodies are buried; the DA better think twice before he pushes me around. I'll find his soft spot. By God, I'll push on it, too. He'll come screaming to us, begging for a deal."

"There isn't going to be a deal," Barbara said.

"What?" Martin Post said, slowly turning toward her.

"You heard me. There isn't going to be a deal. You're not going to call anyone or take care of anything. I want you out of this. I want you as far away from this case as possible."

"Are you mad?" he asked in a growling whisper.

"If you mean crazy, no. If you mean angry, yes. I'm mad as I can get. Mad as hell, frankly."

Martin Post clenched his teeth and stared at the upstart young woman seated across from him. The veins in his temples throbbed and his hand shook as he pointed a finger in her direction.

"Listen, young lady," he said, carefully controlling the tone and pitch of his voice. "I didn't ask for your permission. I don't *need* it. You'll do as I say. I don't give a damn how you feel about me. You can think and feel whatever you wish. Frankly, I couldn't care less."

Barbara stared back at him. Her expression never changed, but her mind was in high gear as he continued.

"I knew who the prosecutor was already. I know all about Bernie Fine. And I know all about the two of you, too. How the hell do you think he got this assignment? Not on his merits, I'll tell you that."

"How in the world?"

"This is war. I'll do whatever it takes to win."

"Is Bernie Fine in your pocket like everyone else?"

"Not yet, but he will be if I want him."

"You underestimate him," Barbara said.

"Everybody has a price. It's all a matter of finding it out."

"You know I could have you put in jail for this." Barbara was totally incredulous.

"Who'd believe you?" Martin Post was smiling now. "Especially after they found out that you're the one who's been giving him the *real* favors. No, I repeat, you do nothing till you hear from me. I'll get the trial date moved in the morning."

Barbara rose from the chair, tossed her coat over her arm, and stepped up to the edge of the writing table. Martin Post looked down and continued writing on his checklist. She stood there. He kept on smiling and kept on writing. She reached down, slowly and deliberately tore the top sheet from his pad, crumpled it up, and tossed it on the table in front of him. His head slowly lifted. He was no longer smiling as he peered at her from above the rims of his reading glasses.

She swallowed hard, tightened her fists to help maintain control, and stared right through him as she spoke.

"Mr. Post, Bernie Fine isn't the only one you have underestimated. Apparently you are a slow learner, so I'm going to go over it one more time. You didn't hire me, you can't fire me, and you can't control me. Whatever I decide to do, it will be between Baxter and me. You have no authority to tell me what to do. And if you try to interfere, if you make *any* attempt to get to me or to Bernie Fine or to anyone else, I'll blow the whistle on you so fast that it will make your head swim."

Her expression was grim and serious, but her knees were shaking. Beneath her blouse, beads of sweat ran down her sides.

"Where the hell do you think your fee is coming from?"

"As far as I am concerned, it is coming from Baxter Post. Where he gets it from is his business; what arrangement he makes with you is his business, too, and yours. If you expect me to do something dramatic like quit this case and throw your money in your face, you are in for a real disappointment. I'm doing a job, and I expect to be paid. Whatever goes on between the two of you is none of my affair. What goes on between you and me, and whatever else you try to do behind my back, is very much my affair. You're not going to keep me from doing my best for my client."

Martin Post was unaccustomed to giving orders and having them rejected; he found this whole scenario perversely fascinating.

"Let me try one more time to make it clear," Barbara continued. "You don't have any idea how tough this assignment is. I'll not bore you with details. You wouldn't understand anyway. But things are tough enough without having to contend with you.

"This is the second major conflict we have had," she went on, surprised that he hadn't tried to stop her. "You didn't want me in this case in the first place. That was tough, real tough. Perhaps I shouldn't have stayed in, but I did. Next day you're apologizing, telling me how great I am, telling me you're with me all the way. Now you call me in and tell me that you are going to take over and involve me in something that sounds damn close to bribery. You treat me like some kind of dog that has dumped on the carpet. I'm surprised you didn't threaten me with a rolled-up newspaper. Or is that coming next?"

Martin Post said nothing. Barbara stuffed her hands into the sleeves of her coat, wrapped her scarf around her neck, and started to say good-night to Mrs. Post. The sofa was empty. Arlene Post had slipped out while the two of them were talking. Barbara turned back to the elder Mr. Post, who remained stony faced and motionless behind the table.

"If you will excuse me, Mr. Post, I think it would be best if I leave." Still he said nothing, and did nothing.

"I want you to know that I am sorry I didn't think to call you," she continued. "It must have been a shock, reading about the indictment in the paper. I'm sorry that happened. I owed you that courtesy, if nothing else. I'm sorry. I also know how important all of this is to you. I'm going to forget about what has been said here tonight. But let's not have any misunderstanding about our relationship, or our roles. We want the same thing. If there is anything you can do to help, anything that is legal and ethical, then I welcome that help. But *I'll* plan the strategy, and *I'll* make the decisions, not you. Until Baxter tells me otherwise, or until I quit, I'm his lawyer, and I'm in charge. That's the way it is, and the way it's going to have to be."

She thought about adding "Do you understand?" or perhaps "Is that clear?" but she stopped herself.

"You will excuse me if I don't see you out?" he said.

"Of course," she replied, trying to sound natural and calm.

The cold air struck her full in the face as she stepped out into the night. The front walk was covered with new-fallen snow. Barbara picked her way along with care and reached her car without incident. As she rummaged through her purse for her keys, she became aware of a movement nearby. A figure emerged from the shadows.

"Miss Patterson ..." Arlene Post began.

"Yes, Mrs. Post."

"Are you going to stay on Baxter's case?"

"That's not a fair question at this moment, Mrs. Post. As you can imagine, I'm not feeling especially charitable. Let me sleep on it."

Barbara found her key, unlocked the door, and started to pull it open. She felt Mrs. Post's hand on her shoulder.

"Mrs. Post, I don't mean to be rude ..."

"Hear me out, please."

In spite of the darkness Barbara could see Arlene Post's face very clearly. She was an attractive woman, almost regal. Her skin was smooth; her nearly perfect features were only enhanced by lines of age. There was something very warm in her expression and Barbara felt sorry for her.

"Let's get in the car," Barbara suggested.

Mrs. Post nodded. "Thanks, I'm about to freeze."

Once inside, Barbara turned on the engine and adjusted the heat.

"Miss Patterson—"

"Look," Barbara interrupted, "you might as well call me Barbara."

"Thank you, Barbara," the older woman responded, but did not reciprocate.

"Barbara, I won't keep you. Thank you for listening to me. I just want you to know that I hope you will stay with Baxter. He needs you. He trusts you. In fact ..."

There was a pause. Arlene Post looked down at her folded hands for a moment before continuing.

"You may be the only person who believes him right now," she finally said. "Please don't leave him alone."

"It's not easy. I'm sure you know that."

"Of course I do. I've lived with Martin for more than thirty years. I know him well. And that's part of why I want you to stay on, because I really believe that you are good for Baxter, and I know, deep in my heart, that all Martin wants is what is best for his son."

"He has a funny way of showing it."

"He's only human. He's had a tough life. Everything he has ever had, he's had to fight tooth and nail to get, and then fight even harder to keep. There's a hard surface there. I know that. A rock-hard surface. He's obnoxious, pushy, and demanding. You're not the first person who's found him impossible to deal with, and I'm not asking you to try again. Believe me, you did exactly the right thing in there.

And you should stick to your guns. But don't punish Baxter because of his father, and don't lose sight of the human side of Martin Post either. It's there. It really is."

"The human side of your husband is not easy to see, Mrs. Post. There are plenty of people who don't think there is one."

"I can tell you one thing for sure. Inside that house there sits a man with a broken heart. He isn't angry, though that's how he acts. He isn't mad or mean or brash or even dishonest. I know that. He wouldn't do half of what he says. Those are just the fronts he puts on. That's all they are, fronts. False faces to keep the world from knowing the truth, that he is scared, and very much in pain. This is his son, his only son. And all he wants, in his own inept way, is to help. Believe me, that's true."

Barbara looked out of her side window, back up the walkway, toward the imposing mansion with its impressive columns and massive front door. Beyond the porch she could see the bay window in the den. In the bay window was the shadowy figure of Martin Post seated at the writing table, his head bowed, his face in his hands.

"Let me think about it for a while, Mrs. Post. I can't make you any promises right now. Let me think about it."

"That's all I can ask. Thank you." Mrs. Post grasped Barbara's hand, squeezed it, then quickly let go. Barbara turned on her car lights and watched the older woman make her way back up the driveway through the gently falling snow. Then she eased her car back down the drive, into the street, and out into the cold, snowy night.

Several days later Barbara made her way up and down the steep slopes of Cameron's Bridge Road.

The house she was looking for was set far back from the road, but its number was clearly marked and visible from a distance, even through the snowflakes. She slowed down, made the turn safely, and headed up a long driveway.

"Dr. Farrar?" she asked as the door opened.

"You must be Ms. Patterson," the doctor responded, without returning Barbara's warm smile. "Please come in. May I take your coat?" Barbara let him. "Mrs. Farrar is waiting in the living room."

Barbara exchanged pleasantries with an attractive middle-aged woman, then sat down on a plush chair in the warm, inviting room.

"It was nice of you to see me on such short notice," Barbara said.

"We'll do anything we can to help," Mrs. Farrar said warmly. Her husband was still standing, half leaning against the mantel, looking down into the smoldering ashes of the fire.

"You represent young Post, do you?" Preston Farrar asked.

"Yes, I do."

"Just wanted to get that straight. Are you with a firm or something like that?"

"I practice alone," Barbara answered perfunctorily, clearly sensing the coldness in the doctor's voice.

"You're young," the doctor said.

"What you mean is that I am an odd choice for such an assignment," Barbara interjected.

"You read minds, do you?" the doctor replied, still no trace of warmth in his voice.

"You're not the first person who has thought that," Barbara said. "I hear it all the time. Baxter Post and I are friends. From school."

Why am I justifying my existence to these total strangers, Barbara thought as the doctor spoke.

"I would think Martin Post could afford whomever he wanted. The very best."

He has the best, she thought.

"Would you like some coffee, dear," Mrs. Farrar interjected, trying to make things smoother.

"Of course you're not any younger than that young man who represents the state," Dr. Farrar continued.

"General Fine?"

"That's the one. The assistant district attorney."

"You've talked with him?" What a stupid question, Barbara thought. Of course they have.

"He was here several days ago," Mrs. Farrar chimed in. "So were the police."

"They told us to expect you," the doctor added.

"Did they tell you not to cooperate with me?"

Preston Farrar glared at Barbara. "Of course not. But let's make ourselves clear, shall we? There isn't anything to tell. Neither of us knew anything about what happened on that hill until after it happened. We can't help you, and we can't hurt you. But there's no love lost in this neighborhood for the Post family, and there's no sympathy for your client. None whatsoever."

Barbara shifted uncomfortably.

"Thank you," she said, for lack of anything better to say. "I understand what you are saying." She took a small pad from her purse. "But if I may, there are some questions that I do need to ask."

Twenty minutes later Barbara emerged from the Farrar home, having nothing more than what she had had when she arrived, except for a clear understanding of the hostility that Martin Post had left in his wake during a lifetime of wheeling and dealing. Over the next few nights she would personally visit every home on Cameron's Bridge Road. When she was through, she would be no better off than when she started.

CHAPTER
Twenty

"Well, can I sit down, or not?"

Barbara stared up at Bernie Fine. She had been so lost in thought, and so engrossed in her notes, that she hadn't seen him approach her booth in the crowded cafeteria.

Bernie smiled broadly. "Look, I could get one of those false faces ..."

Barbara laughed. "Sure, sit. I'll be leaving in a minute anyway." Bernie put his tray across from her on the black tabletop and slid himself into place.

"I hardly think anyone is going to be shocked to see us together in the courthouse cafeteria, for goodness' sake," Bernie said as he peeled off his jacket. "I mean, don't you think you are taking this thing a bit too seriously?"

"I didn't see you. I was thinking."

"I'm not going to ask you what about. I know better." Bernie pulled the fancy toothpick out of a section of his club sandwich and took a big bite.

"How'd you ever get a booth in this place anyway," Bernie asked, glancing around. The cafeteria was the melting pot of the justice system, the repository for all news and all rumors, true or otherwise. "I heard these booths were passed down from generation to generation."

"Can't divulge my secret. Sorry," Barbara said with a smile.

Bernie took another bite. A small piece of burned bacon jumped from the edge of the sandwich, barely avoiding being consumed. Bernie put it back into its rightful place.

"Okay, so you're sitting here," Barbara said. "So what are we supposed to talk about?"

"The weather?"

"You amaze me, Bernie."

"How's that?"

"You can turn it off and on like a switch. One minute you are the hired killer, programmed to be as rude and obstructive as possible, and the next minute you act like nothing is going on."

"It's the nature of the beast, Barbara."

"It's an ugly beast. It's hypocritical."

Bernie put his sandwich down. "Is this the way it's going to be every time we talk from now on?"

"Maybe I'm unrealistic. But somehow I expected better."

"Better than what, Barbara?" Bernie leaned back against the vinyl backrest.

"I've run my butt off for two weeks now. And everywhere I've been, you've already been there."

"You want me to slow down?" Bernie asked, grinning.

"Everywhere I've been, you've had nasty things to say about me."

"About your client. I never said a thing about you."

"That's not how I hear it."

"Look, Barbara. We have two more weeks. As far as I am concerned, I want to be a step ahead of you the whole time. But I'm honest, and I have integrity. That has never changed, and it never will. I may knock the hell out of you in court, but you'll always be able to see the punch coming. Trust me."

Barbara hesitated for an instant, then plunged ahead. "Can I trust you, Bernie?"

"Absolutely," he said, looking in her eyes.

"Then I want you to do me a favor. I want to ask you one question. I want a single answer, yes or no. And I don't want any follow-up. That's it. Promise?"

"What's this about, Barbara?"

"It's your turn to trust me. I can't tell you."

Bernie studied his friend's face. "Every favor has a price."

"What's your price?" she asked, not really wanting to know the answer.

"Dinner," Bernie said, smiling. "You have to promise me that after all of this is over, you will go to dinner with me at least once, so I can have a shot at convincing you that I'm not the jerk you think I am."

"Dinner?"

"Take it or leave it," Bernie demanded. "Dinner for two, alone, my choice of places."

"You're on."

"What's your question?"

Barbara sighed deeply. "Have you had any contact with Martin Post, or anyone acting on his behalf, since you took this case? Any at all?"

Bernie stopped smiling. "You're serious, aren't you?" It was more statement than question.

"I'm in bed with these people, Bernie. I need to know if any of them are cheating on me."

"Questionable analogy at best."

"No it's not. What's the answer?"

"One word?"

"One word."

"No."

"Any suspicions at all? Even the slightest inkling of a problem?"

"None at all."

"Good." Barbara leaned back and began to relax.

"And I'll go a step farther, too."

"How's that?" Barbara asked.

"If anything happens, anything, that makes me think something is amiss, I'll come to you."

"Thanks."

Bernie's smile returned. "Of course that kind of service may cost you more than dinner ..."

Barbara ignored that remark. "I've got two tough weeks ahead, Bernie. I'm going to work my tail off, too. I want to beat you on this one. I want to beat you bad. But I want to do it out on the table, where everyone can see it. Understand?"

"Like I say, when the knockout comes, you'll see it coming."

"How does it look at this point?" Martin Post asked. "Anything new?"

They were all seated at the dining room table; it had become a kind of command central, a place where meetings took place, where reports were given, where encouragement was shared. Today, however, discouragement hovered in the air like a blanket of invisible smoke, choking off optimism whenever it dared to appear.

"I've been at this twenty-four hours a day for more than three weeks, and I still don't feel like I have anything more than I started out with."

"Where are we?" Arlene Post asked. "Would it help to sort of recap?"

"We've done that so much, I could recite it all by heart," Baxter interjected.

"Yeah, but it's helpful. It really is," Barbara said. "You can look at a set of circumstances ninety-nine times, and on the hundredth try, you'll see something that's been there all along, only you somehow missed it."

"Okay, so let's do it," Martin Post said, turning his chair around so that he could lean against its back and still face the others. "What do we have?"

"We have the problem with the search warrant," Arlene Post suggested as she poured Barbara a cup of steaming coffee. "Don't forget that."

"That doesn't count," Barbara said, accepting the cup. "It might help us on appeal, but Cullen Whitehurst is going to let it in. For the jury's purpose, all the evidence will get in."

"We have the other car that was out there, and the informer," Arlene added. "Somebody else was definitely at the scene."

"But we don't know nearly enough for that to help," Barbara replied. "I mean, how many large dark cars are there in this town?"

"We have Baxter's testimony," Martin Post said.

"That doesn't count either." This time it was Baxter doing the talking. "Nobody's going to believe me anyway."

"I haven't even decided to put you on the stand yet," Barbara chimed in. "I will if I have to, though. There is a certain amount of common sense in what you will say."

"Then there's the expert," Martin Post added.

"An outside chance at best," Barbara said. "We don't know what they've come up with yet."

"It's outside, but it's a chance. If we could show that the absence of blood on the car means something . . ."

"Yeah, but he's having to work with theories and speculation. We couldn't get the court to exhume the body," Barbara reminded them. "That's another notch in our gun for the appeal, but I wouldn't bank too heavily on anything's coming out of that before trial."

"Well, it was a good idea, anyway," Baxter mumbled.

"Worth a try," Barbara agreed. "I have an appointment set up."

"Besides, it's the one idea I've had," Martin Post said, halfheartedly laughing. "When are you going to see him?"

"I'm supposed to be at the university first thing in the morning."

"Good luck," Arlene Post said.

"Yeah, I'm gonna need it. I always need it, and precious little has been available lately."

The meeting at the Post home, fruitless as it was, lasted until well into the night. By nine o'clock the next morning, exactly seventy-two hours prior to trial, the fog had not fully lifted from Barbara's sleep-short brain. She nonetheless presented herself at the office of Dr. Raphael Townsend, deep in the bowels of the laboratory wing of University Hospital.

Dr. Townsend, a portly, bearded man who exuded an aura of intelligence and an odor of chemicals, greeted Barbara with the same coldness that had been her lot for days.

"Yes, I got your letter," the doctor said.

"Can you help me?"

"The problem is not 'can' I help you. Of course I can. The problem is 'will' I help you. And if I do, will you like the kind of help I can give?"

"What do you mean?"

"Unlike you lawyers, I won't prostitute myself. I can perform any experiment you want, test any theory you have. But if it comes out against you, you have to live with the results. It's just that simple."

"I understand."

"If I report anything to you, I report the same thing to the other side. I work for no one. Just for justice."

"I assume justice will be paying your exorbitant fee?" Barbara mumbled her words intentionally.

"What?"

"Nothing," she quickly said. "Do you handle all of your court-room work this same way?"

"I avoid the courtroom like a plague. The courtroom will be the downfall of this country. For everyone except the lawyers, that is."

"Not a new position, exactly, but you certainly express it with grace."

"You didn't come here for grace. You came here for help, help in getting a drunk driver out of a very serious jam. Kindly don't bore me with sanctimonious speeches."

"It's a jam he doesn't belong in," Barbara insisted.

"So you say. So they all say. Espouse any position, believe any position, in the name of the sacred advocate system."

Barbara could see that this was going nowhere.

"Look, Doctor. I have a job to do. You may not like it, but that doesn't keep me from doing it. All I want from you is the answer to one question. The truth. That's all I want. You're the only expert in town, so I guess I'll have to take a little verbal abuse. But I've paid the price. Now let's get down to business."

"I take it I've been hired?"

"You've been hired."

"You're persistent. I like that."

"How soon can you give me an answer?"

"Let me be certain that I have the question. You want me to look at the forensic evidence, especially the skin fragments that the police took from the bumper, and tell you if the person was alive or dead at the time of impact, based upon the condition of the fragments and the absence of blood."

"That's it."

"Will the state try to keep me from seeing the evidence?"

"I have a court order. The evidence will be delivered at your convenience. A policeman will stay with it at all times."

"I can have you an answer within twenty-four hours, provided an answer is possible. I can't guarantee anything. I trust you un-derstand that?"

"I understand," Barbara said.

"Verbal abuse, fun as it is, isn't the only price you'll have to pay. I charge two hundred fifty an hour for the work and the report, and one thousand a day, or any part of a day, for coming to court."

Barbara whistled. Even with Martin Post's money to draw on, this seemed ridiculous.

"And I want a grand in advance, before I start."

"Did you say something about lawyers?"

"Surely you know where I learned about getting retainers in advance," the doctor said, smiling.

"The money will be here this afternoon."

"The report will be on your desk in twenty-four hours. And the DA's desk, too, don't forget."

"Fair enough," Barbara said, hoping she hadn't made a terrible mistake.

Within minutes Barbara Patterson was back outside, retracing her steps from the medical school research complex to the parking lot where she had left her car. "I hope we meet again, Dr. Townsend," she muttered as she unlocked her car. "Worms do turn, you know."

CHAPTER

Twenty-one

"You'll need to turn at the next block, Daddy Beckett," Lynn said, pointing ahead.

"Are you sure you have time?" George Beckett asked. "Court starts at nine o'clock."

Lynn smiled. "I don't think they'll start without me. I'm their star." She glanced at her watch. It was just a few minutes after eight in the morning. "There's still plenty of time."

"I wish one of us could be up there instead of you," George Beckett said.

"I don't mind. At least I'll feel useful. Besides, the district attorney wants me on display in front of the jury." Lynn breathed a deep, painful sigh. "This is all so cold, so calculated. It's almost as if there are no real people or real feelings. It's just a numbers game, played out on a stage. Randy is a statistic. One victim. I'm a statistic. One widow. Now we need a statistic on the other side. One conviction, to balance the scales."

The sad little group drove along in silence.

"Anyway, I'm their 'widow,'" Lynn added sarcastically. "They won't start without me."

She pointed toward a side road that jutted off to the left. "This is it. Turn here."

George Beckett pressed lightly on the brakes and signaled for a turn.

"You sure you want to do this?" Lynn's mother asked from the backseat.

"Yes, I owe it to him. It's the least I can do."

George Beckett turned onto the side street, past parallel rows of neat, well-kept homes, all nearly alike, yet each distinctive in its own way. Lynn stared at the houses as they slipped quietly by.

The music on the radio stopped.

"Highlighting the news today, our reporter Carolyn Ferguson is standing by at the city courthouse, where in less than an hour, the vehicular homicide trial of Martin Baxter Post, Jr., will begin. Young Post, son of wealthy industrialist Martin Post, is charged in the December sixth death of—"

George Beckett pushed another button, then turned down the volume. Music once again filled the car.

"It's a shame we don't have little buttons we can push in our hearts," Lynn mused, addressing her remark to no one in particular. "How nice it would be to change emotions whenever something happens that we don't like."

No one said anything in response. The car rolled along.

"The back entrance is just ahead," Lynn said as they approached a long, low, moss-covered stone wall on the left side of the road. George Beckett began to slow the car down. "Unfortunately," she continued, "I know the way by heart."

She did, too. By now she knew every nook and cranny of the old cemetery nestled in one of the city's slowly declining areas. She had been a regular visitor for more than seven weeks.

Lynn talked to Randy in this quiet place. She believed with all of her heart that he could hear what she said. When she was with someone else, her words existed only in her heart. But when she came alone, which was as often as she could, she spoke out loud and stood in silence waiting for the feeling that would let her know that he had heard.

She had kept him abreast of all that had happened since his death and had promised him faithfully to do what she could to avenge his death. Now, on the morning of the trial, she felt the need to renew that promise.

Daddy Beckett drove the car along the winding drive, twisting and turning among the huge trees and staggered rows of headstones mottled with age. Now and then a slab of crisp white marble stood out in mute testimony to a recent tragedy. In the distance the ground rose softly to a crest, capped by the bare, spindly limbs of a young maple tree outlined against the sky.

"It's up there," Lynn said.

George Beckett pulled up to the curb at the base of the hill; Lynn stepped out into the chill morning wind.

"Wait here," she said. "I won't be a minute."

The walk up the hill didn't take long. Lynn stared down at the grave site. A new marble headstone glistened in the morning sun. Brown squares of sod covered the mound of dirt like a checkered quilt. The colorless pattern was broken only by the crimson petals of a single rose, carefully placed in the center of the mound. As she had done several times before, Lynn tossed it aside, as if to question its right to be there.

A gust of cold wind picked up a dried leaf and whipped it against Lynn's leg. She stared for a moment at the headstone, then turned her eyes away. She couldn't stand to read that name, now chiseled in stone, so cold and lifeless. She preferred remembering the vibrant image of the man who carried that name through his days on earth.

"I'm here, Randy," she said.

"I miss you so. I love you. I'll always love you.

"I know you're here. I can feel it.

"Little Randy is fine. He's growing so fast. I wish you could see him. I'd give anything . . ."

She took a tissue out of her purse and wiped her eyes.

"Your mom and dad are here. Your mom is staying with Randy for me. Daddy Beckett is so sweet. Just like you."

Lynn heard the brief blast of a car horn. At the base of the hill she could see a thick white cloud of smoke drifting from the car's exhaust.

"I've got to go, honey. I'm going to do my best to take care of everything. You'll see."

She closed her eyes.

"Dear God, please take care of my Randy. Please love him like I do."

The horn blew again.

"Amen."

She hurried down the hill and jumped into the waiting car. As soon as the door closed behind her, they roared off toward the front gate.

CHAPTER

Twenty-two

"What was that all about?" Baxter Post whispered in Barbara's ear when she returned to her seat at the defense table.

"I'll explain it in a minute," she said, leaning close to him. "I think the judge is going to take a break before we start picking the jury." She straightened up as Judge Whitehurst started to speak.

"Anything further for the defense before we begin?" he asked.

"No, Your Honor," Barbara answered, rising to a half-standing, half-crouched position.

"We're going to take a ten-minute recess before we start picking the jury. Sheriff, please assemble the jurors. Mr. Costello, we'll be in recess for ten minutes."

"All rise," Tony Costello barked out.

Baxter Post stood at attention next to his lawyer. The preliminaries were finally over. His trial would begin in just ten minutes.

His trial. He felt numb, as if he had been mysteriously transported to another place and time and forced to participate in a scenario that had nothing to do with reality. But it was real, and he was there. Now, the best he could do was to survive. He would simply follow his lawyer's instructions, and pray.

For Baxter, the past four weeks had dragged on forever, but for Barbara Patterson, they had passed with lightning speed. Her days had evaporated into thin air, each week starting out with hope and expectation and ending up with emptiness and frustration.

The days and weeks leading up to a trial are always filled with activity. There is much to be done. Good lawyers, Barbara knew, win their cases on preparation. Plans are made, carefully evaluated, then cast aside in favor of some better approach. Avenues are explored, strategies mapped out, all with the meticulous care of the most skilled tacticians. No stones are left unturned. As the time approaches, the passion for preparedness merges with the desire to win and the two become all-consuming. Every waking hour is occupied with thought and effort; sleeping hours become fewer and farther between.

When progress is visible, when success seems attainable, the process feeds on its own energy. Barbara had had cases such as that. But when every road is a dead end, every idea has a flaw, and every effort results in nothing but failure, the effort alone can eat a lawyer alive.

By the morning of trial Barbara Patterson was completely worn out. She had tried everything. Hours had been spent on analysis, planning, and preparation. She and Baxter Post had all but lived together. She had hammered away at Bernie Fine, pestering him unmercifully and burying him in motions and arguments in order to gain access to his investigation files, only to find nothing there. She had studied for hours, even days, preparing and educating herself before questioning the forensic pathologist on the issue of the time of death. But again there was nothing there. The state's case seemed airtight. No flaws. Nothing.

Her attempts to discover the identity of the person who first struck Randy Beckett, if there *was* such a person, had proven fruitless as well. Armed with little more than intuition and the vague description of a "large dark car," she had explored every flight of fancy and followed every harebrained idea to its illogical conclusion, in hopes of finding that magic answer, only to realize that the possibilities she had seen were very likely illusions, created by hope, fostered by youthful enthusiasm.

Four weeks of work. Intensive, backbreaking work. It was an exercise in futility. Almost.

She had, in fact, found one thing. One small thing. She had found it quite by accident during her desperate final days of preparation; she still didn't know for sure where it might lead, or what it might mean.

This morning she could have used it, bringing it up before the court during the argument that had just ended. Possibly that would have been to her advantage. But she had elected not to do so. She would save it for later, when the jury had been selected. She wouldn't waste it on Whitehurst. Her opportunity would come soon enough, and she knew that her only chance for victory was with the jury. Judge Whitehurst wanted blood. She expected nothing from him. So she saved it.

"Now, explain it to me," Baxter Post insisted, as the two of them pulled chairs up to the well-worn table in a room off the central hallway reserved for defendants and their counsel during trials.

"I was making a record," Barbara responded. "I still believe the search of your car was illegal. I'll never sell that theory to Judge Whitehurst, but I want to reverse him on appeal, so I have to be absolutely certain that the record is clear. I have to be sure he understands why I think he is wrong, and I have to give him a chance, every possible chance, to correct his mistake."

"Isn't that the same thing you fought about at the preliminary hearing?"

"Yes."

"That's what I thought," Baxter said. "I cringed when you started up again. I thought the judge would let you have it. I was surprised at how calm he was about the whole thing. He seemed awfully patient, not like himself at all."

"You were surprised, too?" Barbara smiled. "You could have knocked me over with a feather when I heard him. I had both hands on my legal pad so I could use it as a shield. I expected him to throw something at me. Literally, I mean."

"He seems a little foggy," Baxter observed.

"He does, doesn't he. Almost like he's on something. I remember when I was in college, and everyone was popping pills and smoking pot, some people would just sort of glaze over. It was as if their eyes were made of plastic, and their brains turned to automatic pilot. They would function, but not really be there. The spark would be gone. That's what the judge was like this morning."

"Thank God for small favors."

Barbara heard a light tap on the glass door. She got up and opened the door to Martin and Arlene Post.

"Come on in," Barbara said, as Baxter pulled two more chairs up to the small table.

"How do you think it's going?" Martin Post asked.

"Well, we did what we needed to do this morning, I think," Barbara responded. "We set up the basis for an appeal. Now the real trial begins."

"You almost have to handle two cases at once, don't you?" Arlene Post asked.

"Just about. You have to play to the jury, but be constantly aware of the Court of Appeals, almost as if those appellate judges were looking over your shoulder."

"Only in this case they are even more important than this judge, or this jury," Martin Post said, repeating what Barbara had told him earlier.

"Yes, but we're going to give it our best shot at this level," she said. "Believe me, we want to win here if we can."

Suddenly there was another knock at the door, much sharper and louder. The door opened and Tony Costello leaned inside. "Time to go, Ms. Patterson."

"We're coming, Mr. Costello," Barbara replied. "Just a minute."

Barbara gathered her papers, then looked at Martin Post. There was something different about him. She couldn't tell what it was, but it was similar to the quality she had seen in the face of Arlene Post four weeks ago when they had talked in the driveway of the Post home. Her relationship with Martin and Arlene Post had changed after that night. Although she didn't know what Arlene Post had said to her husband, or what else might have happened, Barbara welcomed the change.

"Mr. Post," Barbara said. "I want you to know that I am going to do the very best I can for your son, and for you. I know what this means to you. And I want you to know how sorry I am about the problems we have had. There is no such thing as one person's being totally at fault. Two people make up every conflict, and for my part, I'm sorry."

Martin Post blinked back the tears that were creeping up behind his eyelids. It was a new feeling for him, one he hadn't felt in many years. He clamped his mouth tightly shut and fought against the rising lump in his throat. Then he took Barbara Patterson by the shoulders and pulled her close in an awkward embrace.

When they separated, he was smiling.

"You are the first woman I ever hugged in front of her," he said with a nod toward his wife.

Martin Post pulled open the door and held it as Barbara and his wife walked through. As Baxter followed them out into the hallway, Martin slipped his arm around his son's shoulders and looked into his eyes for the briefest instant. He patted Baxter on the back, then let his arm slip back down to his side.

It was as close as he would ever come to saying what he felt.

CHAPTER

Twenty-three

"Call your first witness," Cullen Whitehurst demanded as he stared down from the bench.

Bernie Fine picked up a single folder from the stack of files cluttering the table in front of him and carried it with him to the lectern, where he adjusted the gooseneck microphone. Finally he was ready.

"May it please the court, the state calls Police Captain Albert G. Osborne."

The much publicized trial of Martin Baxter Post, Jr., was under way.

Al Osborne rose from his seat in the front row of the gallery and walked slowly up to the witness box. As he made his way forward, Barbara Patterson gazed around the massive old courtroom. It was jammed. Along the first row of the gallery she recognized several police officers and investigators. Martin and Arlene Post were seated there, too, as were several other people she didn't know.

Seats on that row were reserved for involved parties and allocated by assignment. The next two rows were occupied by the working press. Beyond that, the public had snatched up all available seats on a first-come, first-served basis.

The unassigned rows had been filled since early morning. If admission had been charged, she knew this trial would have been the hottest ticket in town.

Inside the rail, Baxter Post sat at the defense table next to Barbara. Lynn Beckett was alone at the table on the other side of the lectern, next to the chair just vacated by Bernie Fine.

Barbara looked at Baxter Post as he sat in silence, cloaked in an aura of fear and apprehension. Lynn Beckett, recently deprived of the man she loved most in this world, also sat in silence, cloaked in the black garb of mourning. Baxter Post and Lynn Beckett. Worlds apart, and unlikely to meet had those worlds not collided with a violence that had shattered both of their existences.

"Raise your right hand and place your left hand on the Bible," Tony Costello said when the veteran officer reached the witness box.

"Do you solemnly swear or affirm that the testimony you are about to give will be the truth, the whole truth, and nothing but the truth, so help you God?"

"I do."

"Be seated please," Costello concluded. "Speak directly into the microphone."

"State your full name to the court reporter," Judge Whitehurst instructed, nodding toward the stenographer, who was once again in place at the small table in front of the bench, hands poised and fingers curved, ready to press the keys on her little black machine.

As Captain Osborne pronounced his name for the reporter, Barbara made a small notation on the left-hand side of her yellow legal pad, three fourths of the way down from the top.

3:30 P.M., Osborne—direct.

She habitually kept a meticulous log of the events taking place in the courtroom. It made it easier for her to reconstruct what had happened at a later date. Besides, she just liked to know how long everything took. It was one of her quirks. The only other notation on this particular sheet was at the top. *11:10 A.M., Jury Selection.*

On a separate sheet she had written a series of names in twelve boxes. Some of the names had been written and then scratched through; twelve names remained, one in each box. Twelve good citizens and true. The jury. The late-morning hours had been occupied with its selection.

Prospective jurors had been brought in one at a time and placed in the witness chair to be questioned first by the court, then by the state, and finally by Barbara, representing the defense. Her questions had centered mainly on the matter of pretrial publicity. Her greatest fear was that prospective jurors might already have made up their mind because of what they had learned from the press about Baxter Post and the events of that fateful December evening. She wasn't concerned about the question of guilt or innocence. But if any impression, however negative, had already been formed, that would be difficult to overcome.

She had chosen her questions with care. Her interrogation of the first prospective juror, a retired postal worker, had been intended to set the tone for all her subsequent efforts.

"Mr. Kerrigan," she began, "do you own a television set?"

"Yes, ma'am, I do."

"Do you read the newspaper?"

"Yes, ma'am."

"I assume, then, that you get most of your news from the newspaper, and from the television news programs—is that right?"

"That and what my wife tells me," Mr. Kerrigan replied, to the amusement of the judge and most of the spectators. After the laughter died down, Barbara resumed her questions.

"You try to keep up with what's going on, don't you?"

"Oh, yes, ma'am," came the quick response. Of course he did. That's what any right-thinking citizen would say. Barbara had intentionally framed her question to evoke just that kind of self-serving response.

"And while you might not necessarily read every page of the paper and listen to every story on television, you do keep up with the big events that affect our community, don't you?"

"Yes, I do."

"And you discuss these events with your friends, your co-workers, and as you have already mentioned, with your wife, don't you?"

"Yes, ma'am," he answered, quite truthfully.

"Of course you do. And like every other concerned citizen who keeps up with what is going on in the community, you sometimes form opinions about people and events that make up the news, don't you?" Again he answered in the affirmative, as she knew he would.

Slowly but surely she tried to bring him around to where she wanted him to end up, skillfully encouraging him to follow, while closing off the less desirable alternatives. As she continued, she noticed that Judge Whitehurst had leaned forward in his chair and had placed his elbows on the bench in front of him in a "ready" position. It was a gesture she would come to recognize and dread.

"Back in December this case was big news, wasn't it?"

A perfect question. Short, simple, and direct.

"Yes."

"And you read all about it, and saw news stories about it, on the day it happened, and for several days thereafter, didn't you?"

"Oh, yes," he replied with some pride. He had just admitted to being a solid, conscientious, well-read citizen, exactly as she had known he would.

"And you formed an opinion about Baxter Post, didn't you?"

"Ms. Patterson," Judge Whitehurst interrupted, "a person would have had to have been in a coma back in December to miss the publicity about this case, and they would have had to be unthinkingly inhuman not to form some kind of an opinion. That doesn't disqualify them from service on this jury, however. I trust you know that to be true."

She didn't answer his rhetorical question. There was no time, anyway. Having cut her off completely, the judge then directed his remarks at the unsuspecting prospective juror. Barbara simply stood and watched, trying not to let her irritation show.

"Now, Mr. Kerrigan, of course you heard about this case. We know that. But what we really need to know is this: Whatever your opinion may have been then, or whatever it may be now, you can lay all of that aside and give this defendant a fair trail, can't you? A fair trial based only upon what you hear in court? You can do that for us, can't you?"

"Yes, sir, Your Honor, I can."

"Good. I thought so. Now, go on to your next line of questioning, Ms. Patterson, or we'll be here all week."

Dammit! Barbara thought to herself before plowing ahead.

After more than three hours of such exchanges, a jury had been seated. Twelve good citizens and true. The microcosm of society that would, by its vote, decide how Baxter Post would spend the next years of his life.

Barbara had survived the selection process. And she had managed but one solitary victory—to keep her composure and hold her tongue. Thus, she had won a small battle.

Now she sat and listened as her opponent worked.

Bernie Fine's direct examination of Al Osborne took slightly more than thirty minutes. It contained no surprises. The two men worked well together.

Al Osborne took the jurors with him as he awoke once more to the sudden ringing of a phone. They stood with him on the snowy roadside and stared at the crumpled, lifeless body of a fine young man as flakes gathered on their shoulders. They heard with him the click of steel against steel as handcuffs once again closed around the wrists of Baxter Post, a wealthy ne'er-do-well. Later they would hear the technical side, such as the matching of fibers and skin, but none of that would have the impact of this simple story, told by a man who called upon his years of police experience and countless hours in court, this grim tale of death, real death, right there in their own backyard.

The jurors sat on the edges of their chairs and watched Al Osborne with fascination and respect; they embraced Lynn Beckett with their eyes and hearts, reaching out to comfort her; and they looked at Baxter Post with icy eyes of sheer contempt.

Finally, the direct examination was through.

"You may ask," Bernie Fine said, glancing Barbara's way. He picked up his papers and returned to his seat.

Barbara made another notation on her legal pad: *4:12 P.M., Osborne—Cross.*

This won't take long, she thought as she gathered her notes.

It didn't either. It doesn't take long to play your cards when you only have one ace.

She reached in her purse and pulled out a small tape recorder, then went over to the lectern.

"Captain Osborne," she began, "your involvement in this case began with a single phone call to your home, late at night, did it not?"

"That is correct," the captain answered with unexpected coldness and formality.

"You have told the court earlier that the informer was a reliable source with whom you had developed a relationship of confidence. Was the caller, the informer, someone who called you often?"

"I knew who it was, but I haven't heard from him often. Not in a good while, in fact."

Captain Osborne struggled to sound relaxed as he put together facts about this nonexistent person from the top of his head. He searched his memory to recall what he might have said at other times. Consistency is vital; he knew that well.

"I want to ask you a few questions about this informer," Barbara continued.

This brought Bernie Fine to his feet. "Your Honor, I object," Bernie groaned, trying to sound disgusted. "The court has been over this several times. This area of questioning is inappropriate under the law."

Barbara didn't wait for the judge to respond.

"Your Honor," she said, addressing her remarks to the court, "I understand the rule of confidentiality. I do not intend to ask this officer to violate that rule by identifying the informer. But if you will permit me to continue, I believe the relevance of this will be apparent very shortly."

"You may proceed," the judge stated. He, too, was curious.

"Now, Captain Osborne," Barbara went on, "this informer you relied on was not a member of your family, was it?"

Osborne hesitated and looked over at the judge.

"Answer the question," Judge Whitehurst said.

"No, it wasn't."

"I take it that it also wasn't a personal friend?"

"No."

"Or a fellow member of the police department?"

"No, it wasn't," Captain Osborne replied, somewhat curtly.

"You are probably wondering about these questions, Captain. Let me get to the point. Informers are usually people with whom you have dealt in the past, either personally or professionally. People who, for one reason or another, don't wish to be identified publicly, and can trust you to honor that wish. That's true, isn't it?"

"Yes, usually that is the case."

"Is that true in this case?"

"Yes, it is."

"If the caller had been family or a friend or a fellow officer or anyone like that, anonymity would not have been necessary, would it?"

"That is correct, Ms. Patterson."

"Now, Captain Osborne, when you moved from the Criminal Investigation Division some thirteen months ago, you had accumulated more than twenty years on the force as an investigator, hadn't you?"

"Yes, I had. Twenty-one years, in fact." Captain Osborne tugged at the stiffly starched collar of his shirt.

"I assume you had also accumulated a fair network of informers by that time, hadn't you?"

"Yes, I had."

Barbara Patterson picked up her small tape recorder and stepped away from the lectern.

"May I approach the witness?" she asked. Judge Whitehurst said nothing, but motioned for her to come ahead. She walked up to the witness box and placed the recorder on the rail in front of the puzzled officer.

"May it please the court, during the course of my investigation, I attempted to call Captain Osborne at home to discuss this matter. Specifically, two days ago at eight-thirty in the evening. I looked his number up in the book. This recorder contains the results of that effort. May I play it?"

Captain Osborne turned white as a sheet. Bernie Fine quickly stood at his place.

"Your Honor," Bernie said, "I fail to see the relevance—"

"Overruled, General Fine," the Judge said without taking his eyes off Ms. Patterson. "You may proceed."

Barbara pushed the play button on the recorder and held it up to the microphone on the witness box.

The courtroom was silent as the recorder began to run, emitting at first only the hum of a tiny electric motor and the scraping of a blank tape across the recording heads. Then there was the sound of a push-button phone—a series of harsh beeps, followed by a click, and the electronic sound of ringing.

The ringing stopped. It started again almost instantly, but in a slightly different tone. Then another click, and a familiar female voice.

"I'm sorry, but the number you have reached has been changed. The new number is unlisted."

Barbara turned the recorder off.

Beads of perspiration gathered at Al Osborne's temples. His eyes widened in shock. But Barbara didn't notice; she wasn't watching him. She kept her eyes constantly on the judge as she turned the recorder off.

CHAPTER

Twenty-four

*B*arbara soon focused her attention back to the task at hand.

"When did you have your number unlisted, Captain?" Barbara asked. The veteran officer squirmed in the wooden chair. She was enjoying his discomfort.

"I assume you know already." Osborne shifted around, crossed and uncrossed his legs, cleared his throat, and tugged once again at the stiff collar on his shirt.

"Of course I do. Mr. Miller from the telephone company is in the courtroom with the records. I have him under subpoena." She glanced toward the back of the courtroom. "Care to save me the trouble?"

"I had it changed last March."

"Indeed. And you had it changed ... let me guess ... because so many people had your number that you didn't want to be bothered with the kind of calls you had continuously received when you were actively investigating crimes. I'm just guessing. Tell me the reason in your own words."

Osborne's silence was conspicuous. Seconds ticked by.

"Ms. Patterson, let me explain—"

"Certainly, Captain," Barbara interjected, "but please answer the question first."

"Okay, you are right. That's why I had the number changed. And I'll save you the trouble of asking the next question. No, I haven't given the number out to anyone but family, friends, and a few police officers. I have no idea how the informer got my number. This whole thing about the unlisted number totally slipped my mind. I'm so used to getting calls ... But wherever he got it from, that call was real and the information he gave me was solid. It checked out. The license number belonged to Baxter Post, and Baxter Post ran down Randy Beckett. So you can throw up all the smoke screens you want to, but my informer was right. Dead right."

Barbara waited until Captain Osborne had finished his speech, then paused for effect.

"Are you through?" she said.

"Yes, I am."

"Do you still refuse to tell this court who your informer was?"

"OBJECTION!" Bernie Fine shouted.

"Objection sustained," bellowed the judge, whose calm demeanor and benign expression had disappeared. He was clearly agitated. "We've been over this before, Ms. Patterson. I've already ruled on that."

Barbara wheeled around to face the judge.

"Your Honor, I wish to renew my motion to quash the arrest and search warrants in this case, and to strike all of the evidence gathered as a result of those warrants."

"Denied!" the judge snapped out, slamming down his gavel.

"Your Honor, this testimony brings the entire matter of the informer into dispute." Barbara's voice was rising, demanding to be heard. "I respectfully request—"

"Young lady, I have heard enough," Judge Whitehurst growled. He stood up and rapped his gavel down with a resounding crack. "You motion is denied. Take it up with the Court of Appeals. Are you through with this witness?"

"I have nothing else, Your Honor."

"I assume you have no redirect, General Fine?"

Bernie got the message. "None, Your Honor."

"Good," the judge bellowed. "Officer Osborne, you may be excused. Mr. Costello, adjourn court until nine o'clock tomorrow. Counsel, be ready to proceed on time. I want to finish this case this week. Without fail."

Black robe billowing, Judge Whitehurst stormed down the stairs and bolted through the door. Tony Costello closed court. As soon as the last word had escaped his lips, the courtroom broke into pandemonium.

Barbara Patterson eased down into her chair, leaned back, and breathed deeply. Her pulse was racing, her blouse was damp; a sudden chill ran down her back. Her client was smiling.

Cullen Whitehurst pulled open the lower drawer on his desk and took out a bottle.

"Damn! An unlisted number!" he mumbled to himself. "And I knew it all along! How could I have forgotten?"

He took a glass from the tray on his desk, filled it halfway, and took a sip of the lukewarm liquid. The door to his office suddenly opened. Tony Costello walked in.

Whitehurst started to speak but stopped short when he saw his colleague's face. Costello looked as though he had seen a ghost. He pulled off his jacket and threw it in a chair.

"I'll have one of those, too," he said.

Cullen Whitehurst was stunned. He stared dumbly at Costello then reached for another glass.

Back in the courtroom, Barbara Patterson finally managed to pull herself together. She looked around the imposing room as she gathered up her papers. Most of the spectators had been ushered out. Baxter Post still sat next to her.

"This may be a dumb question, but how do you think things went?" he asked.

Barbara stacked papers up in one of the two briefcases she had used to haul her file into the courtroom.

"I can't say. There's really no way to tell. I know what I feel, but who knows what the jury is thinking?"

Martin and Arlene Post came up behind their son as she spoke.

The rest of the courtroom was empty, except for a police officer who waited patiently at the door.

"We got a good jury," Barbara continued. "Not great, but good. They're paying attention; that's the best we can hope for. Al Osborne's testimony hurt, of course. We knew it would. That last part should help ease the sting. I hope so."

"Can I help you carry something?" Martin Post asked.

"Yes, but we need to talk." She looked at her client. He seemed so vulnerable, so unlike the brash, cocky young man she had first met on the college campus so long ago. Back then, she had been the one who needed bolstering. When they first met she had been the one unsure of herself; he had exuded just the right confidence. They had been fast friends then, and they still trusted each other. But now she was the one in control, and he the one in need.

"It's time to decide whether or not you will testify," Barbara said. "My guess is that the state will finish by noon tomorrow. They don't have much left except for their technical people. Those witnesses should be on and off in no time. We don't want to have to decide in haste."

"What do you think?" Baxter asked.

"You're the lawyer," Martin Post added.

"If you want my opinion, I think Baxter should take the stand," she said. "The jury expects it, and if he doesn't, they will think he is hiding something. Besides, he is the best witness we have. The jury will like him, as much as they can under these circumstances."

Martin Post looked at his son.

"Let's go with it," Baxter said.

Barbara breathed a sigh of relief. That was remarkably easy, she thought. "Okay, then, that's settled. Let's go on over to my office. We can send out for some burgers while we go over your testimony." She glanced at Arlene Post, then at her husband. "You two are welcome to come."

Martin Post stood up. "No, we'll go on home. Unless you need us, we'll get out of the way."

"Let's at least go out together. There's a crowd at the door." Barbara pointed toward the large double doors leading to the hallway.

The struggle was as bad as they had expected. When Barbara and her client finally stepped out into the hallway, they were immediately accosted by reporters and photographers. Bright lights glared in their eyes; microphones were thrust in their faces.

"Ms. Patterson, this is Channel Two News."

"Baxter, how to you feel right now?"

"Ms. Patterson, any comment on the day's proceedings?"

"Ms. Patterson, when did you find out about the unlisted number. How long have you known about it?"

"Why did the judge seem so upset?"

Without comment, they fought their way through the crowd. They wedged their way to the elevator, where a waiting policeman created a path so that they could get on. When they finally reached the parking garage, they went their separate ways.

"I'll see you guys later," Baxter called out as his parents headed for their car.

"I'm glad we are going to work alone," he said to Barbara when they were out of earshot. "I don't like to talk about all of this in front of them." Barbara stared at him incredulously as the two of them walked past the judge's huge black Lincoln.

Cullen Whitehurst didn't fight the crowd; he waited for the courthouse to clear before leaving.

Tony Costello had stayed just long enough for one drink. It had been an uncomfortable time for the judge. Costello had surprised him. More like shock, actually. It had been so casual, so matter-of-fact, like one friend joining another for a nightcap at a local bar.

"I'll have one of those, too." That's what he had said. Came in without knocking, as if he had known what was going to happen behind that door.

He did know, Whitehurst thought. Of course he did. Whitehurst ran his fingers through his hair. My God, how much does he know?

The minutes had dragged by. There had been no small talk, no conversation of any kind. Judge Whitehurst had simply poured a little of the tepid liquid into a glass and handed it over. Not even a thank-you. Costello had sipped at it, worked it slowly down, then left.

Whitehurst's hand shook as he poured another glass from the flask. He put the silver top back on the flask and started to turn it. It jammed. He loosened it up and tried again. The top spun off and rolled across the top of his desk.

"Dammit," he cried out as it rolled off onto the floor. He fell to his knees, retrieved the top, and put it back on.

He sat back down in his desk chair. His stomach burned. He looked at the brass clock perched on a stand on his desk. Margaret had given it to him years ago when he was appointed to the bench. He checked his watch; the time on the clock was wrong. Whitehurst picked it up and put it to his ear. There was no sound.

"Shit. I must have let the battery die," he muttered.

I've got to call Margaret, he thought. He lifted the phone off its cradle and punched out the number of his home.

"Unlisted," he said as he heard the notes playing out his own private number. The irony wasn't lost on him. "A goddamned unlisted number."

Out on Cameron's Bridge Road, Margaret Whitehurst sat alone in the chair by her bedroom window. A book lay open in her lap, but she wasn't reading. Her mind was full of thoughts, her heart was full of concern. Tiny throbbing pains pierced the back of her neck and radiated down her shoulders. She reached back and tried to rub away the tension, but it did no good. Tension had been her constant companion for weeks.

She kept on rubbing as she stared out the window into the darkness. The telephone rang. Her heart jumped into her throat. She picked it up almost immediately.

"Hello," she said softly.

"It's me," came the familiar voice. Her heart hammered away inside her chest. Every time the phone rang, she expected bad news.

"Where are you?"

"I'm still at the office."

"When are you coming home?"

"I'm leaving here now. I'm on my way."

"You don't sound good. Are you okay?"

"Yes, I'm fine," the judge replied, trying very hard to speak distinctly.

There was silence for a few seconds.

"Be careful." Margaret didn't know what else to say.

"I will."

Margaret Whitehurst put the receiver down in its cradle and sat alone in the quiet stillness. Sharp pains continued to radiate through the muscles in her neck and shoulders. She closed the book and reached for the small black notebook on the table next to her chair, the notebook she had found in her husband's desk drawer.

Her eyes skipped down the rows of names and numbers in the notebook as she flipped through its pages. Finally she came to the entry she was looking for.

Osborne, Al—724-4618.

She pulled a small piece of paper out of her pocket, unfolded it slowly, pressed it flat against the surface of the table, then held it next to the notebook.

The paper was wrinkled and worn, but the numbers printed on it were clear and legible. She pulled the desk lamp closer, to get a better look.

Her eyes darted back and forth as they had dozens of times already from the notebook to the scrap of paper, from the scrap to the notebook, looking for some difference in the writing. There was none.

She closed the notebook and placed it in her lap, then carefully folded the scrap of paper, put it on the table, turned off the light, and closed her eyes.

CHAPTER
Twenty-five

M argaret Whitehurst's eyes opened wide the instant her husband turned on the overhead light.

"You frightened me." Her heart raced. "I guess I must have drifted off." She looked at the clock; it was eleven-fifteen.

"I'm sorry, I didn't mean to scare you. Why aren't you in bed?" Cullen sat on the front edge of a chair and began to loosen his tie.

"I drifted off." Margaret's muscles were stiff; her head buzzing. She felt drugged. Her eyelids were coarse and heavy as though she had some foreign object in her eyes. She blinked once, twice, then a third time. The feeling wouldn't go away.

"Where have you been?" She tried not to sound too aggressive. "You told me you were coming home hours ago."

"There were things I needed to do at the office." He untied first one shoe and then the other. "I just got involved and lost track of the time. I'm sorry. I should have called." He stared down at the floor, deliberately taking his time.

Cullen Whitehurst didn't want a confrontation. He hated con-
frontations. It seemed to him as if that were the only kind of com-
munication they were able to have anymore. Meaningless small talk,
or head-to-head confrontation. Margaret was so demanding! He
avoided looking at her, hoping to undress quietly and slip into bed
without saying anything to start her up. He spoke calmly, lacing his
voice with hypocritical kindness.

"I called the office." She hadn't, but she knew he wouldn't know.

"I guess I didn't see the button light up," he said quickly. "The
phone rings in Lorene's office, not mine."

She knew that with no one else in the office he couldn't have
missed the incessant buzzing of the phone.

"Where have you really been?"

"What's that supposed to mean?"

He unfastened his cuff links and slipped out of his shirt, acutely
aware of Margaret's constant gaze. Seconds ticked away as he struggled through the motions of undressing, trying to remain as steady
as he could. Finally she spoke.

"We need to talk."

Dreaded words. Threatening words. Words that signaled the
beginning of a long, long night.

"Shit," he muttered.

"What?"

"Nothing." He stepped out of his trousers. He threw them on
the ever-increasing pile of clothes and walked into the bathroom,
pulling the door shut behind him. Temporary relief. He knew she
would be waiting when he came out. He leaned forward and gripped
the sides of the vanity. The nausea was getting worse.

Wonder what in the hell this is about, he thought.

He studied himself in the bathroom mirror. The face looking
back at him was that of a stranger, not the vibrant, vigorous man
he remembered himself as being. Deep, flabby pockets of flesh hung
below his eyes; his nose was red and blotched with tiny purple veins.
Deeply etched lines crawled out of the edges of his mouth and spread
out along his jaw. He didn't like what he saw. He was wearing out.

Whitehurst splashed some cold water in his face, dried himself
off, and slipped on his pajamas.

"Might as well get it over with," he muttered as he buttoned
the final button. Just as he expected, she was sitting in the exact
same position she had been in when he left.

"What do you want to talk about?" he asked.

"This." She pointed to the table next to her chair.

His heart stopped beating and jumped up into his throat. His breath rushed out in an audible gasp.

"Where did you get that?" he snapped, staring incredulously at the slip of paper.

"I took it out of your suit pocket the night that Al Osborne came over here, after you had gone on to bed. I have had it ever since." She stared right through him.

He wanted to ask her if she knew what those numbers were, but he didn't. Of course she knew. Why else would she have been lying in wait, ambushing him like this?

"I assume you have tried and convicted me," he said.

"Of what?"

"It doesn't matter what. Whatever your suspicious mind has conjured up. You always assume the worst. Especially when I am involved."

"I haven't assumed anything, and you know it. This is Baxter Post's license number. I read it in the newspaper tonight."

"So?"

"And this book has Al Osborne's unlisted number in it." She held up the little notebook. "Do you need me to show it to you?"

Cullen Whitehurst said nothing.

"You came in with your lights off. And you had been drinking. I could tell. Then Al Osborne came. Later that night I found this note. I thought it was just a coincidence, but now I know better."

Judge Whitehurst's hands were shaking. He clamped his palms tightly together.

"You called Al Osborne and gave him this license number, didn't you? Where did you get it from?"

The judge's shoulders started to rock rhythmically as he began to cry. He fought it, but it was no use. Softly at first, then with more intensity, the sobs came. He collapsed back across the bed, covered his face with his hands, and yielded to the flow of tears.

Margaret stared at him impassively as he delivered up the devils within his soul.

CHAPTER

Twenty-six

Barbara Patterson was already standing on the crest of Roller Coaster Hill when Baxter Post arrived.

She saw him coming when his jeep topped the rise some half-mile or so to the east. As he had been instructed, he drove his jeep on past her car, which she had parked at the bottom of the dip between the two hills, at approximately the spot where Randy Beckett's truck had been situated on that earlier December evening.

She had parked there on purpose, driving to that spot from the same direction that Randy Beckett had taken. As Beckett had done, she had left her car and come back the other way. She wanted her impressions to be as close as possible to his on the night he had died. She had walked up the long hill, slowly and deliberately, trying to imagine what Beckett had seen, heard, and felt on that cold winter evening.

The morning sun had barely risen by the time she had arrived.

A cool breeze had immediately encircled her as she stepped out of her car. As she neared the top, the sun's earliest rays splashed against her back, warming her up, throwing a shadow out ahead of her along the quiet roadway.

Now, as she watched Baxter Post drive up the hill, the warmth of the sun was already giving promise of the balmy day that was to come. The grassy fields on each side of the roadway sparkled with reflections of sunlight bouncing off thousands of droplets of early-morning dew.

Baxter Post was immaculately dressed in a dark suit, white shirt, and maroon tie. His shoes were neatly polished. He looked more like a businessman on his way to work than a defendant on the way to testify in a murder case.

"I hope I'm not late," Baxter said.

"Not at all," Barbara responded. "I just got here. Thank you for coming. I really appreciate it."

She looked at her watch. It was six-thirty.

Baxter breathed deeply, smelling the fresh, crisp country air. He looked around at the quiet, pastoral hillsides.

"This is a remarkably beautiful area, isn't it?" Barbara asked.

"I suppose so. The beauty is lost on me, though. This is my first trip out here since that night. I've gone out of my way to avoid it. I guess there hasn't been a reason to come here. I didn't know how I'd feel. Tell you the truth, I still don't know."

"This is hard for you," Barbara said, "and I'm sorry. That was a thoughtless question for me to ask. I never should have dragged you out here."

Baxter waved his hand as if to dismiss that idea. "Don't apologize. I'll do anything that will help. Anything."

"I really don't know what this is going to accomplish. Not for sure. But I never try a lawsuit without soaking up the atmosphere at the scene. And today is an important day for you, too. I thought it might be helpful for both of us to come out here and check things out."

"Fair enough," Baxter said. "What do you want me to do?"

"Why don't you show me where Randy Beckett's body was when you ran back up the hill."

"I'll have to give you my best guess. It all happened pretty fast, and it was dark."

"Just do the best you can."

Baxter Post pointed out a spot on the pavement on the eastern side of the crest, about twenty feet or so from its apex.

That grisly task accomplished, the two of them walked down the hill along the edge of the roadway. They went about three-fourths of the way down. Baxter pointed out the approximate location of the large dark car, then they turned around and started walking back up in silence.

"Is there a big clock somewhere that measures out our minutes and deals out our time?" Baxter mused. "If we could find it, would we be any better off?"

"How many minutes did that poor boy have left," Barbara whispered to herself as she approached the crest. "How many seconds? What could he have done?" Lynn Beckett's face slipped into her conscious mind; just as quickly, Barbara sent the image away.

They reached the top. Barbara looked in both directions. Nothing remarkable. They both stood aside to let a car pass. It was headed eastward across the hilltop; it rumbled and bumped noisily as it passed over the infamous crest, slamming down heavily at about the spot that Baxter Post had marked as the location of Randy Beckett's body.

"That was a pretty good demonstration of what happens when you take that hill too fast," Barbara commented.

"It sure is, and that person didn't really seem to be going very fast."

They watched the car as it drove out of sight over the next hill. Only then did they step back out into the roadway.

"I want to try something else," Barbara said. "Let's get your car cranked up."

She climbed into the passenger side of the jeep and closed the door. Baxter jumped in on the other side and slipped his key into the ignition. The engine roared to life.

Baxter wheeled around and headed in the opposite direction and drove westward to the next hill. He then turned around again and slowly headed back toward the spot where the tragedy had occurred.

As they crept slowly upward toward the top of Roller Coaster Hill, Barbara asked him to stop. He put the jeep in park and tightened the emergency brake and got out. Barbara climbed behind the wheel.

"You've gotta be kidding!" he exclaimed.

"Trust me," she said. He walked a little way down the hill toward the east while she backed the jeep down in the other direction. She couldn't see him any longer.

"Ready?" she called out.

"I guess so," he hollered. "For Pete's sake, be careful!"

She put the jeep in gear and slowly began to rumble forward toward the spot on the other side of the crest where Baxter Post, suit and all, was now lying in the roadway.

She crested the hill and came to a stop right in front of him. He got up and brushed himself off.

"Well?" he asked.

"I saw you, but only because I knew you were there. On a snowy night, I would have missed you. No question about it."

"Now do you believe me?"

She was surprised at the question. "Of course I do. I have always believed you. But I've got to make twelve strangers believe you. If I am going to describe it to them, I need to see it myself. That's all."

"I'm sorry. I knew that."

"Why don't you go get some breakfast?" she suggested, brushing some dirt off the shoulder of his suit.

"I think I'll go home and change."

"You don't need to change."

"I'll feel better."

"Well, maybe something fresh would be nice ..." Barbara threw up her hands in exasperation. "My gosh, I can't believe I did this. I'm so sorry. You look fine. Just fine." She started brushing him off again.

"My lawyer told me that 'just fine' wasn't good enough," Baxter said with a smile. "She told me I had to look perfect. She even picked out the colors. Now I'm going to have to change to her second choice!"

"Will you have time to get something to eat?"

"No problem. I've got plenty of time. And I'll look just right. I promise. What about you? Want some breakfast?"

"I'm too nervous. Thanks anyway."

"I'm the one who is supposed to be nervous," Baxter said. "Let me take you down to your car."

"No, you go ahead. I still have some thinking to do. I'll just walk."

"Okay," he said as he pulled away. She watched his jeep roll on down the hill. He stuck an arm out the window and waved; she waved back. Finally he topped the next hill and was gone.

Barbara walked down the incline. The breeze wasn't as chilly now, but it was hitting her head-on. Her hair bounced and flipped as she walked. Every so often a strand crossed over in front of her face. Her heels clicked on the pavement. She walked slowly, trying to replay the events of that night in her mind.

What could have happened? Who else could have been there? She looked from side to side. The ground dropped off sharply on both sides, right at the edge of the pavement. The drainage ditches on the sides of the roadway were clear and well trimmed. On her left a long white fence stood in stark contrast to the green field beyond; on her right a thick, bristly hedge ran down the hillside, daring any stray horse or cow to try to pass through. In the distance she could see some of the stately homes, the very ones she had approached days earlier, one at a time, in search of some tiny sliver of information.

A deep sense of frustration haunted her as she walked slowly down the hill.

What could it be? Where was the answer?

She was deep in thought, almost completely preoccupied. So much so, in fact, that she almost walked right by it.

It was in the grass, partially hidden. The sun hit its metallic casing just right, the light bouncing toward Barbara. The glint of reflected sunlight hit her squarely in the eye.

She was immediately drawn to whatever it was. A coin? A treasure of some kind? She took a step or two into the grass and reached down.

It was a pen. A slim, expensive gold pen. A lucky find.

Was luck really involved? What about the months of thought and anxiety? What about the weeks of perseverance? What about others who had tried and failed? What about the decision to come to this place, to be in this spot, to do that little extra something that separates the winners from the losers?

Barbara wiped the pen off with a Kleenex and held it up for closer inspection. It had the unmistakable mellowness of real gold. But whose was it?

She turned it in her fingers. It was scratched somewhat and partially smeared with grime, but as she rubbed its surface with her finger, the tiny monogrammed *W* on its golden face slowly began to appear.

She tossed it in her purse and headed on down the hill.

CHAPTER
Twenty-seven

The next morning promptly at nine o'clock Tony Costello burst through the paneled door and entered the courtroom. No one had expected him to be on time; the place was in a state of general disarray.

"All rise," he commanded.

Barbara was seated in the first row of the gallery next to Arlene Post. Baxter was still out in the hall with his father.

Judge Whitehurst came through the door. His lips were set in a thin, grim line. He looked at no one but strode up the small staircase with determination, plopped his file onto the desk, and stood at attention behind his black leather chair.

"Open court, Mr. Costello," he said in a voice barely loud enough to be heard.

"Oyez, oyez, oyez ..."

Judge Whitehurst stared straight ahead until the ritual was finished, focusing on nothing, avoiding all eye contact.

Barbara noticed a difference in the judge the instant she saw him. Something had happened. It showed in the way he walked, the set of his jaw, the vacant stare.

"... be seated, please."

Tony Costello finally finished. Martin and Baxter Post hurried through the doorway. She held the gate open for Baxter and followed him up to the table. Bernie Fine trailed in after them. He, too, had been wandering about the hallway, fully confident that court would start at least fifteen minutes late, as usual.

Finally the players were in place. Barbara stood and waited for the acerbic comment that was bound to come from the bench. Cullen Whitehurst wouldn't let this opportunity pass, and she knew it.

"He probably started on time just so he could embarrass us all," she whispered to Baxter Post.

"Call your next witness, Mr. Fine," the judge said calmly.

Barbara looked at Bernie and instinctively raised her eyebrows in surprise. He shrugged slightly. "The state calls Dr. Lakin Pierce," he said.

A pleasant-looking, red-faced man with a tousled head of white hair approached the witness stand. Michael Lakin Pierce, MD, was more than just a medical examiner. He was a forensic pathologist in the finest sense of that term; a superb medical sleuth. No file of his was closed until the crime was solved and the fate of the perpetrator resolved. Yet in spite of his penchant for overemphasizing the investigative aspects of his work, he was eminently fair, easy to work with, and completely honest. Barbara had been gratified to discover that he was involved in this case.

His direct testimony took just under an hour. He held the jury's attention, using charts, slides, photographs, and illustrations to effectively dramatize his words.

Putting things in such a way that even the most unsophisticated layman could understand, he clearly established the cause of death as complications from blunt trauma to the skull, and then he slowly fashioned a noose for Baxter Post's neck using the raw materials of his trade—scraps of human skin and cloth fibers taken from the victim or removed from the underside of Baxter Post's car.

Dr. Pierce's testimony served as perfect counterpoint to the more mundane investigative legwork described by Al Osborne. It also served as the ideal contrast to the human agony of Lynn Beckett, who sat in stone-faced silence while the doctor described her beloved husband in cold, objective terms. Lynn Beckett's husband, for the moment, became a number, a cold, lifeless form tagged for identification and examined for evidence.

The effect of this was not lost on the jury.

Nor was it lost on Barbara either. When she rose to begin her cross-examination, she knew full well that she needed to be extremely careful not to antagonize this witness or to cause the jury to feel any worse about the Beckett situation than it already did. She looked down at her notes. Her questions were well thought out, safe, and predictable. And she had a surprise in store as well.

"Dr. Pierce," she began, "I have a few questions. I'll try not to cover any ground you have already covered in direct testimony, but if I do repeat something, please bear with me."

"Okay."

"Dr. Pierce, you have indicated that Randall Beckett died of blunt trauma, and you have placed the time of death as some time between twelve A.M. and one A.M. on the night of this incident, more likely between twelve-twenty and twelve-forty. That was your testimony, wasn't it?"

Barbara intentionally used the name Randall instead of Randy, and she always used his last name as well. It sounded less personal, less familiar. Small point though it was, she felt that any effort to dehumanize the unfortunate victim, and humanize her own client, was effort well spent.

Dr. Pierce confirmed his testimony. She went on with her questions.

"Now, Doctor, you have testified as to the cause of death, and within a certain range, as to the time of death, but of course you know nothing about who was involved in that unfortunate incident. That's true, isn't it?"

"That's true. I only know what I am told about that."

"You also don't know of your own knowledge where Randall Beckett was killed, do you? Bear in mind, I'm asking you about your own personal knowledge, not what someone told you."

"No, I don't, not from my own personal knowledge. Just what I was told."

"You also cannot tell us, based upon your own personal knowledge, whether Randall Beckett was run over by one vehicle, or more than one, can you?" Again the choice of words was intentional;

"vehicle" had a cold, emotionless ring to it and really described nothing.

"No, I can't."

"Or for that matter, if he was run over by more than one vehicle, you don't know whether he was killed by a blow he received during the first incident or the second, do you?"

"No, there's no way to tell."

"Dr. Pierce"—Barbara stepped away from the lectern and walked along in front of the jury—"Baxter Post will be taking the stand in a while. He will admit that he ran over the body of Randall Beckett."

A soft murmur arose from the gallery. It quickly subsided; the courtroom once again grew still.

"He will also testify, Doctor, that he never saw Randall Beckett, although his eyes were fixed on the road in front of him the entire time. He will tell this jury that he believes that when he struck Randall Beckett, the young man's body was already on the ground, already put there by someone else, or by something else. Now, I know that this theory cannot be medically proven. But my question to you is this: Is there anything in your report, or in your investigation, or for that matter in your knowledge whatever the source may be, that is inconsistent with this theory?"

"No, there is not."

"In other words, Doctor, from a medical viewpoint it could have happened just the way he described, isn't that correct?"

"Yes, it is."

"Thank you, Doctor."

It wasn't much, but at least she had established that Dr. Pierce's testimony didn't link her client with Randy Beckett's death. Hopefully she had established some credibility with the jury at the same time, perhaps had even planted a small seed of doubt. She moved on to more dangerous waters.

"Dr. Pierce, do you know Dr. Raphael Townsend?"

"By reputation, of course."

"What is that reputation?" She decided to risk this series of questions even though she couldn't predict what his answer might be. She couldn't conceive of anything negative that he might say in response.

"His reputation is excellent, of course."

Barbara interrupted. "I'm talking about his professional reputation."

"So am I. Dr. Townsend is an internationally renowned re-
searcher. He literally wrote the book in his field."

"What is his field?"

"The study of tissue, in layman's terms. That's how it would
relate to this case, I suppose. I believe you have consulted with him,
haven't you?"

"Dr. Pierce, I'll ask the questions." Barbara tried her best not
to sound curt. "You have described Dr. Townsend's reputation as
excellent. Would you give his opinion full faith and credit when
rendered under oath in a court of law?"

"Of course," Dr. Pierce responded in a firm voice. "Absolutely."

"Thank you, Doctor."

"That doesn't mean that I would agree with him, though."

Barbara's face reddened as the witness continued. She was wishing she had stopped, but it was too late now.

"Thank you, Doctor," she repeated, then returned to her chair,
acutely aware that Bernie Fine was probably licking his chops at
this moment. She was right.

"Dr. Pierce," he asked, beginning his question before reaching
the podium, "you said that you didn't agree with your eminent colleague, Dr. Townsend. I take it you have seen the report that he
prepared at Ms. Patterson's request, the one he sent my office a
copy of as a courtesy?"

"Yes, I have."

"In what respect do you disagree with it?"

"Objection," Barbara said, somewhat halfheartedly. "Outside
the scope of cross, and it assumes facts not in evidence, Your Honor."

"Do you plan to introduce the report of Dr. Townsend?" Barbara
could swear that Judge Whitehurst was smirking as he addressed
his question to the assistant district attorney.

Bernie Fine approached the witness, handed him a document,
and asked him to identify it.

"Yes, that's the Townsend report," Dr. Pierce stated flatly.

"It's in evidence now, Ms. Patterson," the judge said as the court
reporter marked the document. "Objection overruled. Proceed,
counselor." Barbara sat back down and tried not to betray her feelings.

"Now, tell us what it is that you are referring to in that report,"
Bernie said, leaning cockily against the podium and looking at the
jury as the doctor read the conclusions which Barbara's expert had

reached. Barbara died on the inside as the key findings of Dr. Townsend were recited. It wasn't at all what she had planned and was the worst possible way for that key evidence to be presented.

"Now, how do you disagree?" Bernie asked when the doctor had finally finished.

"Well, Dr. Townsend has suggested that the absence of blood on the tissue sample taken from Baxter Post's car supports the proposition that he may already have been dead when Post hit him. I would suggest a more plausible theory, however."

"And what is that?" Bernie asked.

"The temperature was below freezing. The windchill was much lower than the temperature. Based upon the distance from his own truck to the point of impact, Randy Beckett was apparently exposed to those conditions for some time prior to his being hit. The skin samples were clearly from one of the exposed areas. I suggest two possibilities: Either circulation in that part of the skin had been reduced dramatically, or more likely still, the skin was frozen. Just plain frozen."

Barbara wanted to bury her face in her hands. The whole thing simply made sense, and she knew it.

The state's proof proceeded at a rapid clip after Dr. Pierce finished. Bernie Fine and his witnesses all seemed infused with newfound energy. One by one the officers at the scene reported their findings. One by one the investigators at the Post home filled in the gaps. Piece by piece the picture became clearer.

Barbara Patterson's cross-examinations were brief and predictable. She dared not wander away again. While the circumstantial evidence was almost overwhelming, she tried her best to point out that none of this was inconsistent with the story that Baxter Post would later tell.

Through it all, except for his one glimmer of emotion during the Pierce testimony, Judge Whitehurst remained the same. Placid, seemingly disinterested, almost sedated.

Finally, Bernie finished with his case-in-chief. The last witness came and went, the last document was stamped; the last exhibit was tagged, marked, and handed to the jury. The state's case was built, as much as it could be. A cage had been constructed around Baxter Post. Now it was time for Barbara Patterson to see if there were any way out.

"Call your first witness," Judge Whitehurst directed.

Barbara was surprised. She had expected a moment or two in which to collect her thoughts, psych herself up mentally, and give Baxter some encouragement.

"The defense calls Martin Baxter Post, Jr."

As Cullen Whitehurst watched the young man approach the witness stand, his thoughts wandered back to that December evening and to the expression on Baxter Post's face as he hovered over the body of Randy Beckett. The judge's heart felt heavy; his breathing became more difficult. He looked away.

Baxter Post stood straight and tall. In the harsh fluorescent lighting of the courtroom he appeared pale, drawn, and haggard looking, with dark circles under his eyes.

He placed his hand upon the Holy Bible and swore that he would tell the truth.

"State your full name, please," Barbara said as Baxter settled into the wooden chair in the center of the witness box.

"Martin Baxter Post, Jr."

"How old are you?"

"Twenty-eight years old."

"You are the son of Martin and Arlene Post, who are seated here in the courtroom, aren't you?" Barbara gestured toward Baxter's parents.

"Yes, I am."

"I believe at the time of this incident you were living at home with your parents, is that right?"

"Yes, but I have since moved to my own apartment."

Barbara left the lectern and positioned herself at the end of the jury box opposite the witness's chair, so that when Baxter answered her next few questions, he would be looking at her and also facing the jury.

"Baxter, we will talk some about your background and family later. I want the jury to know you as well as I do. But first I want to ask you some very direct questions about yourself, and about this case. The jurors want these answers, and they have a right to hear them from you, without delay."

The jurors straightened up, some of them edging forward in their seats, anticipating what was coming. Twelve pairs of eyes were riveted on Baxter Post.

"Do you have any kind of criminal record?"

"No."

"Have you ever been charged with a felony before now?"

"No, I have not."

"Have you been charged with a misdemeanor?"

"Only driving charges."

"Tell me about those."

"I have been arrested twice for drunk driving. The charges were dropped both times."

"Were you guilty of drunk driving?"

"Yes, I was."

"Then, why were the charges dropped?"

"My father handled that."

"Are you saying that your father used his influence to have those charges dropped?"

Baxter looked at his father in the back of the courtroom.

"Yes," Baxter said, so softly that it was difficult for some of the jurors to hear.

Bernie Fine stood up. "Your Honor, could we have the witness repeat that last answer? It is important that the jury hear it, and some of them appeared to be straining."

"Please speak up," Judge Whitehurst said.

"Baxter, let me repeat the question," Barbara interjected. "Did your father use his influence to have those charges dropped?"

"Yes, he did," Baxter repeated, louder this time.

Silence hung over the courtroom like an awesome cloud. No one had expected this, least of all Bernie Fine. He had spent hours in the library researching the law, trying to find a way to get this very testimony into the record.

Barbara let the impact settle. It was a gamble and she knew it. Her second gamble of the day, and she had been burned on the first one. But the most important thing was for the jury to understand that her client was trying to do the right thing. The only way to accomplish that was to tell the truth. All of it.

"Baxter, did you know what your father was doing at the time?" she asked.

"Yes."

"Did you ask him to take care of those charges?"

"I didn't try to stop him."

"That isn't my question," Barbara said, gently steering her witness back onto the course she had chosen to follow. "Did you approve?"

"Yes, I did."

Barbara turned to a different subject. "Baxter, do you use drugs?"

"No, I don't."

"Have you ever used drugs?"

"I smoked pot in college. I mean marijuana. I experimented some with drugs in the dorm. But I stopped all of that after I dropped out of school."

"Have you ever been treated for chemical abuse?"

"Yes. My family sent me to a treatment program."

"For drugs?"

"No, for alcohol. I am an alcoholic. Drugs never were a problem. I spent eight weeks in an intervention program. That was four years ago. I had dropped out of school and wasn't working. It was right after the second DUI arrest. My dad and mom agreed to get that second charge dismissed and keep me out of jail if I would submit to treatment, so I did. I went to Wisconsin, to a place called Pendleton Hills. My family kept it quiet. I did, too."

Tears were streaming down Arlene Post's cheeks. Cullen Whitehurst felt a wave of nausea. He put down his pen, leaned back in his chair, and closed his eyes.

"Baxter, did the treatment work for you?"

"Not at first. I didn't want to be there. I started out trying to con everybody, including my parents. But after a while I finally came to grips with reality. By the time I left there, I was clean, and determined to stay that way."

"Did you stay that way?"

"For a while. Maybe for a couple of years. But I started up again. A little at first, then more and more. Always in secret. Never in public. I would go to out-of-the-way places, take great pains to hide everything. Under the seat of my car, in the back of a drawer, behind books on a shelf; I went to a lot of trouble. I didn't think my parents knew. I didn't think they realized what was happening until that night the police showed up to arrest me."

Cullen Whitehurst thought about the glass container in his desk drawer, and the one behind one of the rows of books on his shelf.

"Had you been drinking on the night when Randall Beckett died?"

"Yes, I had. I had been to a tavern, a beer joint, really, on Highway Forty. It was one of the places I went, way off the beaten path. I had had four beers. I would have had more, but I got scared when it started to snow. I didn't want to get in trouble, so I stopped, and headed home."

"Baxter, there was a flask in your car, under the seat. It was vodka. Had you had any of that to drink?"

"No. I didn't even remember that was there. I had hidden that there and forgotten it. I never even thought about it. I had been drinking beer, and I don't usually mix things up. It makes me sick. That's the truth."

"Were you under the influence of the beer you had been drinking that night?"

"I had drunk four beers over about a three-hour period. I didn't feel anything. I know it isn't possible to drink four beers and not be affected some. But I was alert, and completely in control. I swear it."

Barbara walked along the front of the jury box, looking at the jurors' faces as she passed them by.

"Baxter, this jury has to decide if you are guilty or innocent of vehicular homicide. That's a murder charge, Baxter. They need to hear the truth from you." She turned to face her client. "Baxter, did you run over the body of Randall Beckett?"

"Yes, I did."

Barbara paused before asking the next question. Even Cullen Whitehurst felt a twinge of sadness as he watched Baxter struggle with his answers.

"Did you see him in front of you?"

"No, I did not."

"Were you looking?"

"Yes, I was. It was snowing. The going was rough. I was alert. The only way to drive in snow is to pay attention. That's what I was doing. I couldn't possibly have missed seeing him if he had been standing in front of me."

"But you did run over him?"

"Yes, I did."

"After you ran over Randy Beckett, did you stop?"

"Yes, I did."

"Did you stay at the scene long enough to know that you had run over a person?"

"Yes. I stopped, got out of my car, and ran back to see what I had hit, because I hadn't seen anything. I thought it was an animal. I knew it was large. Then I saw it was a man."

"Why did you leave?"

"Because I panicked. I had been drinking. With my history, I knew I didn't have a prayer. So I ran. I didn't think about it, I just ran."

Barbara moved up to the witness box and stood next to her client, as if to signify her support to him and to the jury.

"Baxter, did you kill Randy Beckett?"

"I don't think so."

"Why not?"

"Because he wasn't standing in front of my car for one thing. He had to be already on the ground. And when I reached him, he was already dead. The blood on his head was dry. I touched it. He was cool, not warm at all. There wasn't anything I could do. I could tell that instantly. I knew no one would believe me, so I ran. I wish I hadn't. More than anything, I wish I hadn't. But I did. I got back in my car as quickly as I could and drove home. My head was spinning. I went up to my room and tried to sort things out, to decide what to do. That's where I was when the police came later that night."

Barbara watched the jurors. They were totally involved in what Baxter was saying. She gambled again.

"I have no more questions. You may ask."

CHAPTER

Twenty-eight

"Mr. Post," Bernie began in a solicitous voice, "I only have a few questions. I just want to be certain that the jury heard what I heard on your direct examination. Now, for openers, I believe you testified on direct that you had been arrested twice before for driving an automobile while under the influence of alcohol or narcotic drugs. That is what you said, isn't it?"

"Yes, sir, it is," Baxter answered, remembering his instructions well. Don't argue, don't get angry, don't show any hostility or irritation, no matter what he says, or how bad he makes you feel.

"On those two occasions, was there an accident?"

"Yes, both times."

"Tell me about those accidents."

"The first time I ran my car off the road and hit some parked cars. The second time I crossed the center line and hit a lady in the other lane."

"The police came both times, is that right?"

"Yes."

"Both times you were given a ticket?"

"Yes, sir."

"And both times your daddy had the ticket fixed," Bernie said, drawing out the word "daddy" for emphasis.

"I wasn't prosecuted in either case. The charges were dropped."

"Are you telling us that the tickets weren't fixed?" Bernie Fine asked, raising the volume just a bit.

"I don't know the details. I just know that the charges were dropped."

"You were content just to let your daddy take care of things, without knowing how he did it, is that right?"

"I . . . I suppose so," Baxter stammered.

Bernie stepped up closer to the witness box. "The woman you hit, and the owners of the other cars you smashed into, I suppose daddy paid them off, too?"

"Their damages were paid. That was only fair under the circumstances."

"Fair?" Bernie asked with mock incredulity. "How much were they paid?"

"I don't know."

"Then how do you know if it was fair?" Bernie snapped.

Baxter hesitated. "I guess I don't," he finally said.

"I thought not. Now," Bernie continued, "after all of that took place, as I understand it, you stayed out of college, and never went back, but went to Pendleton Hills, the high-priced treatment center in Wisconsin, where you underwent treatment for alcohol and drug abuse. That was how many years ago?"

"Four years. And my treatment was for alcohol dependence. I wasn't doing any drugs."

"You admit you used drugs, though?"

"Yes, I tried a few."

"Your parents paid for that treatment, too, didn't they?"

"Yes, they did."

"And you rewarded them by coming back home and continuing to drink, only this time you cleverly hid all the evidence from them. Is that what happened?"

"Not exactly . . . I really tried. You don't understand—"

Bernie Fine interrupted him, his voice laced with sarcasm. "Then suppose you explain what happened, please."

"It didn't happen overnight. It took a while. I was clean for two years after I got back. I began to get overconfident, thinking I was in control when I wasn't. I started back gradually. I thought I could handle it. I found out I was wrong, but I couldn't stop myself. Then there was no turning back. I was right back where I started, as if I had never left off."

Cullen Whitehurst listened intently.

"And you hid it from your parents, successfully so, until they finally found out about it at the time of Randy Beckett's death. That's correct, isn't it?"

"Yes, sir."

Bernie Fine was on a roll. He tossed caution to the wind and gave it all he had.

"And on the very night of Randy Beckett's death," he said, his voice rising in volume, "the *very* night you sneaked off to a tavern, way out from town, and swilled beer all night, fully intending to lie to your parents about where you were, and what you were doing. Isn't that true?"

"I suppose so," Baxter said. "Only I wouldn't say I was exactly 'swilling' beer."

"Call it what you will," Bernie said, glaring at the jurors. "The jury knows what you were doing."

The young prosecutor approached the witness, assumed a stance with his hands on his hips, and bellowed out the next question.

"The fact is, Mr. Post, for the past two years your entire life has been nothing but one big lie, hasn't it?"

Barbara sprang to her feet. "Your Honor, I object. General Fine is badgering this witness."

"Sustained. Try to tone it down, General."

"All right, Your Honor. I'll rephrase the question. Mr. Post, for the past two years, you have lived a life of deception, haven't you?"

"I don't know what you mean," Baxter said.

"You have lied—excuse me—'made up' stories about your drinking, stories about your whereabouts, and generally lived a life of deception and deceit, haven't you?" Bernie Fine was face-to-face with the witness.

"Your Honor, I object," Barbara said again, still on her feet. "Mr. Fine is continuing to badger the witness."

"I apologize, Your Honor," Bernie said as he turned toward

Barbara Patterson. "I certainly wouldn't want to upset the lad. I withdraw the question."

The jury didn't need to hear the answer anyway. They knew it.

"All right, Mr. Post," Bernie continued, much calmer. "Let's move on. You did, in fact, run over Randy Beckett, didn't you? There isn't any question in your mind about that, is there?"

"No, there's no question. I told you that. I ran over Randy Beckett."

"And you stopped, according to your story, and ran back up the hill to see what you had hit?"

"Yes, I did."

"Tell the jury what you saw."

There was silence for a moment. Baxter Post looked at Barbara Patterson.

"I'm not sure I understand."

"Of course you do." Bernie waved his hand at the witness as if to coax out the words. "It's a simple request. Tell the jury what you saw."

"I saw a man. He was lying in the road. He didn't seem to be breathing. There was blood on his head, but he didn't seem to be bleeding right then."

Another pause. "Are you finished?" Bernie asked.

"Yes."

Bernie Fine left the lectern once again. He walked around to the back of the prosecution table and stood behind Lynn Beckett. Her face was red; tear tracks marked her cheeks.

"Baxter, do you have any medical or life-saving training?"

"Well, I learned some first aid a few years ago. Not much, but some."

"What kind of first aid did you try out there on Cameron's Bridge Road that morning?"

Baxter squirmed in the hard wooden chair. "None."

"None at all?"

"None."

"Did you take Randy Beckett's pulse to see if he had a heartbeat?"

"No, sir. He was already dead. I could tell."

"You think you could tell, but you don't really know if he was or not, do you?"

"I think he was."

"But you don't really know?"

Baxter swallowed hard. "I believe he was, but I can't say for sure."

"Dead or alive, you just left him there, and ran off to protect yourself. That's true, isn't it?"

Fresh tears streamed down Lynn Beckett's face; several jurors were blinking back tears of their own.

"Yes, sir, that's true."

Bernie Fine sat down next to Lynn Beckett. "I believe that's all."

Barbara Patterson stood. "Nothing on redirect," she said. "And the defense has no further witnesses."

Judge Whitehurst turned his attention to the jury.

"Are there any members of the jury who could not work this evening? The state will provide an evening meal; we can work out transportation if necessary. But I would like to finish this case tonight if possible. Any problems?"

All eyes turned toward the jury. All of their faces were somber, but no one responded to the judge's request.

"I take it there is no problem." He turned toward the lawyers. "What about counsel?"

"The state is available," Bernie Fine responded.

"So is the defense," Barbara Patterson said.

"Good," said the judge. "Mr. Costello adjourn the court for one hour. When we resume, we will hear arguments from both sides, and then I'll charge the jury."

"All rise," Costello chanted.

CHAPTER

Twenty-nine

"Well, what do you think?" Martin Post asked as the waitress poured a second cup of coffee. "How does it look?"

"Who can tell?" Barbara answered. It was a lie. She knew full well how things were going. Badly, that's how. Very badly. But why say that to those poor people? They already knew it, anyway. They couldn't have looked at that jury during the cross-examination of their son without knowing full well how things were going. Nothing she could say would make it any better, or any worse. She stirred her coffee and thought about what she might tell them to boost their spirits.

"That thing with the Townsend report hurt," Barbara admitted. "He would have covered the same ground on cross-examination anyway, but still, it hurt."

"Why didn't you go ahead and put Townsend on?" Martin Post asked. "He's a pretty impressive guy. Might have done well."

"The report is in. So are his qualifications. Frankly, I was scared to try anything. That would just have given Bernie another shot at cross-examination."

Nobody said anything. Barbara wondered if they understood, if they could possibly understand what it was like to be alone at that podium, having to make those decisions in an instant, with no advance warning.

Finally Arlene Post changed the subject. "I thought that was a low blow, his standing behind the widow like that during cross-examination, putting her grief on display. That was unnecessary."

"But not unexpected," Barbara suggested. "That's all part of the show. Pretty effective, too. Juries are more sophisticated than that. If they wanted to look at her, they knew where she was. It probably didn't have much effect."

Another lie.

Barbara glanced out of the front window of the small café. Across the street she could see lights on the fourth floor of the courthouse, in the jury assembly room, where twelve people were trying their best to eat dinner, preparing to make an awesome decision.

"I'll say one thing, there's nothing phony about the Beckett woman," Baxter said. "I nearly cried myself."

"Have any of you had contact with the family?" Barbara asked.

"Only through my lawyers," Martin Post answered. "It didn't seem appropriate to make contact, under the circumstances."

"I suppose that's right," Barbara said.

"Maybe when this is over there will be something I can do," Baxter said. "I doubt that she would want to hear from me."

"I don't know," Barbara mused. "It's hard to say. You never can tell. People are suddenly thrown into these circumstances and they stay away from each other, acting like they don't care, as if it would somehow tip the scales of justice or demonstrate weakness to show compassion. Yet people care. *You* care. I know you do. What's the right response? I don't know. No one knows. So most of the time people do nothing."

"Maybe a note later on?" Baxter said.

"Maybe so," Barbara agreed.

The four of them sat in silence.

Barbara glanced at her watch. "Time to go. We had better be

on time. The way the judge is acting, I don't want to be late." She
slipped out of the booth. The others followed; Martin Post left some
money on the table.

"What do you make of Judge Whitehurst?" Martin Post asked.
"Is there something wrong?"

"I don't know," Barbara said. "I've never seen him like this. So
quiet. Almost as if he isn't there. It scares me. And working at night
... it's so unlike him. At least when he's being a jerk he is predictable."

They stopped at the front door to bundle up.

"Well, I suppose a huddle wouldn't be inappropriate," Barbara
said. "I feel like it's fourth down, and we are calling our last play."

"Hang tough," Martin Post said as he held open the door and
let her pass. "We'll be cheering you on in our hearts. You can count
on that."

"Thanks," she said.

Across the street, Cullen Whitehurst stared out of the window
of his darkened office. He watched as the café door opened and
the foursome stepped outside, immediately surrounded by reporters and curious bystanders. He followed the group as it
struggled to cross the street, its progress hampered by the rudeness
of the press as reporters grabbed and snatched for bits of news
like vultures picking at a carcass. His eyes remained riveted to
Baxter Post as they approached the courthouse. The young man
finally disappeared from sight. Whitehurst sank back into his leather
chair, reached for the half-filled crystal glass on his desk, and took
another sip.

"May it please the court, members of the jury, I take no pleasure
in this assignment. I did not seek it, but I won't avoid it."

Thus began the closing argument for the state.

Bernie Fine did a remarkable job. He was brief, to the point,
and sincere. He dissected the proof piece by piece, spread it out for
the jury to see, then put it back together in a narrative form, weaving
a cohesive story from start to finish.

The jury followed him from start to finish, consuming every
word with a passion, a passion fanned into flames during the two
long days of evidence and testimony. It was obvious to everyone
that the jurors were in total agreement with Bernie as he completed
his summation.

"The past two days have been difficult for you." He walked slowly up and down the length of the jury box, looking each juror in the eye, one at a time, as he spoke. "You have been taken from your homes, separated from your families, and have had your schedules totally disrupted. You have responded to the call of your state, and now you sit here, ready to decide the fate of a fellow human being.

"Some of you may wish you weren't here. Some of you may wonder how it is going to feel to vote 'guilty' when the time comes. You may wonder if you are going to be able to do it, if you are going to be able to bear the burden of this responsibility. I know that feeling. Believe me, I know it, because I used to struggle with the burden of being a prosecutor, just as the judge undoubtedly struggles with the responsibility of being a judge, and having to pass sentence."

He stopped pacing and stood in front of the jury box, hands at his side.

"Let me tell you something, ladies and gentlemen. I need not suffer over this. And you need not feel bad about voting for guilty if you believe, as I think you should, that the evidence cries out for such a verdict. The judge needn't have sleepless nights after passing sentence. We can all do our job with a clear conscience."

God, I wish that were true, Cullen Whitehurst thought.

"We can rest easy tonight," Bernie continued, "because we are not the authors of Baxter Post's fate. He made his own decision. He did it to himself. He is an adult, totally responsible for his own actions. *He* decided to get drunk that night, and *he* decided to drive. *He*, and he alone, decided to leave a fine young man lying in the middle of a remote, snow-covered highway, his life's blood dripping away, and *he* decided, on his own, to run home and hide, to continue to perpetrate on his parents and his community the deception and deceit that have characterized and dominated the last few years of his life."

Baxter Post stared blankly into space.

"Baxter Post killed Randy Beckett, and thus wrote an end to that young man's life story. But at the same time he wrote a chapter in his own life story. And your job, the one you were selected to do and the one that you promised to do, is to follow the law, and render unto Baxter Post the guilty verdict that he himself earned, by his own free will."

Bernie sat down. Barbara moved with deliberate slowness toward the lectern, composing her thoughts as she went.

Finally ready, she looked at the jury. Her eyes met nothing but cold, impassive stares.

"May it please the court, members of the jury." She paused, looked down, then fixed the jurors once more. "What can I say on behalf of Baxter Post? I have worried so much about that. If only I had the words to tell you what is in my heart. If only you could talk to him as I have done, get to know him as I have done, understand him as I have done, then perhaps you, too, would believe as I believe, that for all of the mistakes in his past and for all of the uselessness that his life may represent to you, he did not kill Randy Beckett. I believe that. I believe it because it is true."

She really did believe it. The jury listened attentively. Her sincerity was coming through.

Playing off Bernie's argument, she went back through the litany of evidence in the same order in which he had presented it, emphasizing how circumstantial it all was, and how equally consistent it was with Baxter's innocence as with his guilt.

She reminded the jury that like most crimes, this one had not been committed in a stadium in front of spectators who could report what they had seen. There was no eyewitness. The time of death was uncertain. The absence of blood at the site of the body was unusual. The story told by Baxter Post was, indeed, logically possible.

But would the jury believe it?

A lawyer must believe in his or her client, or all is lost. Hypocrisy is impossible to hide. Jurors sense insincerity long before they identify it.

"Members of the jury, I ask only this on behalf of my client. Weigh the proof in your minds, and also in your hearts. Look at it with the kind of care and scrutiny you would want jurors to use if your own son were called to account. There has been a death. It is tragic. Vengeance would be sweet, but before you vote to destroy a second life, ask yourself this: Am I certain? Do I still have a doubt? For that is what the law requires of you. You must be certain, beyond a reasonable doubt. If you are not certain, absolutely certain, then you *must* acquit Baxter Post."

Barbara stood behind Baxter, borrowing a trick from her opponent.

"Beyond a reasonable doubt. That's the phrase. You have heard it all your lives. What does it mean? The judge will define it for you. And when he does so, listen carefully. Understand what he is staying. Then ask yourself this: Am I sure? Do I still have a lingering doubt, however small?

"If you do, and I think you will, then in spite of the tragedy of Randy Beckett's death, in spite of what you might feel about Baxter Post, and even in spite of your own desire to see that vengeance is wreaked upon the wrong and that justice is ultimately done, your responsibility, more importantly your duty, will be to say to the state, 'I'm just not sure.' Your duty will be to vote 'not guilty.' "

Barbara sat down. The arguments were over.

All eyes turned toward the judge as he adjusted his glasses and picked up some of the papers on his desk.

"Members of the jury," Judge Whitehurst said, "it is now my duty to tell you what the law is, and it shall be your duty to apply that law to the facts of this case, and to render that verdict which you believe the facts and the law require."

The instructions to the jury took almost twenty minutes. Judge Whitehurst read in a colorless monotone.

The jurors listened attentively. Several leaned forward in their chairs, eyes glued to the judge. One or two took notes. All twelve strained to hear the judge's sonorous words.

Bernie Fine held a pad in his lap. He had listed all of the points that he wanted the judge to address; one by one he checked items off.

Lynn Beckett sat in a trance. She heard all but understood nothing. Her defense system still hadn't let her slip back into reality. And every time the judge said "Randall Allen Beckett" or "the victim" or "the deceased," she withdrew just a bit more, one part of her mind hearing the cold reality of those words while the other part stood aside like a spectator, questioning it all, searching for a way out of her nightmare.

Barbara Patterson was also in a trance, but of a different kind. Having finished her argument, her body's internal systems had all collapsed. For the past two days she had existed almost exclusively on adrenaline and nervous energy. Once through, they abandoned her.

Baxter Post sat upright in his chair, leaning forward slightly with elbows resting on the glass-topped surface, hands clasped. The veins running along the backs of his hands were blue and bulging; white knuckles stood out in stark contrast to the flushed color of his skin.

Baxter heard every mention of Randy Beckett's name, too. He also heard his own name, linked with such terms as "murder," "homicide," "criminal intent," and "willful and wanton disregard." None of it escaped his attention as he sat transfixed, wondering if his last minutes of freedom were ticking away.

Baxter stared at the tabletop and continued to listen.

"The first thing you should do when you enter the jury room is to elect one of your number as foreman. That person is to moderate your deliberations; he or she shall have no authority, and his or her vote shall count no more than the others. Each of you must decide on your own, regardless of what the others might think or say."

The charge was almost over. Bernie's pad was filled with checks. Barbara watched Tony Costello take the verdict form from the judge and hand it to the nearest juror.

". . . when you have reached a verdict, just knock on the door. Mr. Costello will be nearby, and will inform the court that you are ready. Anything else, counsel?"

The two lawyers stood. There was nothing else.

The jurors marched out single file, somber-faced.

It was eight-thirty P.M.; Judge Whitehurst advised counsel that he would let the jury deliberate until ten o'clock, then call them in for a report. Then he, too, marched out. Tony Costello followed through the door.

Now the wait began. Lynn Beckett joined her mother in the gallery; the older woman quietly slipped her arm around her distraught daughter's shoulder. They sat in silence, watching with detached curiosity as Martin and Arlene Post hugged their son. Lynn felt nothing. No sympathy, no hatred, not even dislike. Nothing. There was nothing left to feel.

The Post family also waited in the courtroom, to avoid the clamor of the press and the stares of the curious out in the hallway. An awkward quiet hung over the huge room. Barbara waited with them; every now and then they whispered back and forth, calling on each other for strength. It was uncomfortable, but they didn't have to endure the discomfort long. In exactly thirty-eight minutes

Tony Costello walked through the paneled door and announced that the jury had reached a verdict.

Lynn Beckett's heart raced.

Barbara Patterson's heart sank. A fast verdict is not a good sign for the accused.

Baxter Post's heart stopped beating. For him, time came to a standstill; seconds stretched into eternities.

As Martin and Arlene Post hugged Baxter again, Bernie Fine strode confidently through the door, the slightest suggestion of a smile on his face. The gladiator in him smelled victory. Once he was in place, the jury walked in, single file. None of them looked at Baxter Post. None of them smiled.

Finally the judge and jury were both in place. Everyone sat down, except for Barbara Patterson and her client.

"Has the jury reached a verdict?"

"We have, Your Honor," came the response from a man in the middle of the first row.

"Please stand and read your verdict," Judge Whitehurst said. The foreman stood and unfolded the slip of paper in his hand.

"We, the jury, find the defendant guilty of vehicular homicide, guilty of leaving the scene, and guilty of driving while intoxicated."

Cullen Whitehurst bowed his head for an instant.

Baxter Post slumped back into his chair. A numbness enveloped his body.

"So say you all?" the judge asked. All twelve nodded in assent. The judge turned toward Baxter Post; Barbara Patterson motioned for him to stand once more.

"Then the verdict of the jury becomes judgment of the court. Martin Baxter Post, Jr., I find you guilty of all three counts of the indictment against you. Under the law it is my duty to sentence you. Counsel"—he looked directly at Barbara Patterson—"I will pass sentence on this defendant tomorrow morning at nine o'clock. The defendant may remain on bond until then. Adjourn court, Mr. Costello."

Barbara's jaw dropped. She started to speak, but it was too late. Judge Whitehurst was gone.

CHAPTER

Thirty

Barbara stood behind her desk and faced the window. Her hands were tightly clasped behind her back as she stared out into the darkness and shifted nervously from one foot to the other.

The only noise to be heard in Barbara's office was the bubbling of the coffee maker. The receptionist had been gone for some time now; Barbara had put on a fresh pot only minutes ago. Now she waited restlessly for the pot to fill. It was going to be a long, long night.

Barbara's office was cluttered with the kind of mass confusion that tends to accumulate in a busy lawyer's work space, especially during a time when one case is receiving all of the attention. Files were scattered about in an organized disarray that only Barbara could understand; unanswered letters cluttered the desk, call slips covered the telephone table and spilled over onto the floor. It was a mess, but it was her mess. She knew where everything was, and what was important.

In spite of the appearance of chaos, there was an appealing atmosphere about the place, an aura that gave one confidence. Here was a busy person, the office cried out, one who is in great demand. You have come to the right place.

Right now, however, the condition of her office was the last thing on anybody's mind.

The events of the evening had caught them all up and carried them along in a whirlwind. Now they were struggling for some sense of direction, fighting for some means to turn this thing around. The final pronouncement had been the biggest surprise of all.

"I just don't understand. I know that's not the kind of thing you like to hear from your lawyer, but frankly I'm at my wits' end. I have no answers. I'm not even sure I know the questions anymore. This trial has deteriorated into a circus."

Barbara slipped out of her jacket and sank down into the swivel chair behind her desk.

"I just can't believe it," she continued. "He's going to pronounce sentence tomorrow morning, without any opportunity for briefs, with no chance of our getting prepared, with no character witnesses, and most of all without a probation report. How in the hell is he going to sentence Baxter without a probation report?"

"I thought the law was that he had to turn this over to a probation officer," Martin Post said. "How can he just ignore the law?"

Barbara reached for a large book with dark green binding that lay open on the credenza behind her.

"I thought it was the law, too," she said. "Every case I've tried has been handled that way, routinely. You have a trial. You win or lose, and if you lose, your client goes through the probation process. That's how it works. Unfortunately, as it turns out that's *not* the law."

She flipped through the pages of the book, stopped, turned to another page, then read for a moment.

"Damn," she muttered, slamming the book tight. "The only thing the statute says is that the judge has the power to pass sentence, subject to such procedures as may be established from time to time to ensure that sufficient information is available to him. The rest of it—the probation interview, the report, all of that—that's just what they have decided to do here locally. But apparently the law doesn't make them do it."

"Isn't there some kind of precedent, though?" Martin Post asked. "Doesn't fairness have anything to do with it?"

The gurgling noise stopped.

"I'll get us some coffee," Arlene Post said.

"The cups are in the cabinet under the machine," Barbara called out as the older woman left. "I'm sorry. You were saying something about fairness?"

"I guess I was dreaming," Martin Post said, "but I thought that fairness had a place in our judicial system."

"It's not the system," Barbara responded. "It's Judge Whitehurst. I've never seen him like this. He's gone off the deep end. He's always been hard to deal with, but at least I have known what to expect. I had gotten used to him. Now, all of a sudden, he's completely different."

Arlene Post came back with several cups of steaming black coffee.

"He didn't say anything, all day long," Barbara went on. "He seemed to be in some kind of trance, just enduring the trial, surviving until it was over. He seemed nervous, apprehensive ... something. I can't put my finger on it. But nobody was in charge. It was as if the trial were a runaway train, and his only responsibility was to keep it on track so it could end before it crashed. He didn't seem to care at all about doing anything right. He just wanted to get it over with. Just get it over with."

"Can we appeal?" Baxter Post asked.

"We've got to," Barbara answered with a shrug. "It's our only chance. There are a lot of holes in this record. The Court of Appeals should take a long look at the sentencing procedure. Let's face it. Whitehurst is going to make some kind of grandstand play in the morning. Why else would he be ramrodding this? He is playing his role to the hilt. Crusading judge! Conscience of the community! Watchdog of the public highways! It makes me sick."

Baxter gazed off into the darkness and sighed. His stomach was churning; his nerves were on edge.

"I'm going to be made public example number one," he said, forcing a laugh. "A human sacrifice on the altar of politics." He hung his head for a moment. "How much time do you think he will give me?"

He tossed the question off with the nonchalance of one who was asking the time of day.

Arlene Post felt a chill run down her spine. All through the weeks of intense preparation, all during the two days of trial, she had kept her worst thoughts and fears locked away in the corner of her mind, safely out of reach of her consciousness. She had steadfastly refused to think about jail. As long as there was hope, as long as there was a chance, however slim, she had denied the truth and suppressed even the possibility. Baxter's words hit her like a sledgehammer. All of her fears suddenly rushed to the front.

"It's too early to think about that now," Barbara said. "There are too many possibilities. Whatever he gives you, we will immediately ask for probation."

"Will we get it?" Martin Post asked as he looked at his son. "Is there a chance?"

"There's always a chance," Barbara responded, forcing a note of cheer into her voice. "They sure can't stop us from asking. We'll have time to prepare ourselves, too. We'll put on some witnesses, maybe bring in an expert. And since this isn't a capital crime, we can ask that bond be continued until that hearing. Who knows, once Whitehurst pronounces sentence, maybe his thirst for blood and his lust for publicity will be satisfied and he'll listen to reason."

"I hope so," Arlene Post whispered, pulling a tissue from the deep recesses of her purse. "God, I hope so."

Barbara stood up. "We need to get to work. There's going to be a hearing in the morning, and we have got to put on the best show we can. All three of you must come up with names. We need to make a plan. We've got to get on the phone and call some folks, and get some help." She glanced at her watch. It was almost eleven.

"Call people? In the middle of the night?" Baxter asked.

"Desperate times call for desperate measures," Barbara answered with resolve, handing legal pads to all three of them. "Nobody is going to complain. Believe me, they'll understand, no matter *how* late it gets." She looked at Baxter and winked. "Besides, how many of Baxter's friends would be in bed this early on a Friday night?"

Baxter smiled. "I'll be lucky if I can find anybody at home, much less asleep."

All four felt energized as the pace began to accelerate.

"I'll check the coffee supply," Arlene suggested, "and I'll call around and see if anyone will deliver some doughnuts, or something else for us to munch on. It looks like we may be here all night."

As it turned out, it didn't take all night, but it didn't miss by much. A list was compiled. Calls were made, each beginning with sincere apologies for the ungodly hour of the call, each ending with an enthusiastic commitment to help. One by one, witnesses were lined up for the next morning. A number of possibilities had come to mind, but they finally decided on four people: the counselor who had helped Baxter during his period of recovery, a longtime family friend who had known him as a child, the minister who had counseled the family, and a young contemporary whose friendship had not flagged in spite of all that had happened.

The street was totally deserted when the four of them emerged from Barbara's building at ten minutes after two in the morning. The security guard in the lobby smiled a groggy smile; they had awakened him from his customary half-sleep.

"What's the drill in the morning?" Martin Post asked. "Let's be sure we have our signals straight."

"Your office, six o'clock sharp," Barbara said.

"I'll just meet you at the courthouse," Arlene Post said. "I've got to get some rest. I'm about to drop in my tracks."

"No problem," Barbara said.

"Well, I guess that's it," Barbara added. "Except maybe a prayer or two. That's about the only base we haven't covered."

"That's been done, too," Arlene Post said. "Believe me, that's been done."

"What do you pray for in a case like this?" Baxter asked. "What do you say to God when you are in my shoes? What do you ask for? I've thought a lot about that. A whole lot. And I've thought about the other side of the coin, too. What does Lynn Beckett pray for? Vengeance? My soul to burn in hell? And which one of us does God listen to?"

"I can only tell you what I have been praying for," Arlene said, taking Baxter's hand. "I pray every night that the truth will come out, and that God will love us anyway, and have mercy on us all."

"Amen," Barbara whispered. "Amen."

About fifteen minutes later, at approximately the same moment that Barbara Patterson unlocked her front door, a telephone was ringing some forty-five miles away. The jangling sound fell on deaf ears for several rings. Finally the thick blanket of sleep was pierced, and Richard Maxwell fumbled for the receiver.

Instinctively he sat up in bed. Calls such as this one, in the middle of the night, were not unknown to him.

"Hello?" he said quietly. Then he listened. Whatever fog might have shrouded his senses was quickly burned away by the strident panic in the voice that he heard. Dr. Maxwell glanced at his still-slumbering wife.

"You hold on," he said when there was a break. "I'm going to change phones. You will be on hold for a moment; don't hang up. Okay?"

"Okay," Margaret Whitehurst answered from the quiet solitude of her own bedroom, the bedroom that had been her self-imposed prison for the past several hours.

Richard Maxwell hurried to his study, flicked on the light, found a pad and pencil, and reached for the telephone on his desk. All the while, everything he knew about crisis management ran through his mind.

"Mrs. Whitehurst?" He began by making certain that she was still there.

"Dr. Maxwell, I'm so glad you are there."

"Do I need to call anyone? Are you okay?" So many of his middle-of-the-night calls were suicide related that his first thought was always to get someone there as quickly as possible.

"I'm not okay, but I'm going to be all right, I think, now that I've called you." Dr. Maxwell knew what she meant.

"Where's your husband? Are you alone?"

"I don't know where he is. I think he's at his office. No one's answering the phone. I don't really know where he is at all."

"Take your time, Mrs. Whitehurst. Tell me what's wrong."

There was silence for several seconds.

"Mrs. Whitehurst?"

"Dr. Maxwell, it's started all over," Margaret Whitehurst managed, and then she burst into racking, breath-stealing sobs. Richard Maxwell tried to soothe her, to keep her as much in focus as possible.

"Let it come, let it all come on out," he said quietly as the woman at the other end of the line released the tensions that had held her in a death grip for so long. "Crying is the best thing now ..."

After what seemed like an eternity to them both, Margaret Whitehurst calmed down enough so that she could begin putting words together again and could understand what the doctor said to her in response.

"Now, I want you to talk to me, Mrs. Whitehurst," he said slowly and deliberately. "You have all the time you need. Don't rush it. Don't force it. You're in shock right now, emotional shock. Just take your time."

"I have so much to tell you," Margaret said between lingering sobs. "So much has happened . . ."

As he listened, Richard Maxwell wanted to ask questions, but he didn't. Some of them would have been unkind, questions such as why she hadn't called sooner, why she hadn't done something when all of the signs began to appear again, why she had once again allowed herself to be a part of the problem. Such thoughts were irrelevant. The immediacy of the crisis became crystal clear in the words that tumbled out of Margaret Whitehurst's battered heart.

"I need to see you, Doctor," Margaret said in a few minutes. "I can't handle this alone. Can I come?"

Richard Maxwell had made his decision several minutes earlier. As he listened, he busily scribbled instructions to leave behind for his wife.

"Listen to me, Margaret. I'm coming to you. Tell me how to get there. I want you to stay where you are. I don't want you to try to drive—I don't want you to do anything but wait for me. You understand? It's going to take me about an hour altogether. Will you be okay?" He was talking to her very deliberately now, using the tone a parent might use to be certain that an errant child understood the seriousness of a situation.

Finally the conversation concluded. Richard Maxwell jotted off another note, then headed back to the bedroom to throw on some clothes.

"Good God Almighty," he whispered as he reached for a sweater.

CHAPTER

Thirty-one

Lorene Crosby looked up from her typewriter the instant she heard the door open. Margaret Whitehurst and Dr. Richard Maxwell walked in and quickly shut the door.

"Mrs. Whitehurst?" Lorene's brows rose in surprise. She recognized the man with her, but couldn't remember his name. There was no time to ask before Margaret spoke.

"Has Cullen gone on the bench yet?"

"Tony is helping him with his robe. Should I buzz them? It may not be too late."

Margaret pulled her scarf from around her neck and unbuttoned her heavy coat.

"I don't think so," Richard Maxwell said. "Let me think a minute."

"What happened last night?" Mrs. Crosby asked.

"What do you mean?" Margaret Whitehurst snapped, giving her husband's secretary a sharp look.

"Your husband was here when I got here this morning. He

—225—

looked awful, like he had slept in his clothes, if he had slept at all. I spoke to him as usual, but he cut me off. Snapped my head off, for nothing. I thought about calling you. I know it's none of my business, but ... here, let me take that."

She took Margaret Whitehurst's coat and scarf and hung them in the small closet. Margaret stared at the gold-leaf lettering on the opaque-glass door leading to her husband's office.

"Can I get you a cup of coffee?" Lorene Crosby asked.

"No thank you." Margaret paced back and forth the length of the small office, glancing down at her watch every few seconds. Finally the door opened and Tony Costello stepped out.

Margaret held a finger to her lips as the heavy door shut behind Tony.

Tony recognized the other visitor immediately. "Dr. Maxwell."

"Tony, we need to talk to you. It's important. Can you break away?"

Costello glanced at his watch. "We're about to open court."

"Can you get away after that?"

"I could step out for a minute."

"We need longer than a minute," Margaret responded.

"Margaret, I ..."

She touched his arm. "Please. This is important. We've got to talk to you."

Tony knew that Judge Whitehurst was waiting for him.

"Wait here," he said. "I'll be back out as soon as we are through. It's the best I can do. I'm sorry."

Margaret and Dr. Maxwell watched Tony disappear into the passage that led to the courtroom. She heard the echo of his opening words as the door closed.

"Don't press it, Margaret," Richard Maxwell said. "There's time. This has got to be done right."

Inside the courtroom, everyone stood as Judge Whitehurst entered. His face was drawn, his lids heavy, his face blotched and covered with stubble.

"Oyez, oyez, oyez ..."

Barbara Patterson and Baxter Post looked little better than the judge after their night of toil. Lynn Beckett appeared pale and tired herself. Only Bernie Fine appeared to have managed any sleep.

"Be seated, please."

Barbara Patterson remained standing.

"May I address the court?" she said from her position at the defense table.

"Go ahead," Judge Whitehurst mumbled resignedly.

Barbara moved to the lectern. She had no notes.

"May it please the court," she began, "for the record, I would like to enter the defendant's objection to the court's decision to have this sentencing hearing this morning. It is Saturday morning—"

"We all know what day it is, Ms. Patterson," the judge interrupted, his deep voice rumbling in obvious irritation.

"Yes, Your Honor. I recognize that. However, I am not only addressing these remarks to Your Honor, I am also addressing them to the record, and I want the record to reflect that it is now shortly after nine o'clock on a Saturday morning, and we are assembled for the purpose of having this court pronounce sentence on my client, who was convicted by a jury in this very room only twelve hours ago."

Barbara moderated her voice and paced herself carefully. She knew that she was walking a very thin line. The slightest miscue might result in a tirade from the judge. But nothing happened.

"I know that, Ms. Patterson," the judge said in a calm voice. "Are you taking the position that this court is required by law to wait any given time before pronouncing sentence? If so, the court would appreciate your authority."

There was none, and she knew it. "Your Honor, it is not the time lapse that causes us concern. It is the fact that this court is departing from the procedure that it usually follows in criminal cases. As far as we know, there has been no probation report on Baxter Post. No investigation, nothing. While such procedures may not be required by statute, they are certainly suggested by tradition and mandated by fundamental principles of fairness."

Martin Post's word. Fairness. It couldn't be put any more succinctly than that.

"Our constitution guarantees a fair trial," she continued. "The sentencing procedure is as much a part of the trial as the opening statement or the direct examination or anything else. All we are asking for is fairness; all we are suggesting is that without the presentencing procedures and safeguards ordinarily employed by this court, it isn't possible for Baxter Post to receive fairness in this matter."

Barbara stood back from the podium and waited. Cullen Whitehurst spoke slowly, almost thick-tongued.

"Ms. Patterson, are you telling me that you don't believe I know enough about Baxter Post to be able to render a fair decision regarding his punishment at this time?"

Barbara swallowed hard. "Yes, Your Honor. Technically, that is what I am saying."

"What do you mean by 'technically'? Are you saying it, or are you not?"

"Your Honor, of course I am not able to put myself in your place and make a judgment about what you know and don't know. But I—"

"You might be surprised at what I know," the judge said.

"I beg your pardon?"

"Never mind, it's not important." Judge Whitehurst waved his hand as if he could cast the whole subject aside with the flick of a wrist. "Your exception is noted. Whatever power may stand in judgment of my actions today, it will just have to decide. Now, could we please get along with today's proceedings?"

Barbara Patterson was taken aback. "Your Honor, we are prepared to offer proof in support of our plea for mercy on behalf of Baxter Post."

"Proof?" The judge groaned. Of course they'd want to do that, he thought.

"Yes, Your Honor. We have witnesses here who are prepared to testify on behalf of the character and integrity of Baxter Post and the entire Post family. With the court's permission, we would like to present those witnesses."

Cullen Whitehurst leaned back in his leather chair and folded his arms over his chest.

"Go ahead," he said curtly. Barbara went back to the table and picked up her notes.

The case for the defense took less than fifteen minutes. All four witnesses were surprisingly brief, and Bernie Fine asked no questions at all. Tony Costello went through the motions of his various tasks, but he was in turmoil inside, forcing himself to look as normal as possible.

"Call your next witness," Cullen Whitehurst said as Baxter Post's longtime friend Alan Hargrove stepped down from the witness stand.

Barbara Patterson looked down at her list. "The defense has no more witnesses."

"What says the state? Anything in rebuttal?"

"Your Honor, the state would like to put Lynn Beckett, Mrs. Randall Allen Beckett, on the stand, if you please."

For the first time that morning Judge Whitehurst didn't appear irritated.

"Come around, please, Mrs. Beckett," he said as Lynn rose from her chair.

What Lynn Beckett said really didn't make much difference. Her mere presence on the stand spoke volumes.

She sat forward, on the front edge of the wooden chair. Tony Costello adjusted the microphone, then stepped out of the way. Lynn held a handkerchief tightly in one hand; with the other she brushed aside a wisp of hair that trailed down in front of her eyes.

"Mrs. Beckett, I am going to ask you a few questions," Bernie Fine began. "I know this is difficult, and I'm sorry. I will do what I can to make this as easy as possible. If you need to take a break, please let me know."

"Thank you," Lynn said softly, almost in a whisper.

"Mrs. Beckett, do you understand what this hearing is about?"

"I think so."

"Then you know that the judge here has got to decide what to do about Baxter Post, the man who has been found guilty of murdering your husband. You understand that, don't you?"

He's milking this for all it's worth, Barbara thought. But she kept quiet as Lynn Beckett once again assured the assistant district attorney that she understood.

"Mrs. Beckett," Bernie continued, "the judge has a right to do whatever he wants to do, but he wants to hear what you have to say. Now is the time. If you have any opinion, anything at all that you want the judge to hear, now is the time."

Bernie Fine was satisfied that he had set the scene as dramatically as he was capable of doing. He stepped back and let Lynn Beckett do her thing.

Lynn leaned forward and spoke into the microphone with all of the presence and impact of one who was not accustomed to the spotlight, but who was expressing the truth as best she knew how.

"I loved my husband," she whispered softly into the microphone. "I still do. If anything would bring him back, I would do it. But that's not possible. The only thing that can be done now is for the person who did this to pay for what he has done. All I ask this court to do is what's right. The person who took my husband from me deserves to be punished. Severely punished."

She was looking right at Baxter Post as she spoke. He was staring straight ahead, acutely aware of her gaze. There were no dry eyes in the courtroom. Not any. Not even those of Baxter Post or Judge Whitehurst.

Lynn turned in the witness seat and looked directly at the judge.

"Your Honor, Randy and I have two little boys. One of them never saw his father; the other is too young to remember him. Someday they are going to have to ask me questions, and I'm going to have to answer them. They are going to ask me about their father, and I will tell them as best I can. They're also going to ask me what happened to the man who killed their father, and whether justice was done. Your Honor, I want to be able to answer yes, to tell them justice really, truly was done. You are the only person who can make that happen. The only one."

Silence fell over the courtroom. Lynn Beckett was through. She slumped back down into the wooden chair and started to cry softly. Bernie Fine held out his hand and helped her down.

CHAPTER

Thirty-two

Barbara marched to the lectern as Judge Whitehurst glared at her every step of the way.

"I would like to address the court one last time."

Cullen Whitehurst rolled his eyes and leaned back in his chair. He was clearly nearing his wits' end.

"Ms. Patterson," he drawled, "what else can you say that I haven't already heard?"

"You haven't heard anything I have said, so far." She looked determined; her knees were shaking. "You haven't heard anything at all. If you had, you would have realized by now that this entire proceeding is a disgrace!"

Judge Whitehurst's eyes opened wide in shock. He appeared lost, almost disoriented, but only for an instant. He stood straight up and slammed his gavel down on the wooden surface.

"I've heard all I need to hear, Ms. Patterson. I assure you of that. I will render a decision in a few minutes. I am going to retire to consider this matter. Court will be in recess. In the meantime, I want to see counsel in my chambers. Immediately. Adjourn court, Mr. Costello."

"All rise!"

Judge Whitehurst stepped quickly down the small stairway that led to the door to his private office. Barbara and Bernie followed Tony Costello through the other doorway, on through Lorene Crosby's office, then into the judge's private chamber.

Both of them glanced at Margaret Whitehurst as they hurried past. Neither spoke or even acknowledged her presence. Neither of them knew Richard Maxwell.

Once inside the judge's office, Tony Costello offered to take the judge's robe. Judge Whitehurst waved him off, closing the door behind himself.

Cullen Whitehurst was in front of his desk, leaning back against the wooden surface, half-sitting on its edge. His hands were tightly clenched. He was obviously working very hard to restrain himself.

"Ms. Patterson," he finally said. "I am tired of fighting with you. I don't have any fight left. So I'm just going to have to spell it out for you, in black and white. Please listen. And if for some strange reason you don't understand, please tell me. Okay?"

"Your Honor, I . . ."

Judge Whitehurst held up his hand. "No explanations, please. And don't waste your breath on apologies. They don't mean anything. Just tell me whether or not you are listening, and when I have finished, kindly tell me whether or not you understood."

Barbara's cheeks reddened. "I'm listening."

"Ms. Patterson, you have deliberately and intentionally attacked me in open court. You have accused me of judicial misconduct. You have done so in a most sarcastic and disrespectful way. As far as I am concerned, you are utterly and completely in contempt of court, and deserving of punishment. The only question now is what to do with you. Do you have any suggestions?"

Silence hung like a pall over the small office.

"Well?" the judge asked again.

"I have no response," Barbara finally managed. "You and I do not agree, so whatever you decide to do is up to you."

Judge Whitehurst stared intently at the young woman. Bernie stood silently, his eyes darting back and forth between the two of them.

"Your Honor?" Barbara said, trying to get the judge headed on another track.

"Yes?" he responded curtly.

"I would like to have the court reporter brought in here to record these proceedings. I want a record of this."

'Atta girl, Bernie thought, stifling a smile. Fortunately his outward expression never changed.

"To what purpose?" Whitehurst asked. The mildness of his voice surprised both of the lawyers.

"Because ..." Barbara hesitated. She swallowed hard. This wasn't going to be easy.

"Your Honor," she said, "I am an advocate. I represent a client. I have a serious responsibility. The manner in which this hearing has been conducted is more than just unusual, it is barbaric. It smacks of Star Chamber or other oppressions. It is unfair, and it affects my client's rights. He deserves better than that. He is *entitled* to better than that!"

Barbara gained confidence as she worked up a full head of steam.

"You can do as you will with me," she went on. "I am not important. Neither are you. We are only part of a system that exists to serve the people. Like it or not, Baxter Post is one of those people. He may be guilty and you may find him personally distasteful, but he has a right to be treated fairly by this system. That isn't happening. He is being railroaded, and you are driving the engine. I want all of this on record. I'm going to take this to the Council on Judicial Ethics!"

Whitehurst's face reddened, but he still didn't move. If anything, a trace of sadness appeared in his expression. Bernie Fine, at this point a spectator, looked on in amazement.

"Look, Judge," Barbara implored. "I'm sorry. I really am. Everything I have said in the last few minutes has come out wrong. I didn't mean to be disrespectful. I didn't intend it that way. But forget about me. You can do what you will to me and it won't matter. I can take it. But I beg you not to let your feelings about me affect your decisions about my client. That would be the gravest injustice of all."

After an interminable wait, Judge Whitehurst stood erect. He walked over to the door that led back into the courtroom, all the while staring at Barbara Patterson. He adjusted his robe, then placed a hand on the doorknob, his eyes still fixed on hers. When he finally spoke, his voice was empty, flat and lifeless.

"Ms. Patterson, I don't think we have communicated at all. I have no more time for this. Kindly leave. I will deal with you in time. In the meanwhile, I want to be alone while I consider what to do with your client."

Tony Costello opened the door and held it.

Bernie scooted through the opening first. As he walked past the elderly jurist, his face reflected the extreme seriousness of the situation, but when he emerged into the courtroom, a wide smile of relief spread across his face.

Barbara couldn't move. She felt helpless and totally frustrated.

Finally she walked toward the judge. She neither spoke nor looked at Tony as she passed. In the doorway she stopped suddenly. On an impulse, with practically no thought whatever, she wheeled around and faced Whitehurst.

She tugged at the purse that was hanging from her shoulder, unsnapped it with one hand, and jammed her hand down in it. After closing her grip around a slender metal object, she quickly pulled it out.

"Here. I believe this may be yours." She thrust a gold pen at him. "I found it off of Cameron's Bridge Road."

He took it from her and looked at it.

His eyes, wide with surprise, met hers.

Barbara wheeled around and walked away as the door closed behind her. She walked directly to the first available chair and sat down.

Oh, my God, she thought.

Back in the judge's office, Cullen Whitehurst looked down at the gold pen. His face was ashen when he looked back up at Tony.

"Go on, I'll be out in a minute," the judge said quietly.

Tony glanced at the door to Lorene Crosby's office, but quickly elected to go on out into the courtroom.

CHAPTER
Thirty-three

"I don't give a damn about what you need to be doing," Barbara Patterson said to Tony Costello. "This is important. We have got to talk. Right now!"

It was the second such plea he had heard in the last few minutes, but the decision was easy. Costello could see the fire in her eyes.

"The judge is in his office, working on his decision," Costello said. "His wife is in the reception room. Where can we go?"

"What about Al Osborne? He was here a few minutes ago. We can use his office. See if you can find him."

Barbara found Baxter Post seated with his parents.

"Something has come up," she said. "Something very important. I am going to be downstairs in Al Osborne's office. If the judge gets ready to come out, they'll come get me. I'll tell the deputy. Just don't worry, and don't leave here. If you go outside, the press will eat you alive."

Tony waved for her to come on. In a few minutes the two of

them were following Al Osborne into his cramped office on the second floor.

"Come on in," Al said as he pushed open his office door and switched on the light. "Hope you can find a seat." As he spoke, he cleared stacks of paper off the vinyl side chairs, piling them unceremoniously on the floor.

"I'm glad you were here," Barbara said. "I was afraid you might be headed home."

"Tony said it was important. What's up, Barbara?"

"I'll get right to the point. I have a strong suspicion that Judge Whitehurst might have been involved in the death of Randy Beckett."

The two men sat in stunned silence.

"That's a pretty heavy accusation," Osborne said. "What makes you think that?"

"I've been suspicious for some time. Lots of little things have been piling up, things that don't mean much alone ..."

"Like what?" Osborne asked.

"For openers, on the night of Beckett's death, the judge left the Cambridge Club drunk, driving his own car, alone. The route he would have taken, the most direct route, would be right through the accident scene. The next day when the news broke, that jumped out at me. Then, once I had a chance to talk to Baxter Post, I believed him. I know he ran over Randy Beckett, but he's convinced that he wasn't the first, and I believe him to this very day. There had to be someone else. But who? It's been eating at me."

"That's not much to go on," Osborne said.

"That's not all. That's just when I had my first gut feeling about this. I hesitate to use the word 'intuition,' but I guess that is what it was."

Tony Costello stared blankly ahead, but he was listening to every word.

"Anyway, I didn't think about it much until the matter of the unlisted number came up. There again that didn't really say much to me, not right then. But I knew that you and the judge were friends, and certainly that was a possibility."

Osborne looked puzzled. "He had that number. He was one of the first ones I gave it to. But still ..."

"When I found out from the telephone company that your old number was changed just a few months before Randy Beckett was killed ... How many people could have had that number?"

Osborne rubbed his chin and searched his memory.

"What kind of car does Whitehurst drive?" Barbara asked. "Baxter Post saw a large dark car at the scene."

"What about it, Tony?" Osborne asked.

Tony Costello rose from his seat and walked over to the window. "He drives a black Lincoln. So what?"

Tony bit his lip and stared out at the gray, rainy sky hovering over the city he had called home for so many years. His eyes suddenly became moist; he wiped at them with the back of his hand as Barbara continued her litany of circumstances.

"Yesterday morning I took Baxter Post back to the scene where Randy Beckett was killed. After he left, I walked down that hill, trying to make some sense of this whole thing. I found a gold pen in the grass, next to the roadway, about halfway down the hill. The pen belongs to Judge Whitehurst."

Al Osborne stared in disbelief. "How do you know that?"

"It was monogrammed with a *W*. I didn't know what to do with it. Then I took a chance. Just a few minutes ago, in his office, I gave it to him. He recognized it. That puts him at the scene. So does the car. He was probably the anonymous caller. He had to be; he was one of the few with the number. At the very least he shouldn't be trying this case."

Al Osborne let out a low whistle.

Barbara Patterson sank back into her chair, exhausted.

Tony Costello took a deep breath, held it for a few seconds, then allowed it to escape slowly into the atmosphere. Then he turned back to Barbara and Al with a calm, almost placid expression.

"All of that may be true," he said, "but I can tell you that Judge Whitehurst didn't run over Randy Beckett."

There was silence for a moment.

"How do you know that?" Osborne asked.

"Because I did," Costello replied.

CHAPTER

Thirty-four

*B*arbara didn't take Tony Costello seriously. Anger rose within her. "What are you talking about? If this is your idea of a joke, it's not very funny."

"It's no joke," Costello whispered. "I wish it were."

Barbara was stunned. So was Al Osborne. Neither of them knew what to say next.

"Why don't you tell us about it?" Osborne finally managed.

"I ran over Randy Beckett," Tony said quietly. His voice revealed no emotion as he looked at the startled expressions on their faces. "I should have spoken up sooner, but I couldn't. I don't know why, but I couldn't."

Al Osborne instinctively reached for the pad and pencil on his desk.

"The night Randy Beckett died was the night of the Bar Association Christmas party," Costello continued. "Of course you know that. I went with Judge Whitehurst, as I always do, only we took separate cars. Usually I would drive him. But this night we took separate cars. He insisted. I didn't really like it, but I didn't put up much of a fight. I wish I had. The judge was in good shape when we left the courthouse. As usual, I was convinced that everything would be okay, but he got worse and worse as the evening went on.

"I knew the judge had started back drinking. I could tell. He has been back to his old ways for some time. I found out by accident. There was something in his office I wasn't supposed to find. I probably should have said something then, but you know, the judge has been a good friend to me. I owe him a lot. And I refused to let myself be realistic about it. I couldn't accept it, so I didn't."

"How long?" Barbara asked. Her shoulders were slumping. She felt drained. "When did this start?"

"Probably two years ago, maybe a little longer," Tony replied. "Anyway, I didn't say anything, or do anything either. I didn't even tell him I knew, although he eventually found out."

His mind wandered for a moment to the previous evening, and to the shocked look on the judge's face when Tony had walked in on him.

"Like a fool, I thought I might be able to do something about it by myself. I'd been through the whole thing before with the judge, and I knew better, but I did it anyway. It's hard not to try to help when you want to help so badly, when you want to protect someone you love and admire. I knew what it would do to the judge if anyone found out, so I tried to handle it myself."

"You're not the only one who has made that mistake, Tony," Al said. "The signs have been there for months. Longer even. We all have been running away as fast as we could."

"I found all of his hiding places," Tony said. "I watered down whatever he was drinking. It was always either gin or vodka—something that looked like water. I swear to God, I even found the smell of gin one day in the glass he keeps on the bench."

Al Osborne looked shocked. "Damnation," he muttered. "How long has that been going on?"

"I don't know. I only found it recently, a few weeks ago. But heaven only knows how long it was going on before that."

"What did you do about it?" Al asked.

"Like I say, I did what I could. I cut his gin. I went everywhere with him and made him leave parties early. I wouldn't let him drive—and all the time I was trying to figure out what I could do to get him straight.

"At the Christmas party I really was worried about him. He got real belligerent, and was clearly out of control. I should have stepped in, but how do you make someone do something they don't want to do? And I didn't want a scene, so I convinced myself that he wasn't too bad, and I left him alone. I just followed along. I stuck with him all evening. Then I lost him. Just like that. I was distracted for a minute, and I lost him."

Tony recalled his talk with Barbara Patterson, and his feeling of panic when he went to try to find the judge.

"You remember that, Barbara, don't you? I went off to talk to you, and I lost him. You were worried about him. You said that everyone knew, that the judge was the butt of everyone's jokes. That hurt. I got mad at you and cut you off. You were right, though. I guess everyone knew. I was hiding from the truth myself."

"You're not alone," Osborne interjected. "I heard the talk. Everybody did. None of our guys wanted to go into his court. They would bitch and moan and call him all kinds of names. Not all of them knew what was happening, but some did. Of course I denied it. I defended him. Just like you two did. I guess we can't blame each other for that. We all did the same thing."

"I remember the feeling I had, the awful feeling, when I realized that he had left the party alone," Tony said. "I'll never forget it. I was physically sick. It was nearly midnight when I went looking for him. Several people made smartass cracks when I asked if they had seen him. I got to the front door just in time to see him pulling out of the driveway. It was snowing. The drive was already covered. I panicked.

"I got my car. It's a black sedan, by the way. Full size. I figured he would come out Highway Forty. That was his usual route. So I took a chance. I drove fast—too fast—but I never saw him. My car was slipping and sliding all over the place. I lost traction and had to turn around and go another way entirely. I finally made it off Forty.

"I thought about stopping at the market where Cameron's Bridge hits the highway and calling his home to see if he had made it, but the market was closed. So I turned onto Cameron's Bridge. I almost lost control on the slick surface when I tried to turn.

"Then I hit that hill. I know Cameron's Bridge Road like the back of my hand. I have been out there a hundred times. I went too fast. When I crested the hill, I heard a noise."

"Did you see anything?" Osborne prodded.

"No, not then. I just felt this horrible bump and heard a noise.

"I managed to stop without losing control. I got out of my car and ran back up the hill. As I neared the crest, I could see that what I had hit was a person. I'll never forget it. He was all twisted and mangled. He wasn't moving."

"Was he breathing? Did he have a pulse?" Osborne asked.

"I didn't check. I started to, but suddenly I saw the lights of another car on the crest of the next hill, back toward Highway Forty. It was coming toward me. I really pushed the panic button then. All I could think about was saving my own skin. I ran back to my car, turned off my lights so I wouldn't be seen, and drove away."

"Leaving Randy Beckett there to die," Barbara whispered.

"I know that's what it looks like, but that's not the way it was. I figured the next car would see him and stop, and give him whatever help he needed. I know that doesn't seem very rational now, but that's what I thought at the time. I didn't want to be involved."

"Had you been drinking?" Osborne demanded.

"Yes, I had taken a couple of drinks, maybe three or four. I almost never drink when I am with the judge, but I was so pissed off that I just didn't care."

"What happened next?" Barbara asked. "What did you do?"

"I got out of there as fast as I could. I went home. I couldn't think of anything else to do. I just went home.

"I didn't sleep at all. I didn't even try. I didn't think about sleep. I didn't even change clothes. I just walked the floor until daybreak. I read about Baxter Post the next morning. I was overjoyed. It was perfect. Of course I didn't know anything about the warrant and the episode at the judge's house at that time. Anyway, it was perfect. A rich, obnoxious kid with a bad record. An airtight case. It was absolutely perfect. I went home and went to bed. It didn't start eating at me until later."

Nobody said anything for a few seconds.

"I'm more confused than ever," Barbara said. "I hear what you are saying, but the evidence is still there. The phone number, the gold pen . . . I don't know what in the hell to believe, much less what to do next." She looked at Al Osborne. "What do you think?"

Al Osborne stared intently at Tony. "How carefully did you look at Randy Beckett?"

"Not long. Just long enough to panic."

"What was he wearing?" Osborne asked.

"Don't play games with me, Al," Costello snapped, a startled look on his face.

"I'm not playing. I'm dead serious. I don't believe you for a minute. It's too easy, too convenient. You're covering Whitehurst's ass, and I know it. What kind of clothes was the boy wearing?"

Costello looked at Barbara. "That's crazy. I'm telling the truth."

"Look, Tony, we know how you feel about Judge Whitehurst," Al Osborne said, "but don't let your loyalty get out of hand."

"I'm not so loyal that I would sell myself down the river."

"Tony, let's face the facts," Barbara said. "The judge was there. He was on that road, he was drunk, and he is acting crazy in this case. He has to be involved. He's got to be the one who called Al with the license number. You've said yourself that you left. Even if you were telling the truth, your car couldn't have been the one Baxter Post saw."

"In order for the judge to get the Post boy's license number, he had to be there when Post hit the body. He had to be hiding there, waiting and watching," Al chimed in.

"And he had to have hit Randy Beckett himself, otherwise there would have been no reason to frame somebody else," Barbara added. "You can't change that, Tony, no matter what you say now."

Tony hung his head and rubbed his hands together nervously.

"He didn't do it," Tony mumbled. "I just know it. He couldn't have. He's not that kind of man."

"Neither are you, Tony," Osborne added. "If you had run over Randy Beckett, you would have come forward long ago."

Tony slumped down in a chair. Al looked at Barbara.

"Maybe I am that loyal," Tony mumbled.

"The only thing we know for certain is that we don't know anything for certain," Barbara whispered, almost to herself.

"But there is one thing we do know for sure," Osborne asserted, standing up behind his desk. "Baxter Post may be telling the truth. His car really wasn't the first to hit Randy Beckett, and Judge Whitehurst set him up. We can't just sit here and do nothing about that."

"What do we do?" Barbara said.

"We've got to start with the judge," Osborne replied, putting on his suit jacket.

The three of them scurried out of Osborne's office and marched briskly down the hallway, through the reception area, and out into the large central corridor. They went directly to the bank of elevators. Osborne pressed on the UP button again and again. The elevator took forever. Finally the brass doors slid open.

The elevator was empty except for the operator, a genial, gray-haired old man who had been a fixture in the courthouse for years. He spoke to Al Osborne as the threesome climbed aboard. "What floor, Captain?"

"Four. Express if you can. We're in a hurry."

The operator held down the button that would allow them to bypass the intervening floors.

"You're headed for a hornet's nest, Captain," the operator exclaimed as the doors closed. He pulled the brass lever to one side. The elevator began to rise.

"What do you mean?" Osborne asked.

"All hell has broken loose up there. Haven't you heard?"

The old man obviously relished the opportunity to be the first to pass along some juicy news.

"Heard what?" Osborne was getting impatient with this cat-and-mouse exchange.

The operator released the lever and turned toward the threesome just as the elevator arrived at the fourth floor.

"Judge Whitehurst just set that little son of a bitch free, that's what."

CHAPTER
Thirty-five

The fourth floor of the courthouse was a mass of confusion. Hundreds of people milled about aimlessly. Passage was clearly going to be difficult.

The three of them formed a wedge with Tony Costello at the point and forced their way through the crowd. As they approached, the doors to the courtroom opened; Lynn Beckett came through, flanked by Bernie Fine on one side and her father-in-law on the other. The bright beams of television lights bounced off her face; she held up her arms to ward off the glare. She was crying.

"Mrs. Beckett, do you have any comment, any comment at all?" one reporter cried out.

"Mrs. Beckett, how do you feel, now that your husband's killer is a free man?" another asked.

"Mrs. Beckett, do you plan an appeal?"

Costello and Osborne continued down the hall, toward the back entrance to the judge's chambers. Barbara stopped at the edge of the crowd to watch. She was stunned. She wanted to reach her client, but she couldn't force her way through the mass of bodies that blocked the courtroom door.

Bernie Fine was holding his hand up for silence. "Please, please," he said. "One at a time."

The crowd settled a bit. All eyes focused on the distraught woman.

"As you can imagine," Bernie continued, "Mrs. Beckett is quite upset right now. We are all upset. Give us a break. She will not be making any kind of statement or be answering any questions. Perhaps later, but not now. I hope you understand."

A reporter interrupted. "General Fine, what do you think of the judge's decision to put Baxter Post on probation? How do you feel?"

"I'm terribly disappointed. And confused. I don't understand any part of it. I think it is a mistake. A travesty. That's all I will say."

"Do you think Martin Post used his influence again?"

Bernie paused for a moment. "I have no comment. You heard the evidence; you draw your own conclusion."

Another reporter squeezed her way to the front of the crowd. "General, do you plan to appeal this decision?" She stuffed her microphone up under his nose.

Bernie looked down at the woman with disgust. The other reporters all strained to hear his response.

"That's the saddest part. The question of probation is discretionary with the judge. It's his decision. What Judge Whitehurst has done today is final."

Bernie bit his tongue. He wanted to say more. Much more. But he dared not.

"General Fine, do you think—"

"That's all for now." Bernie cut the reporter off in midsentence. "We'll issue a statement later. Please, let us through. Let us through."

He held one arm out to block off the crowd, put his other arm around Lynn Beckett, and pressed forward.

Barbara stood her ground and watched as Lynn Beckett passed in front of her, not three feet away. Cameras clicked all around, the wildly flashing strobes adding to the carnival atmosphere. The beleaguered young woman looked older than her years; her eyes were reddened and deeply set in blue pockets of fatigue. She looked depressed. Her eyes met Barbara's for an instant, but her contempt showed through clearly.

It was an image Barbara Patterson would never forget.

One of the reporters recognized Barbara. "Ms. Patterson, do you have any comments?"

Another followed suit. "Ms. Patterson, where were you when the judge was reading his opinion?"

Barbara ignored them and walked briskly through the courtroom door. The uniformed officer standing at the door recognized her and let her pass.

Baxter Post was huddled around the defense table with his parents.

"What in the world happened?" Barbara asked.

Martin Post responded, "Judge Whitehurst just burst through the door and called the court to order. You weren't here; I tried to point that out. General Fine offered to wait, but the judge said no. He ordered me to sit, made Baxter stand up, and started reading from a sheet of paper."

Baxter Post picked up the story. "He sentenced me to the maximum sentence he could impose. I thought I would pass out. Then he started in on a speech about law and order, and about doing what is right. He said something about people not always understanding. At the end of his speech he suspended the entire sentence and put me on supervised probation. He didn't even wait for the defense to ask. He just did it."

"He was right about one thing," Martin Post added. "Nobody understands. Not even us. We're grateful, but we sure as hell don't understand."

"This has gone far enough," Barbara said. "Wait here. I'll be right back."

She hurried through the paneled door that led into the back hallway. Without knocking, she pushed open the door to Lorene Crosby's office. Margaret Whitehurst looked up at Barbara as she entered; the judge's wife was ashen faced. Lorene was crying softly.

"Where is the judge?" Barbara demanded.

"He's gone," Al Osborne said. "He was gone by the time Tony and I got here."

"Gone? Gone where?"

"I don't know," Lorene Crosby said. "When he came off the bench, I heard the door in his office open and shut. I started back there to see if there was anything I could do. The minute I opened his door, he came bolting through, right past me, right past Mrs. Whitehurst and Dr. Maxwell."

Barbara looked at the stranger holding Margaret Whitehurst's hand.

"The judge didn't say anything to anybody. He just stormed out into the hall. I followed him. He disappeared into the stairwell. I called after him as he went down, but he never answered."

Tony Costello stepped into the judge's office.

"Since then I have done nothing but answer the phone," Lorene Crosby added. "I finally had to take it off the hook. Even the governor's office has called, and it's only been a few minutes since all of this took place."

"You've heard what happened?" Al asked.

"I already knew," Ms. Crosby answered. "He wrote out his judgment before he went out there. He gave it to me, and I typed it."

"Do you have any idea where he might have gone?" Costello asked as he returned from the judge's office. "His briefcase and topcoat are still there. So was this." Costello held a crystal glass in one hand, an empty carafe in the other.

"I have no idea," Ms. Crosby said, staring at the empty carafe. "He didn't tell me anything. He could be anywhere. I'm worried. I've never seen anything like this. The look in his eyes as he left . . . it was wild. Almost like a madman. I've never seen him so intense."

Margaret Whitehurst buried her face in her hands and sobbed softly; Richard Maxwell slipped an arm around her.

"Where does the stairwell go?" Barbara asked.

"You can stop on every floor. If you keep on going you'll wind up in the basement garage," Costello answered. "He could be anywhere in the building, or already far away from here."

Al Osborne instinctively took charge. "Lorene, why don't you get on the phone and see what you can find out. Check with the clerk's office. Call the other judges and see if he is with any of them. Call whoever you have to, but find him. We'll be in his office. We need to talk."

Dr. Maxwell took Margaret by the arm and led her into her husband's office. Tony Costello and Barbara followed. Lorene Crosby picked up the receiver on her phone and began to dial frantically.

Margaret Whitehurst walked over to the window behind her husband's desk. Outside, she could see the sidewalk below peppered with people. Most were carrying umbrellas; rain had been falling all morning. The dark grayness of the sky added to her depression.

She turned back toward Al Osborne as the office door clicked shut. Osborne looked quizzically toward Richard Maxwell.

"Captain Osborne, Dr. Maxwell is my counselor," Margaret said. "He is here at my request. The others know him; he worked with Cullen and me many years ago. You can speak freely in front of him."

"What do we do now?" Costello asked after a pause.

"Find Cullen," Margaret suggested.

"We're working on that, Margaret," Al Osborne said. "We need to make some decisions."

"Mrs. Whitehurst," Barbara interjected, "something important has come up. I think your husband may have had something to do with the death of Randy Beckett."

"Let me explain," Al Osborne interjected. "Here, perhaps you should sit down." He turned the judge's swivel chair toward the woman, but she remained standing.

"I'm fine," she whispered, looking at her husband's chair.

Dr. Maxwell took over. "You don't need to explain anything, Ms. Patterson," he said softly. "We already know you are right."

"You do?" Tony Costello asked.

"Yes. Margaret called me last night. She already knows that her husband thinks he killed Randy Beckett. I've been with her since the middle of the night. She has told me everything. We have got to find the judge as quickly as possible."

There was a moment of uncomfortable silence as Margaret took a tissue from her purse and dabbed at her eyes.

"Perhaps you had better explain," Al suggested.

"I'll do it," Margaret said. "I can handle it. Just let me sit for a minute." She settled back into the comfortable chair, put down her tissue, reached into the pocket of her jacket, and handed Al Osborne a crumpled note.

"After you came to our house for that warrant, I was cleaning out his clothes where he left them piled in the dressing room, and I found this in the pocket of his jacket."

Al Osborne stared at the scrap of paper while Margaret continued.

"That's Baxter Post's license number. By the time I found it, Cullen had passed out and it was too late to ask him, so I put it aside and forgot about it. Then during the trial, when I read the part about the license number, I went back and looked."

"He could have written that down when I gave it to him," Al Osborne said.

"He didn't have his suit on when you came," she reminded him. "Anyway, why would he write it down and then hide it? Why would he write it down at all? Besides, that's not all I have found."

"What else?"

"When he came home that night, I was still up. I was upstairs in our bedroom with the lights off, sitting in the reading chair by the window that looks over the front of the house, and the driveway. You can see all the way out to the road. He came in with his lights off. Then two days ago I learned about the telephone number."

"What telephone number?" Osborne asked.

"Yours," she said, taking a small notebook from her purse. "I was watching the news. The big story was your unlisted number. I went and checked Cullen's notebook, the one where he keeps his numbers. Here it is. It's the same number."

She opened the small black book to the right page and handed it to Al Osborne. The veteran policeman looked down at the familiar numbers.

"Look at the writing on the note and the writing in the book," she said, pointing to the distinctive jotting that she had so readily recognized. "He wrote both."

"What does this mean?" Osborne said, holding the note and the notebook side by side under the glare of the desk lamp.

"Cullen had Baxter Post's license number before you ever came to our house."

"Have you said anything to him?" Osborne asked.

"Yes. Night before last, I waited up for him and told him everything that I have just told you. The note, the unlisted number, the fact that he had sneaked in with his lights off—all of it."

"What did he say?"

"He told me that I was right. He said he had happened upon

the accident and had seen Baxter Post leave, and had gotten his license number. He admitted that he had been drinking; that was why he had tried to keep his involvement a secret, for fear that word would get out that he had started drinking again."

"How did he explain the lights?"

"He reminded me that when he had run the car into an embankment he had smashed the lights. He had run off the road and messed up the car that evening. It's the same thing he told me before."

"Did you believe him?" Osborne asked.

"He was very convincing. He cried and told me he was sorry. He asked for help. He said all the right things. I held him in my arms and let him cry. I wanted to believe him. We talked all night long. Yet the next morning he was just the same: worried, preoccupied, so irritable I couldn't even talk to him."

"The next day I called the garage that works on our car. The lights hadn't been broken at all. His story fell apart. It was then that I knew for sure. I reached the end of my rope; I didn't know what to do. That's when I called Dr. Maxwell. Thank God he was available. He came. Together we decided to come down here and do something. But we haven't even been able to talk to Cullen."

Margaret's emotions reached the brink and began to spill over. The others watched intently as she cried. It was an awkward moment for all of them.

"Don't blame yourself, Mrs. Whitehurst," Barbara said. "You haven't done anything but try to help."

Margaret Whitehurst bowed her head and continued to sob softly. No one said anything. A foreboding sense of doom hung over the room as Richard Maxwell knelt next to her chair and took her hand.

"There's nothing left now," Margaret whispered.

"Nothing except for the truth," Dr. Maxwell said. "That's the only thing we have left, Margaret."

"We're pretty sure we know what happened," Barbara said, noticing the gold pen that still lay on the judge's desk. "This confirmed it, at least for me." She picked up the shiny object; Margaret stared at her through moist, reddened eyes. "When I handed the judge his pen, it was all over."

"What's that?" Margaret asked. "What pen?" She held out her hand.

"I found it out at the scene, on the side of the road, near where Randy Beckett died." Barbara handed the slim, monogrammed ball point to the judge's wife. "I returned it to the judge this morning. He recognized it immediately. It's obviously his."

Margaret Whitehurst turned the pen in her fingers until the tiny *W* faced her. "It's not his," she said quietly, almost matter-of-factly. "It's mine."

"Oh, my God . . . ," whispered Barbara.

CHAPTER
Thirty-six

*I*t took several minutes for the others to calm Margaret down before she was able to continue.

"Just admitting it has helped some," she said to Richard Maxwell as he handed her a glass of water. "You can't imagine what a burden this has been. I have felt like such an incredible hypocrite, trying to help Cullen, yet hiding the truth. But I just couldn't tell him, not until now. I've been hoping and praying that I could find something that I could use to convince him that he wasn't guilty without having to tell him what really happened."

She stood again, turned to the window, and gazed out at the city she and her husband called home.

"I wonder if he will ever forgive me. I wonder if he will ever get the chance."

Margaret smiled through her tears. "You don't believe me, do you? You think I'm trying to cover for him."

Al and Barbara looked at Tony Costello, but none of them responded.

"I'll never forget it," she continued. "I saw Randy Beckett clearly, right in front of my car. He was on his knees. His face was turned away from me . . ."

She stopped again, sat back down, and tried to pull herself together before going on.

"It's the kind of thing you never forget, though you wish to God you could."

"What were you doing out there?" Costello asked.

"I was alone, angry and depressed. I wanted to do something to hurt Cullen, to get back at him for the way he was treating me. Night after night he was away. He drank too much. After all of his promises, all of the agony we went through the first time, here he was, doing it again. I decided I would leave. Not for good, nothing like that; I didn't even take anything with me. I just thought that if I wasn't there when he got home, well . . . maybe I could scare some sense into him."

"Anyway, I left. I just drove around. I went way out Highway Forty, not headed anywhere in particular. It started snowing suddenly. I had no idea it might snow. I headed home. I was careful. The snow kept getting worse, and I became frightened. I started going too fast; I was close to home; I wanted to hurry up and get there."

Margaret began to cry again.

"That's when it happened. I saw the young man, right in front of me, then heard this awful noise. My car went on forever before it finally stopped. I started to go back toward him, but I had on heels. I even tried going barefoot. It was slippery and wet. I fell, more than once. My purse went flying; I guess that's when I lost the pen. I haven't even missed it! I couldn't begin to get up that hill. Then I saw another car coming. So I drove on home, thinking that car would stop and help.

"When I got to the house, I decided that I just couldn't admit what had happened to anybody. Not then. Not until Cullen came home. I thought maybe he could help."

"Were you just not going to do anything at all?" Barbara asked. "Were you just going to let someone else take the blame?"

"I didn't know there *was* a someone else. Not until Captain

Osborne showed up for the warrant. Then I realized that no one knew anything and that I was home free."

"That doesn't answer my question," Barbara said.

"There is no answer. I never really had a plan. I've been living in hell for weeks, just responding to circumstances, surviving day by day. Besides, your client really didn't worry me. He was drinking. He admitted his own guilt. Why should he be spared punishment just because he was lucky enough not to be the first? He was the last thing on my mind."

Barbara couldn't believe her ears. She bit her tongue and said nothing in response.

"I know you don't like that," Margaret went on. "I know you don't understand. Cullen and I have been married for many years. He's all I have, and when I began to realize what was happening, I was consumed by guilt and worry. He's been getting worse and worse. Last night he didn't come home at all. I sat up all night waiting. I haven't slept in two days. Finally I reached the end of my rope. I called Dr. Maxwell. He convinced me to talk to Cullen. Only nothing has happened like I planned."

When Margaret finished no one said a word. Thoughts ran wildly through each of their heads. Al Osborne stared into space, his well-trained, disciplined mind searching for possibilities, rejecting and assessing with lightning speed. Tony sat with head bowed, his hands clasped in front of him, thinking about the friend he dearly loved. Barbara Patterson continued to stare at Margaret Whitehurst as the older woman clung to Dr. Maxwell's hand and leaned back in her husband's chair, tears streaming down her cheeks.

Finally Al broke the silence. "I guess we have come to the end of the road. It's time to decide what to do."

"What's to decide?" Barbara said. "What choices do we have? We have a responsibility—"

"It's not that simple," Osborne interjected.

"It never is," Margaret whispered. "It never is."

Al Osborne leaned forward and spread his hands on the top of the judge's desk, pressing his weight down on his palms. He looked down as he spoke.

"As far as I am concerned we only have one choice," he said, slowly looking up. "We keep our mouths shut, and do nothing."

Richard Maxwell was incredulous. Margaret Whitehurst stared

at the veteran officer as he came around the desk and sat on its edge, looking into her eyes as he spoke.

"Look, Margaret," Al began. "You know we can't do anything to help Baxter Post. Not really. He's free, and whatever bad publicity he has gotten from all of this cannot ever be erased. Besides, as you say, he's guilty as hell. He's been a problem for everybody, all his life. He is getting no more than he deserves."

Barbara's jaw dropped as she listened. It was as if she weren't even there. She didn't believe what was happening, much less feel a part of it.

"I understand," Margaret said, though she really didn't, not completely. Everything was tumbling in on her.

"This won't work," Dr. Maxwell said. "It won't help anybody, Margaret. You're just going to sink deeper and deeper into this mess. Can't you see that?"

"You're wrong, Doctor," Al Osborne insisted. "This is the only way. Nothing is going to change for Baxter Post. The only person we can help is Judge Whitehurst, and we can't help him by ruining him."

"Sometimes the truth hurts," Richard Maxwell said. "But deceit kills. You've got to know that by now. Think about this, Margaret. Think about where lying and hiding and looking the other way has gotten you so far."

Margaret looked at her confidant.

"Margaret," the doctor continued, "you almost made it once. You almost broke out of the cycle. You were almost free. You can do it; *both* of you can."

Osborne stood up straight, then walked over to the window. He stared out into the gray mist.

"God knows your husband has suffered enough. He doesn't deserve any more punishment. It's your call, Margaret. This will convince him to try to work his problem out again."

The five of them were quiet for a moment.

"We really don't know all that much about his involvement," Margaret added, a coldness creeping into her voice. "We don't know whether Randy Beckett was dead or alive when Cullen ran over him."

Richard Maxwell sighed and released Margaret's hands.

"No, we don't," Tony Costello agreed. "We can't prove anything.

And what good would it do for us to ruin the judge's reputation in the process?"

"None, of course," Margaret responded. "But what about me?"

"What do you want me to do, Margaret," Al responded. "Should I indict and try you so that you can rot in jail? You wouldn't live to get out. So what would that accomplish? Your life would be ruined. Your husband's chances of recovery would be gone forever. And for what? You can't bring Randy Beckett back, and you can't rewrite a word of Baxter Post's life. All you can do is add a meaningless statistic to the district attorney's won-lost record. He would be the only one to gain."

Dr. Maxwell took Margaret by the shoulders and looked deeply into her eyes.

"Is this what you want? Is it going to be worth it?"

Lorene Crosby opened the door and came in. She looked crestfallen. "Judge Whitehurst isn't in the courthouse. He has left. I got in touch with the attendant down in the garage. He saw the judge leave. He drove out without stopping. Just roared on past."

"Keep checking around," Osborne responded. "See if you can find anything else out."

A fresh tear rolled down Margaret Whitehurst's cheek as Lorene Crosby left.

Richard Maxwell stood and went to the window behind the judge's desk. He stared out through the drizzle as the gray, gloomy morning engulfed the city.

Al Osborne turned toward Barbara. "Well," he said, "I guess it's up to you."

CHAPTER
Thirty-seven

S everal miles away, the shiny black Lincoln pulled out of a slow-moving traffic lane and rolled up the entrance ramp to the Northwest Expressway. As it traveled up the ramp it picked up speed; by the time the ramp blended into the outside lane of the expressway, the Lincoln was moving along at a steady clip.

Cullen Whitehurst had no thought for caution. In truth, he had no particular thoughts at all.

He looked down at the glowing green numbers on the digital speedometer ... sixty-four, sixty-five, sixty-six ... and pressed on the accelerator.

Music droned from the radio. The music ended. A rich baritone voice, devoid of any trace of local accent, filled the car.

"Headlining today's news, less than an hour ago, in a shocking move that caught the entire community by surprise, Judge Cullen Whitehurst sentenced Baxter Post to ten years in prison for the vehicular homicide of Randy Beckett last December, and then immediately suspended the sentence. This allowed Post, son of wealthy industrialist Martin Post, to walk out of the courtroom a free man, less than twenty-four hours after a criminal court jury had found him guilty."

The judge pressed harder on the accelerator and glided the car over into the far left lane. The green numbers continued to change: sixty-nine, seventy, seventy-one ...

"The Post family was unavailable for comment. Baxter Post remains cloistered in the courthouse at this hour. FM Ninety-seven's Alice Murray was at the scene as Assistant District Attorney Bernard Fine escorted the distraught widow of Randy Beckett out of the courtroom, and she filed this live report from the courthouse."

Whitehurst guided the Lincoln around a slow curve to the left, up onto a long bridge that spanned the railroad yards. His palms were sweaty; beads of perspiration trickled down his cheeks. He listened intently as the car picked up speed. Seventy-four, seventy-five, seventy-six ...

"Bob, there is confusion and anger here at the courthouse. Lynn Beckett, widow of the slain young man, had nothing to say, but she was obviously upset. The prosecutor, Bernard Fine, was guarded in his comments, but in response to my question, he did refer to the whole thing as a travesty, and suggested by inference that the Post family might have used its influence to change the course of justice once again."

The Lincoln's tires pounded out a rhythm as the big car rolled along the steel-grid surface of the bridge, still picking up speed. Seventy-nine, eighty, eighty-one ...

"What do you mean, it's up to me?" Barbara said. She held up her hands defensively and shook her head. "Oh, no, you don't. You're not putting this off on me."

"I'm not putting anything off on you, Barbara," Al Osborne said. "But you're the only one who hasn't said anything."

"So?" Barbara interjected.

"If you agree, then we leave here with our lips sealed. If not, then you will just have to do whatever you think is right."

"My God," Barbara whispered, almost in a daze. "This isn't the way it's supposed to end. The courtroom is out there. That's where the decisions are supposed to be made, not in some back room where everyone has his own self-interest."

"Do you have a better solution?" Costello asked.

Al Osborne walked over to where Barbara was standing. "Look, Barbara. You were right. The judge was involved in this whole thing. But he didn't kill Randy Beckett. Your client was involved, but he's a free man. You can't make things any better for him. And as for Margaret, I'll ask you the same thing I asked her. Is it going to help anyone for her to go to prison?"

Barbara stared at him, a bewildered look in her eyes. "That's not my decision. I took an oath."

"And you kept that oath," Osborne interrupted. "You did your best for your client. You uncovered the truth. But your job is over. The case is over. Baxter Post has been punished. After all, there are no really innocent people in this affair. Margaret has paid one hell of a price. Her life is in shambles."

"It's your call," Costello said. "Nobody's gonna fault you, whatever you do.

"All you have to do is to tell us you can't do it. Everyone here will understand," Tony Costello added. "But I wish you wouldn't. I wish you would be one of us."

Barbara looked at Margaret Whitehurst. Their eyes met. For an instant Barbara could almost feel the pain Margaret had endured for so many years.

"I guess we'd better stay together until we find the judge," Barbara said. "We'll need to get to him as quickly as possible before he says or does the wrong thing. I had better go make excuses to my client. I'll be right back."

The courtroom door closed behind her. Margaret Whitehurst leaned back, breathed deeply, and said a silent prayer for her husband. Richard Maxwell felt sick to his stomach.

At that moment, Cullen Whitehurst was thinking about Margaret, too. He saw her face in his mind's eye, but he forced the image to go away. He tightened his grip on the steering wheel and focused his attention on the radio as the woman spoke again.

"In a prepared statement read in court when the sentence was suspended, Judge Whitehurst said that he was doing what was right, and that this was what he had to do, regardless of what others might think. Well, I can tell you what others think, Bob. The people here are hostile. Pandemonium has broken loose. We nearly had a mob scene after court recessed."

The Lincoln left the steel surface of the bridge, hit the pavement, and began its descent on the other side. Eighty-four, eighty-five, eighty-six ... The words and music of a long-forgotten hymn, left over from his childhood, wandered into the judge's conscious mind.

I come to the garden alone . . .

The news broadcast continued. "Thank you, Alice. Meanwhile, FM Ninety-seven has learned that Governor Foreman has scheduled a news conference for two o'clock this afternoon. FM Ninety-seven will cover that conference live."

At the bottom of the bridge, the highway curved gently to the right. With consummate effort Cullen Whitehurst gripped the steering wheel, locked his arms, and jammed his foot down onto the accelerator.

. . . and the voice I hear, falling on my ear, this heart of mine discloses.

A truck driver jockeying a giant semi down the long incline glared angrily at the black car as it sped on by on the left. His scowl quickly gave way to wide-eyed shock.

Inside the Lincoln, Judge Whitehurst pressed his back against the seat and tightly closed his eyes.

EPILOGUE

B arbara Patterson and Bernie Fine attended the funeral of Judge
Cullen Whitehurst together. They met for dinner two times
after that and spent a great deal of time talking, in an effort
to make some sense of their relationship. Neither ever felt fully
comfortable with the other again, however, and their relationship
ended. Barbara was right about the value of being involved in a
highly publicized case. Her law practice is flourishing. Bernie was
promoted to Senior Assistant District Attorney. Many regard him as
the heir apparent to the top job.

Lorene Crosby retired to a life of seclusion almost immediately
after the funeral. Tony Costello accepted a job with the judge who
replaced Cullen Whitehurst. Al Osborne did not involve himself further in front-line police work, but he still works for the department
in an administrative capacity. Dr. Richard Maxwell did not involve
himself further in the affairs of Margaret Whitehurst. He still sees
patients on a limited basis, and is in the process of writing a self-

help book, aimed primarily at the problems experienced by spouses of alcoholics and children of alcoholic families. Governor Bradley Foreman won re-election by a narrow margin.

Margaret didn't return to her husband's office at the courthouse until several days after the funeral. Once she felt strong enough, she spent a long, bitter, painful evening in his chambers sorting out the personal effects of a lifetime. She lives alone in her family's home, and is seldom seen in public.

Baxter Post no longer resides in this area. Public pressure was too much for him; he finally chose to leave and start his life anew in another place. His parents, however, are toughing it out. With their complex business and social ties to this community, they do not really have the luxury of choice.

Lynn Beckett has also gone elsewhere. She and her children are living with her mother. The memories were too much.

As of this date, all of the people who gathered in the judge's office on the morning of his death have kept their word. None has ever said anything to anyone about the events leading up to that day, or the bizarre circumstances surrounding their solemn oath of silence.

Richard Speight
January 31, 1988